HOW TO BITE YOUR NEIGHBOR

& WIN A WAGER

D.N. BRYN

HOW TO
BITE YOUR NEIGHBOR
AND WIN A WAGER

Guides for Dating Vampires
Book One

D.N. BRYN

Printed in the United States of America
First Printing, 2022

Print (paperback) 978-1-958051-06-1
Print (hardcover) 978-1-958051-05-4
Ebook 978-1-958051-04-7

For information about purchasing and permissions, contact D.N. Bryn at dnbryn@gmail.com

www.DNBryn.com

Cover design by ThistleArts.
Cover and spine typography by Houda Belgharbi.
Published with The Kraken Collective.

This work is fictitious and any resemblance to real life persons or places is purely coincidental. No vampires were harmed in the making of this story.

This book contains mature content.
Flip to the back of the book for a detailed list.

To Chris DiCocco,
whose brilliant enthusiasm for
these disaster gays gives me life.

1

VINCENT

Vincent Barnes was perpetuating stereotypes, and he knew it.

Any vampire with a firmly placed moral backbone would tell him that sneaking into a stranger's home to drink their blood while they slept was rude, illegal, and, above all, a terrible portrayal of the vampiric community. The problem was, back when Vincent had associated with the vampiric community, none of *those* vampires had turned out to have a moral backbone. And Vincent was starving.

Dealers of bagged blood charged as much as rent—which he already couldn't afford—and existed in tight black-market clichés he didn't have the social prowess to hunt down. Seducing some drunk fool into letting him have a quick nibble went far beyond the limits of his flirting expertise. Straight up attacking a human in a back alley? Vincent could feel his panic rising just thinking about it, not to mention all the *other* terrible vampire stereotypes it would perpetuate.

So that left home invasion: the vampiric equivalent of that old game show with the doors. What's behind door number one? An empty bed, or an elderly lady wearing three bottles of perfume, or an angry naked fireman with an ax? Vincent hadn't realized it was possible to have horny nightmares, but after the fireman encounter he didn't sleep through the day for a month.

He stared at the small suburban house he'd chosen for tonight and hoped for a slightly less angry, less ax-murderous, abs-bared fireman behind tonight's door. With its three-bedroom floorplan and tight side yard, it didn't look like much, but it sat just far enough back from the aging streetlamps that its deep shadows and ancient locks made it a perfect game-show-style hunting ground. Vincent's 'door' in question was technically a large second story window with a slightly bowing screen and an incredibly tiny ledge outside.

If he'd been any taller than five-foot-nine he wouldn't have fit. With one bare foot curled around the sill and the other wedged into a lump in the stucco, he fiddled with the screen. The fraying strings of his fingerless gloves dangled in the starlight and he flicked his head to dislodge a chunk of shaggy hair from his eyes as, with a final finessed pop, the screen slid free.

His bare feet made only the softest rustle as he lowered himself inside. The gentle swish of his dark clothes blended into the white noise of the distant highway. He breathed slow and deep, waiting for the first sign of a twitch in the night. Despite the moonless sky, Vincent could clearly make out the room's contents in his monochromatic night vision. An open closet revealed a tornado of clothing. The desk and dresser held a cluttering of books, games, and other knickknacks. A collage of photos had been pasted across the far wall. And halfway between the window and the door was a queen-sized bed bearing Vincent's prey like a silver platter: a single human soundly asleep beneath the blankets. The man's pillow was bunched underneath him, his head already tipped to reveal the crest of his neck below the lazy curls that flicked around his ears.

This was, undeniably, the best door of the month.

As Vincent stepped closer, he corrected himself. This was the best door ever, or at least since Vincent had become a vampire during his first and only semester of college four years prior. Even the most average humans—those who took regular showers and didn't wear cologne to bed—all tasted and smelled a bit different. In most cases, different meant a unique brand of mediocre. But Vincent could already tell this particular human's blood would be absolutely delicious. He even smelled delicious. The scent wasn't *like* something, not sandalwood or fresh bread or motor-oil, but the natural musk of him was better than any signature fragrance, a dark, lovely aroma that urged Vincent to press his nose to the man's skin and just breathe.

The thought almost made him turn tail and run. He was here, breaking into people's homes while they slept, because not doing so would mean starvation and eventually death. He was *not* here to creepily think about how wonderful they smelled while staring at their perfect cheekbones and the gentle flutter of their long lashes and... oh god he was still fawning over this complete stranger.

Vincent pressed his lips together and steadied his thoughts. *Feed and get out. Feed and get out.*

He eased his weight slowly onto the mattress to reach the delicious man—*feed and get out*, Vincent repeated, *feed and get out.* The scrappy edges of his long jacket hung threateningly, and he held them back as he leaned over the sleeping human. His fangs slipped from above his canines as instinct moved him toward the juiciest curve of the man's neck.

After the initial break-in, this was the most precarious part of the act. If he could nick his prey's skin with just the right dose of venom, then the neurological effect would keep the human slumbering peacefully through the feeding. If the human woke at the first touch of teeth, though, both of them would be in for a wild time, one that usually involved a lot of screaming and throwing things on the human's part and a rapid relocation to another neighborhood on Vincent's.

Vincent's hair fell back into his eyes as he lowered his mouth to the human's neck. He indulged himself with one long, deep breath of the man's scent before piercing his fangs through the man's skin. The man made a little involuntary sound, soft and low, and continued sleeping.

The tension slipped from Vincent's shoulders. He settled a little more deeply onto the mattress, propping one arm against the back of the man's head. Oh god, his hair was so soft—*feed and get out, feed and get out. You can do this.*

Vincent drank.

Becoming a vampire had given him a healthy craving for blood regardless of the flavor. Usually blood tasted alright. There were exceptions, humans so far out of Vincent's palate range that it made them disgustingly flat, or so far into it that each swallow was like a hearty dessert. But blood wasn't supposed to taste this good, he was pretty sure. Nothing was supposed to taste *this* good.

The man's blood was rich and dark and sweet, like his scent but in the form of the best quality maple syrup, the kind Vincent's mom used to buy—and probably still bought—but duskier, as though it had been turned into whiskey or bourbon but without the bite of hard liquor. Vincent forced himself to drink slowly, to savor each drop. When he left this room, that would be it. No repeats, no returns. That was the rule he'd set for himself when he'd finally broken down and jiggled free the lock of his first door; if he was going to take blood from humans who couldn't consent, he would at least not go to the same ones over and over again. He wasn't going to be the stereotypical vampire who stalked a human like it was some kind of game.

But, fucking hell, this particular human was going to make that rule difficult.

Vincent continued to drink, not quite curled against the man's back, but not quite *not* curled against him either, until his mind buzzed with the initial signals of over-indulgence. That was one thing the stereotypes got entirely wrong; it was hard to drain a human to the point of death. Hard physically, because the average adult body contained multiple liters of blood, and hard psychologically, because murder was still murder, and hard because it went against the vampire's natural instinct to keep the human alive so they'd produce more blood for the next meal. But Vincent wasn't coming back to this meal, no matter how tasty.

He repeated this to himself as he withdrew his fangs and pressed his tongue to the side of the human's neck until he felt the skin close up. He repeated it as he checked that the wound had vanished, gently patting the area clean with his sleeve, the taste of that amazing blood slowly vanishing from his tongue. He repeated it again as he slipped out the window, leaving behind the man's frustratingly wonderful scent: no more feeding on this particular human. One time was all he got.

He stopped repeating the thought around late morning, as he finally drifted off to sleep, still thinking of the man's taste, his smell, his dark curls, and gentle sounds of slumber. A week and a half of bland and bitter blood later, Vincent broke his rule of no returns.

He went back for seconds.

2

Wesley Luis Smith Garcia was perpetuating stereotypes.

Again.

"Dude, there's no fucking way. I'm too young and hot to waste my life in a cubicle for the next forty years. Dammit, I auto-spawned in the fourth quadrant again, are you close enough to back me?" Wes kicked his leg over the couch's armrest as he leaned forward, controlling his avatar into a dive roll behind a broken wall.

Over his headset, Kendall cursed. "Nah, I'm pinned down now," she grumbled. "You know most regular jobs aren't all bad though, right? I mean, the starting pay is pretty crap and you do not want to see my health insurance bills, and no matter how much turnover we have there's always someone exploding their lunch in the microwave, but the steady income is nice."

"Are you buying anniversary presents for your retirement fund now?"

"At least I have one!" A gentle barrage of pistol noises came through from Kendall's side, followed by another curse.

As if on cue, a red flare burst from Wes's fictional head, his avatar falling to the ground. The respawn screen reappeared. He deployed again, triggering his avatar to huskily shout *"I'm always up for the hunt!"* as an explosion echoed in the background. "I'm not against getting a job, okay, I just want to like what I do."

"You, Wesley, want to be in love with what you do. You want it to give you fluttery heart feelings and raise your dick at night. Which is why you need a girlfriend. Or a boyfriend. You have so many options! At this very moment, you could be out falling in love with *literally* anyone."

"That's *literally* not what bisexuality means and you know it," Wes grumbled. "I thought you were grilling me about jobs, not partners."

"It's a two-for-one. I'll start grilling you about finding a new best friend, too, if you don't get your ass over to that last house."

Wes glanced at the second, smaller monitor beside his primary TV, where Kendall's screen was currently streaming. A video of her face took up its corner, her dark skin a little shiny and her short hair with its bleached tips sticking up at all angles from running her left hand through it every time she died. She would always complain that the habit fluffed up her rigorously straightened natural curls, but she never stopped doing it. Wes hadn't seen the act in person since they'd both graduated twelve months ago and moved back to their respective hometowns, but after three and a half years as roommates, he had cataloged it at every possible angle, in almost every possible situation. "Right, fine, I'm coming. But you can't claim I'm stealing your assist this time. This is practically charity work I'm doing here."

"Just kill that damn vamp on the roof for me already."

"Bet I can clear the whole house before you get here."

Kendall grinned. "Five dollars says you can't."

"You're stacking yourself against some terrible odds here, you know that."

"I can spare the cash. Unlike some people, I have a job, therefore I receive money."

"I hate you, Kendall," Wes shouted and charged the vamp-laden house.

The game vampires had red eyes, blood blurred along their lips and a sickly pallor to their skin that Wes was pretty sure went beyond the typical lack-of-tan that haunted most vamps in real life. Not that he'd seen many outside the occasional news spotlight or viral social media post, though he was also pretty sure some of those vampires were just regular people looking for attention. In the game, they flailed once as he shot silver bullets through their skulls, their bodies collapsing into pools of unnaturally dark blood that remained after their corpses flickered out. Wes ran through his gun's ammunition and switched to stakes for the last two vamps. His health dropped to five percent as the last one of them caught him with a bite to the arm, but he killed the vamp before it could drain anything more from him.

"*Mission successful!*" popped across the screen.

Wes hollered, letting the game save before tossing down his controller. He bounced from the couch to flip off the console. With the screens black, the house went dark, but he didn't bother with the lights on as he crossed the living room to the kitchen. His phone reconnected him to his video call with Kendall after a momentary lag.

Wes smirked despite knowing he'd only be a flimsy shadow on his friend's screen. "Five dollars?"

"Five dollars," Kendall replied, "But only once you pick something to apply for. Or someone."

"That wasn't part of the wager." Wes leaned his head against the side of the fridge, letting the light wash him in fluorescent tones. "It's just... I'm not ready."

"It's been over a year, Wes." For how softly Kendall said it, it still hurt like a punch to the gut.

Most people didn't take this long to grieve, Wes knew. But most people didn't come home from college to find their mother had vanished the week prior. Most people didn't have to lower her empty coffin into the ground alone while their mother's homophobic extended family demanded to know why they hadn't been invited and their father sent his regards in the form of a note card with their step-family's names neatly printed in swirly cursive. Most people understood how and when and why their loved one had died. Wesley only knew where. And it was a place he couldn't seem to get into.

Dwelling on that fact felt like breaking apart piece by agonizing piece, his soul crumbling to the size of bullets that he might shoot straight through the hearts of those responsible for his mom's death. He was pretty sure he wouldn't live through the process. So he tried to shove the emotion right back where it had come from.

"OJ goes with vodka, right?" he joked, staring into the fridge.

Kendall seemed to take that as a bad sign. "I'm sorry, dude, I'm pushing and I shouldn't be. I just worry about you." She sighed, running her hand through her hair. "You know the spare room at Leoni's and my place is always open if you need it."

"It's fine. I've got the house." It was only luck that his mother had just transferred the property into his name before her disappearance. Luck, or the knowledge that something terrible could happen to her at the fucking asshole pharmaceutical company that was Vitalis-Barron. "I'm good here." He took a long guzzle of orange juice straight from the carton and slammed the door behind him. The magnets rattled. He grimaced. "You owe me five dollars."

"Sending now."

Wes made his way upstairs. The dark of the house was nothing compared to the fifteen years of knowledge he had of the place, fifteen years of just him and his mom, both of them loud enough to make the small home seem full. It never felt that way anymore. But it was paid off, and it was his, and if somehow his mother hadn't died the way he theorized, then this was where she'd come back to.

Not that she would come back. She was dead; Wes knew that. But he still had to see the evidence for himself and get the proof of it in his own hands. And use that proof to burn the people responsible to the ground.

His phone beeped and he clicked the notification. Kendall's image turned to a little side icon as the money transfer app appeared. At the top sat the five dollars from her, followed by the back and forth of a dozen other wagers from that week alone. He swiped away, scrolling mindlessly through his other open apps, and ended up in his emails, staring at his only bolded message. Its subject line *Job Offer Follow-up* with the preview of *Wesley Smith, we look forward to seeing you again...*

He'd opened it dozens of times by now, but his vision still tunneled with each new attempt, and he turned it back to *unread* so fast that he hadn't gotten through the first paragraph yet. It had been so much easier interacting with them in person, where the constant action and reaction of an adrenaline-inducing conversation had blocked out the rest of his emotions and let his natural charisma shine. But while charisma alone might have gotten him the initial offer, there was still one more thing they wanted from him.

"I do have one job I'm looking at." Wes mentioned it as casually as he could manage.

He couldn't tell Kendall that he was only trying to get the position in order to rip the company up from its foundations and hurl it into the sun. Kendall might have been his best friend, but it still felt too ridiculous to say, *"Hey, I'm convinced the largest pharmaceutical company in the country killed my mom but they won't let me into their top-secret research center unless I work for them."* Especially when the only proof he had was a flyer for their research he'd found tucked into her bedside book, her complaints of falling ill two months before, and the fact that a bus ticket had been purchased with her card on the assumed day of her disappearance. His mother hated buses so much that she'd thrown a party when the train system that passed through the city had added a new line. Someone had bought the bus ticket as a cover up. Someone with funds and slightly dangerous research opportunities that his mom had taken an interest in when the symptoms of her illness lingered.

Someone Wes was going to ruin, if only he could get that far.

"I already had an interview, actually. They seemed to like me." He also didn't add that he'd applied with his father's last name to minimize his connection to his mom, or that *liked him* had been an understatement when he'd nailed all three of their grueling interviews.

"Dude, that's awesome." Kendall beamed at him. "Why didn't you say something earlier?"

"Eh, it probably won't work out. It's for a sales kind of deal with that big research company that's always trying to recruit new volunteers, Vitalis-Barron. Except I'd be the one recruiting, and the volunteers they want most right now are vampires."

"Shit, so you'd have to what? Single out vampires and convince them to do medical research?"

"Something like that."

The shine of the interviewer's teeth was engraved in his mind as she had leaned toward him, smiling in a way that sent chills down his spine. *"Our research participants are all volunteers, but we know that research of this kind can be... intimidating. Sometimes participants need a little pressure to get through the doors. Once they're inside and touring our facilities though, it's rare they leave."*

Well, Wes sure knew a little something about people going into Vitalis-Barron Pharmaceutical and not leaving. Right now they seemed to be focusing their attention on vamps and not humans. But how long would it be before their focus swept back toward single mothers with absent children?

"Like I said, I probably won't get it. Their job offer has a clause where they'll only accept me if I can prove I've got what it takes by signing up a vamp for them first." Wes flipped on the light in the bathroom and propped his phone against the mirror, shoving his toothbrush into his mouth dry.

"You know it's shit that they're asking you to do unpaid labor, right?"

"Yeah, I know." Wes popped out his toothbrush, leaning both elbows down to the counter to flick the tip in Kendall's direction. "It's probably why their entry-level salaries are so high." That and their plethora of highly illegal and totally despicable research practices. Wes's gut boiled. He just had to get in there. Had to prove it. "Where the hell do I *find* a vampire on my own, though?"

Knowing Vitalis-Barron's dirty secrets, he wanted it to be a vamp who deserved that fate. Not some poor fool who just happened to get a bad bite and was doing his best not to hurt anyone, but the violent sort of vampires that always made the news. That seemed to be most of them, if the media could be believed. Though Wes had seen enough of his country's finest journalism about humans of his own Hispanic heritage to know the media was as reliable as a gossiping aunt when it came to accurate portrayals of anyone they didn't want as their neighbors.

That would all be beside the point if he couldn't find any vampires in the first place. "I looked up stats, and the predicted number of vampires in San Salud was 'between 2000 and 7500.' Like fuck, man, if the experts don't even know how to find the vampires to count them, what am I supposed to do?" He shoved his toothbrush back in his mouth at the end of the question, brushing so hard his dentist was probably getting goose bumps. The massive collection of beads wrapping up his wrist jangled.

"Hang out in the inner city?" Kendall suggested. "That's where most of them live, right?"

"And poke my head into every alley hoping that I happen to spot one with their fangs out?"

"Or you could go to a bar wearing a revealing shirt and touch your neck a lot. Janice claimed she picked up three different vampires that way. Maybe you'll find a job *and* a date."

"Janice claimed she was a secret descendant of Marie Antoinette," Wes retorted, trying not to think about the time he'd stumbled into their complex's back entrance at four am, somehow already hungover while still half-drunk, and seen a pretty pale boy with blood on his lips and his mouth against Janice's neck. She'd looked so enraptured, relaxed and blissful and serene. The vision still haunted Wes sometimes, late at night when it seemed the only thing that could let him finally fall asleep would be an orgasm. He rinsed his toothbrush and dropped it back into the cup, trying not to look like he was hastily burying a multi-year sex fantasy.

Kendall, at least, seemed preoccupied with something that wasn't his expression. "What's that on your neck?"

Wes scowled at his reflection. He examined his tanned skin, his curls bobbing as he turned his face back and forth. Sure enough, a tiny mark marred the side of his neck. And was that another just above it? Wesley's blood went cold and hot all at once. But they couldn't be. He was overthinking this. "They're just little bruises." Now that he *was* thinking, he was pretty sure some slight discoloration had been there on and off the last couple weeks. "I probably did something stupid in my sleep."

"Knowing you? Definitely." Beneath the forced humor, she sounded almost worried. "You sure they're not fang marks or something?"

"You're only saying that because we're talking about vampires." But they were the right distance apart. And the right general area. Wes laughed. "That would mean a vamp is sneaking into my bed at night, which is ridiculous. You'd think I'd *know* if someone was in my bed."

"I'd know. You'd be wildly oblivious until ten minutes after you'd already come."

"That's unfair!" Wes protested, a little over-dramatically, maybe, but the situation seemed to call for it.

"Not if it's true! In sophomore year, you didn't think to ask if Mel was into you until you'd already spent a full week sticking things up each other's—"

"I regret ever telling you about that!" Though he didn't regret the experimenting, or the orgasms that came with it, even if its subsequent dating attempt had failed miserably. "Or anything from my sex-life, for that matter. I'm abandoning our friendship in favor of the shower, thank you very much." He picked up the phone, but his eyes flicked back to the mirror. To the marks on his neck. He had to stop thinking about them. "We still on for tomorrow?"

"I was going to take Leoni to see this new romance adventure movie that came out last weekend."

"Abandoning me for your girlfriend."

"You could go get your own girlfriend, or boyfriend," she added, "inbetween friend, neither friend. Whoever makes you tingly in your—"

"I'm hanging up now."

"Pingly," Kendall managed to get in before her video officially closed out. Wes's screen turned back to his usual background picture of them from college, Kendall with her tongue stuck out and him smooching her cheek.

Wes shook his head and laughed. As he stripped and started the shower, he couldn't get the thought of vampires out of his head. If by some crazy turn of fate, there was one actually biting him in his sleep, then that would be terrifying and dangerous. And lucky.

A message pinged on his Griffon chat app.

KendallCanoodles
Dude, if there is a mystery neck-nomming vampire, then I wager a hundred bucks that you can't get them to go with you to that research job thing.

LordOfTheWin
Deal.

3

Wesley

Wesley turned off the light, scrunched his pillow under his chin and closed his eyes. Sleep didn't come. In the back of his head, Kendall's bet returned.

"You'd think I'd know if someone was in my bed."

Both of them understand just how unlikely this was. But Kendall had still wagered a hundred dollars. And Wes had still accepted.

It wasn't as though vampires weren't known for this kind of thing: for stealing blood in the dead of night, whether from sleeping victims, or lonely travelers, or blood banks already struggling to find enough donations for their human patients. It wasn't entirely impossible. Wasn't his window screen looking a little more bowed than usual? Hadn't he been sleeping in later, waking up a bit groggier some mornings?

Wes shuddered from the top of his head to his toes. He didn't believe the rumor that bites could randomly turn humans into vamps—if that were the case, he figured far more vampires would lurk the streets at night—but being bitten in his sleep, without his consent, was still a terrifying form of assault. Maybe it wasn't deadly research level cruel, but it was up there.

And it was exactly what Wes needed. A vampire willing to commit these crimes was someone he'd had no regrets turning over to Vitalis-Barron for the chance to take them down. It was almost too perfect, in fact. Like the universe had aligned this for him because it knew Vitalis-Barron had to be dealt with.

As the night wore on, Wes's mind couldn't quite seem to shut off. Every creak and bump in the night flared like a firework behind his eyes, jolting him out of a half-sleep. It was all in his head, he told himself. Just his worries slipping into his dreams. Those, too, were filled with vampires and the dark, things that were half visions and half his own imagination, just conscious enough to be lucid. While there were probably no vampires coming for him, he couldn't stop himself from picturing what it might be like to encounter one now, vulnerable in bed.

It would be the swish of dark fabric spilling through the window, eyes tracking along his sleeping form, the shift of the bed as a monster joined him. Something hungry coming for him, because it wanted him. Because it *needed* him. A gentle breath on his neck, shivering down his spine. Fingers touching his hair, winding into it, holding him in place. His life in the hands of a stranger, an adrenaline rush that no amount of gambling with Kendall could ever match.

Lips on his skin.

The prick of fangs.

Still half awake, Wesley's lungs caught in a little sound that pressed out of him unbidden, and he fluttered back to full consciousness. The half-dream came with him: the pressure of a mouth, the hand pressed against his head and another on his shoulder and—oh fuck, oh fuck, there was a vampire: a real, non-imaginary vampire holding him down and sucking out his blood. And it felt… Wes couldn't think about how it felt, because *vampire* and *here* slammed through his head hard enough to propel him into his lampstand. He flicked the switch.

The light burst on, so bright Wes had to blink. He half expected to be wrong again, that it was still just a hyper-real dream. But hot blood trickled slowly from his neck, and flinching away from the light across the bed from him was an honest-to-god bloodsucker. The vampire's shaggy black hair tangled around his eyes and draped onto the collar of his even shaggier, ratty black coat. Beneath the dark clothing he looked nearly as pale and sickly as the vamps Wesley had shot up in-game a few hours earlier, his irises an icy blue and a trail of scarlet dripping down the edge of his lips.

He narrowed his eyes at Wesley, brows pulled tight and gaze a little distant. As the vampire's focus clicked, fear tore across his face. He scrambled backwards, falling off the bed in a clumsy pile, and lunged for the open window.

A vampire was in Wes's house. A vampire who'd assaulted him in his sleep. A vampire he needed to bring with him to Vitalis-Barron Pharmaceutical. A vampire who was going to run off into the night in the next ten seconds if Wes didn't do something about it.

Wes was shorter, and, even if vampiric strength wasn't in play, probably still weaker than the vampire. He had no weapons at hand and every fighting technique he'd picked up over the years had come from some kind of fictional media. So he did the only other thing he could think of.

"Wait! Wait, come back, you can eat me!" As he said it, the hazy desires of his dream returned in tingles and flashes, forcing him to swallow at the end. It wasn't like he *wanted* a vampire to pin him down and snack on him. If his aversion to the bloodsucker wasn't so outweighed by his loathing for Vitalis-Barron, he wouldn't have wanted this particular vampire near any part of his body. It was just that the idea of being bitten triggered a rush of adrenaline. Like the thought of skydiving. Except that in one of those situations you died, and in the other one a beautiful monster licked your skin and told you how delicious you tasted.

Whatever the case, his wild exclamation worked. The vampire slowed, one hand on the window. His breathing seemed to be coming unusually hard. Or maybe that was Wesley's.

The vampire's eyes dropped to Wesley's neck and his throat bobbed.

Wes lifted his hand to the spot. His fingers slid over a warm liquid. Ah, fuck. Bleeding, right. The top edge of his t-shirt was already wet, the stain spilling quickly down his shoulder in a crimson streak. Wes had lost this much blood before, doing one stupid thing or another— and won something for his efforts most of the time—but the shock of it still turned his head a little woozy. He grabbed the bedpost to steady himself.

"Ah, fuck," he said.

The vampire rested one knee against the mattress across from him, there so fast that Wes wasn't sure when he'd moved. Then he was pressing into Wesley's space, not quite touching him but still somehow pushing him back against the headboard with his presence alone, as though the force of his hunger were a physical thing. He caged Wes in, a palm to the wall above one of Wesley's shoulders and another so near his ribs that Wes could feel the barest brush of his coat's sleeve with every breath. He leaned close to Wes, mouth open and head cocked, face out of view beyond Wesley's periphery.

A tremble ran through Wes. He almost regretted calling the bloodsucker back, but he needed him here, needed not to lose him to the night. Wes would happily give as much blood as he had to, put up with his heart fluttering and his stomach twisting and determinedly turn his fear into a wave of motivational adrenaline, if it meant crushing Vitalis-Barron to dust.

Then the vampire's tongue slid up the side of his neck, and all concept of revenge flitted out of Wesley Smith Garcia's mind, leaving with a gasp that felt a little like a sob and a bright, almost painful ache that slid serpentine through him. It lasted forever and not nearly long enough, an almost agonizingly gentle suck following the tongue-pressure. The vampire pulled away again, slower this time.

Everything in Wesley begged to call him back.

Vincent

"You can eat me," the human had said.

He'd said that. Vincent had absolutely, definitely heard it with his own ears. Which meant that this was okay. It was not just that Vincent needed one more taste, with the scent of all that blood in the air, smelling like ambrosia and nectar and every other mythological delicacy. And the man had been oozing all over the place, so any decent vampire wouldn't have left him there to *keep* bleeding, right? *Right.*

But as Vincent scooted away from him, nearly falling off the bed for a second time in the process, he was still fairly certain that this was the worst thing he had ever done as a vampire. He should leave now, just to make sure it never happened again.

"Wait," the human said. This time his voice was softer, lower. His head leaned against the wall still, his body loose where it had been so tense under Vincent's. The edge of his lips lifted a little. "Please."

Vincent could feel himself leaning toward the open window, but he couldn't quite force his legs to move. In the light of the nightstand lamp, he could finally make out the room in full color, the combination of it all so bright and alive: video game décor and movie posters, old bottles lined across a shelf with a collection of tiny Pride flags propped in them, a collage wall featuring shot-glass towers and absurd food, rooftops and mountain vistas, concerts and skydives. Most of the pictures showed the room's owner at various stages of teenage and adult life, his smile brimming and his posture carelessly happy. It looked like the portrait of a man who ran with the wind and never said no to anything.

He was even more handsome while awake, his skin a warm tan and his brown eyes large and excitable in a square, well-jawed face with high cheekbones that seemed just the right size for the massive smile that filled it in his pictures. Right now, his mouth was growing tight as his eyes wandered over Vincent in a way that made Vincent's skin crawl, the attention a hair to the left of what might have been decent. Vincent couldn't quite tell what the man was looking for, but he could guess it had something to do with stereotypes and the way Vincent had proceeded to perpetuate almost every last one of them. Unlike the human stereotypes, or their real-life basis, at least this man hadn't screamed or come at him with an ax.

"Shit, you're kind of feral," the human said, finally. "It's a nice aesthetic, though. Like a dumpster grunge or something?"

"Thanks?" Vincent had found this particular coat in a thrift store, not a dumpster, but after wearing it most days for the last three years he figured that was probably where it belonged. He glanced back along the edge of the man's shirt, still wet and red. What a waste.

The human followed his gaze and his brow shot up. "I'm not bleeding anymore, right?" He pressed his fingertips to his neck so firmly he seemed to be checking his pulse.

Vincent reached for him on instinct. "Careful!" He pulled back almost as fast, cringing. "The new skin's still delicate there."

The human whistled. "But you healed it? Just like that?" He continued to touch the spot. "Is that why I haven't had much of a mark?"

Vincent swallowed, looking away from the man's fingers—from the way he was so perfectly highlighting his neck while still covered in his own delicious blood. Vincent really needed to work through whatever the hell had gotten into him before this became his personal fantasy for the next month. He swallowed yet again and managed to say something that sounded an awful lot like, "I'm not here *every* night," except it definitely came from the mouth of someone quite a lot less stable and far more breathless than him.

The man's lips quirked. "Seeing other humans, are you?"

Vincent wanted to die. If someone could come stake him right there, he'd probably say *thank you* and *have a nice day* after. Though, who was he kidding, that would be his response no matter what. At least politely depressed vampires weren't also a stereotype. "I should really just—"

"I'm Wesley. Or Wes." The human held his hand out, fingers still crimson from where he'd initially touched his bleeding neck bites.

Vincent stared at Wesley's elbow, trying to look somewhere on his body not currently covered in an aromatic delicacy. He swallowed. Again. "You have blood on that hand."

Wesley pulled the arm back. "Oh shit, is that a vampire faux pas or something?"

Vincent couldn't find a courteous way to say *no it just makes me want to suck on your fingers* so he opted for, "I'm Vincent."

Wesley grinned and nodded, his curls bobbing lazily around his ears. "No way. There was a kid whose family lived down the street from here in elementary named Vincent; we used to call him Vinny the Vampire because he was always lurking behind the curtains and wouldn't hang with us." The smile faded, but it turned into something almost brighter, a wide exuberant thing that seemed to shine out of him. "Oh fuck." He cackled. "Vinny Barnes? Is that *you*?"

Vincent fought not to give into the dread coiling in his gut at the thought of this human—this breathtaking, larger than life human he could now vaguely recall as an annoying, larger than life child—remembering him so shy and miserable. "Barnes, yeah. No one's called me Vinny in years."

Not since his parents had told him he had an hour to collect his things. They were adamant that he wouldn't burden them with this, not after all the complaining he'd done growing up, all the sick days he'd made one of them take off to watch him mope on the couch when he wasn't even ill to begin with. This was the last straw, they'd said; he was an adult now, and if he couldn't make his way on his own then he didn't deserve the life they'd toiled to give him.

Except he didn't think they'd used his nickname for that lecture, either. One of his sisters, maybe, in the couple scattered phone calls he'd exchanged with them before their reprimanding pity had grown too much to bear. That had still been three years ago, at least.

Wes kept watching him, his gaze sharpening. "But you weren't actually a vampire *then*? You were just a kid."

"I got turned in college."

"Rough."

Vincent glanced back at the window. He shifted one leg off the bed. "I should really be—"

"No, wait." Wes leaned forward, a hand out like he was going to grab for Vincent.

Vincent flinched, but Wes had already stopped, halfway.

His hand tightened, blood-tipped fingers curling in. Carefully, like each motion was an effort, he sat back. "I mean, you should come back. I know we weren't friends or anything, but it would be cool to catch up. Besides, I have blood. You need blood. It's a win-win."

"You would let me bite you?" It sounded like a joke. It had to be a joke. "Voluntarily?"

"No, you'd have to catch me first." Wes snorted. "Yeah dude, voluntarily. But only if you ring the doorbell. My screen is looking like hell and you really don't know what I might be getting up to during all hours of the night."

Vincent didn't *know*, but he was pretty sure he could *imagine* some of those things. Had been imagining them. Was imagining them now, picturing himself slipping into the room to find Wes with his head tipped back and his hands moving in time to the same kinds of gentle sounds he made when bitten, and… oh dear god, Vincent really had to stop thinking like this. He was fairly sure now that Wesley had been that obnoxious eight-year-old who wouldn't stop blaring Disney music off his mom's iPod as he scootered down their street, and he was definitely a very real person currently sitting across the bed from Vincent, staring at him like he might be able to see into Vincent's brain if he looked hard enough.

Vincent opened his mouth, and his fangs slid out. He closed it again.

"So that's a yes?" Wesley asked, brow raised.

It shouldn't have been. Somehow, Vincent knew that agreeing to come back was just setting himself up for disaster, or at least emotional mayhem. But he did need to feed, and now the person he'd been feeding on more and more over the last month was offering himself up on a silver platter. "Why?"

Wes's gaze slid toward the wall with all his photos. "I've always kind of wanted to do this."

It matched with everything Vincent could piece together about him, and it sounded genuine. That the man was only inviting him back for kicks felt a little disheartening, but Vincent couldn't actually say no to an opportunity like this. The word wouldn't physically come out of his mouth even if he wanted it to. He nodded. "Yeah, I'll be here. At the front door, I mean."

Wesley's lips parted, his smile a crooked, cocky thing that reminded Vincent of movie stars and adventure heroes. "Then we're on. See you at eight tomorrow?"

"I have a job then." Half a job, really, and possibly illegal. Vincent hadn't bothered asking. "Thursday?" That was three days away. After the couple days he'd already gone without blood and the incomplete meal he'd just had, he'd need to find someone else to feed on in the meantime, but it was probably better not to come to Wesley so hungry for their first time anyway.

Wes didn't even hesitate. "Thursday, then."

Vincent leaped down from the window, still not quite sure how he had gotten this lucky. This unlucky? Was it a good thing to have your breathlessly handsome, less-than-consensual snack turn around and offer his neck to you while also telling you he'd thought you were a weird, lonely vampire even before you became a weird, lonely vampire?

It had to be, Vincent decided, because otherwise why would his chest feel like it was full of helium and his feet like they could carry him to the moon? He had to keep reminding himself that it was just going to be a few nibbles. Wesley would eventually get bored and learn to lock his windows at night. This wasn't going to change Vincent's life. But it could be nice. It could be nice to talk more with someone who already knew he was a vampire and didn't give him odd looks when he came too close to their personal property. It would *definitely* be nice to have even a few stable blood meals accounted for, so he could focus on putting regular old food into his body and fresh clothes on his back.

This would be good for him.

And that meant he was allowed to be excited.

5

WESLEY

Wesley had found a vampire. A real life, honest to god vampire, who had agreed to return in three nights. Which meant in three nights he was getting into Vitalis-Barron. In three nights, his mother's death would be confirmed, then avenged. If he could just distract himself enough to keep from falling apart until then.

Vincent was, unfortunately, a distraction all on his own.

Half of Wes's brain kept replaying the way the vampire's hair had fluffed as he jumped out the window, dark jacket fluttering and ice-blue eyes meeting Wes's one last time. Wes shook his head. Vincent wasn't *that* cute, and no amount of enigmatic charm could make up for the fact that he'd been breaking into Wes's room, violating his private space and taking from his body without his consent.

It didn't matter that he was the shy, awkward kid Wes had briefly been acquainted with in elementary, or that he seemed no less shy or awkward as an adult. Whether he acted like a monster or not, he had done something monstrous. Vincent didn't seem like the serial assault type, but looks could fool. Wes knew that well enough; he'd just used his charm and enthusiasm on the vampire in order to cover up his real intentions. He felt no worse about that than he did for all the charismatic lies he'd given the Vitalis-Barron interviewers.

He still felt a lot of other things though, his nerves shivering with the memory of Vincent's tongue and the intrusive bliss it had forced upon him. The vampire had to be inflicting him with some kind of inhumane thrall. That was the only thing that could explain why, after cleaning himself up and climbing back in bed, Wes kept slipping into dreams that were half memory, half desire. He bolted upright more than once, slapping the light back on to find his room empty, window shut tight, the phantom breath on his neck only his imagination. His skin tingled where the dream vampire had pinned him down, one knee pressed to his inner thigh and fangs shining despite the dark of the night. They had looked like Vincent's fangs, had felt like Vincent's as they drew gently across his skin. He'd squirmed in the dream, but he hadn't fought it.

Because it had been a dream, after all. It wasn't even the weirdest adrenaline rush, almost wet dream he'd ever had. That was what dreams were for—getting you horny in circumstances that made your waking self reevaluate your sanity.

Not that he would ever tell that to a therapist, despite being pretty sure it was what they were for. Who knew what kind of clauses they had for a patient planning to turn the vampire giving him weird wet dreams over to the pharmaceutical company who probably killed his mother. Maybe they would applaud him. One less home-invading assaulter out there, terrorizing society.

One less Vincent Barnes sneaking into Wesley's bedroom.

❧

LordOfTheWin

Dude the vampire was REAL call me asap.

KendallCanoodles

Did you just wake up?

LordOfTheWin

I told you a vampire has literally been biting me at night and you want to know about my circadian rhythm?

KendallCanoodles

I'm trying to decide where to put you on my revised friends list.

Somewhere between a friend who'd tell me a vamp was sucking him right after it happened and a friend who'd wait to tell me a vamp was sucking him until the next afternoon?

Also I know that if anything bad had happened your text would've had an entirely different tone.

LordOfTheWin

Alright yes, I went to sleep but I knew if I messaged last night you'd be in a state of sheer unadulterated anticipation for the entire day until I woke up.

I am a very good friend thank you so much.

Also, for the record, "a vamp was sucking him" could be interpreted exactly the wrong way.

KendallCanoodles

Or exactly the right way ;)

KendallCanoodles

But yeah okay I forgive you. Leaving the office at 330 today, call me then.

KendallCanoodles

I demand the juiciest sucking details ;))))

KendallCanoodles

And I mean all the sucking ;)))))))))

~✦~

"Wait, I lost track," Kendall said, her voice a little choppy from her hands-free system. "Is this vampire helping you with the pharma job or with your lack of a partner?"

Wes snorted, shoving his own cell on speaker as he booted up his console. "Were you even listening?"

"Oh, I was listening. That's the problem."

"Fuck you, sincerely."

"I love you too, Wes." The line went quiet for a moment, just the soft click of a blinker. "Really though, dude, he sounds cute, and you sound interested."

"Interested in using him to get me this recruitment job!" Wes tucked one leg beneath him and kicked his other over the couch armrest, scrolling mindlessly through his downloaded games. "You should be happy for me. You're the one who's been pushing me to apply." Not that he would be keeping the job for long, because he didn't intend for there to be a functional Vitalis-Barron left once he revealed the depths of their depravity, but what was the point of emotionally manipulating your best friend if you didn't also lie a little?

"I am glad! You've just talked more about this vampire than you have about the job you're saying you'll use him to get to, and that sounds kind of suspicious to me."

Wes could tell her. He could still tell her everything, or at least the very little everything there was to tell. But his mother's death felt like it belonged solely inside his chest right now. It had grown so large there, shaped into something pointed and a little nasty, and he didn't want to drag her into that, not until he'd speared it through the heart of the people who'd let his mother die.

"Wes? You there?"

"Yeah. I'm here." He clicked away from his downloaded games, browsing through the newer releases just to give himself something to do that didn't involve having an angry breakdown he couldn't tell Kendall about. "Maybe it'll all be a bust. The vamp might not even come back."

"I think he will," Kendall replied. "Who can pass you up, Wesley? You're highly biteable."

"Very funny." He hovered over a new multi-route RPG, tapping his finger to the side of his controller. Night Of Blood: date, kill, or feed? Judging by the previews it seemed to have some kind of romance aspect

41

mixed in with a murder mystery component, including playable and datable vampire options.

Wes hit buy.

6

Vincent

Vincent stopped beneath the overhang of Wesley's house, tugging at the frays on his fingerless gloves. Light streamed between the curtains of the large living room window to his right, spilling slivers of orange onto the flowering bush below it. He used the tip of his toe to nudge aside an overlong branch that had begun creeping onto the walkway. The duct tape under his sole caught on the tops of the little decorative tiles that flanked the cement. He shoved it back into place with a hop, nearly falling into the potted cacti beneath the wall-mounted mailbox.

He just had to get it over with. The longer he stood there, the more his nerves flared every which way and his rather empty stomach churned in a flurry of butterflies. He should not have been this damn anxious; he knew what would be behind this door.

Get in, feed, get out. Nothing had changed. Vincent was just here for blood, and Wesley for the curiosity or the rush or the story—for another beaming picture to hang on his collage of wild memories—and that would be that.

Vincent lifted his finger to the doorbell. And held it in mid-air. He swallowed.

Get in, feed, get out. That was all he had to do. That, and not focus too much on the bob of Wesley's curls or the curve of his neck or the way his smile could fill the very edges of his face. Oh god.

Vincent pressed the doorbell. It chimed a quaint jingle. From inside the house rang a curse, then a shout.

"Coming!"

Vincent shifted between his feet. He could still leave. Break into some random victim's bedroom like he had the last two nights. Be satisfied with bland blood from complete strangers and hope they all slept through it. He could still—

But then the door swung open. Wesley leaned against it, just as delicious as ever, an arm propped distractingly over his head and a grin on his face that seemed to light up the darkness. A set of teal and gold beads was wrapped ten or twelve times up one of his wrists, accentuating his strong fingers. His loose t-shirt was just a little lopsided over his shoulders and his tight pants sculpted his thighs in ways that made Vincent have to deliberately stop himself from staring. The man swept his gaze over Vincent, and his expression stiffened a little, the smile growing slightly forced.

Vincent adjusted his jacket, trying to ignore the way that tiny shift rattled him. He'd changed his shirt to his spare, even though it was a little warm for the season and the hole under one shoulder had grown so large that his armpit hair was poking through it. Maybe he should have stuck with the original. "Hi."

"Hey!" Wesley launched off the door, waving him into the house. "You're early, I was just eating. I guess that's perfect timing?"

"Only if you want to risk fainting into your food." It was a joke, technically, and after a moment's hesitation, Wes seemed to take it as such.

"Ha! Well, then, I should probably finish eating *before* you eat me."

Vincent looked at the doorstep, then back at Wesley's retreating form. For once he was being invited inside, so why did this feel harder than breaking and entering?

"Vinny?" Wesley leaned around the wall of the kitchen, head cocked and brows raised. He looked like he was debating whether to return for Vincent's coat like some old-time butler. Based on the neighborhood's average income, Vincent was fairly certain he would be the first butler ever to work in a five-mile radius.

"Coming." Vincent slipped inside and closed the door behind him.

The house smelled of Wesley. It was faint and a little tangier than the musk Wes gave off directly, but it seemed ingrained in the space, like a bakery after hours of cooking or a greenhouse in full bloom. Warm and dark and sweet, it was such a contrast to Wesley's personal jubilance, and somehow just right for him, too.

The scent made it even odder how instantly familiar the house's floorplan was, the living room to Vincent's right a mirrored image of his childhood one. Wesley's stairs on the left were wood where Vincent's had been carpet and the first-floor bedroom beside it was closed up where his had always been kept open, his parents hoping it would get him to come out more, be a real part of the family for once.

As if that had ever turned out well for them when he actually made the effort.

The similarities between their houses ended there. More than merely smelling of Wesley, his home had a life of its own that far outshone Vincent's old, sterile family dwelling. Here the laundry lay folded sloppily on the blue recliner and every inch of shelf space held clusters of adorable, animated figurines or fantasy statuary. A few spaceship models had been mixed in, as well as a crucifix, though the nearby dangling rosary made Vincent suspect it had nothing to do with outdated vampire superstitions. Both seemed a bit dusty. The main couch faced away from the foyer, and photos of scenic ruins and elegant cathedrals had been pinned to the back of it around a weathered map. A sock stood like a hat on the banister's end post.

As Vincent crossed the foyer, one of the wooden floor panels creaked under his foot. He scooted away from it, wrapping his arms around himself. It stopped complaining the moment he left.

He slipped through the living room, absentmindedly counting the brightly colored array of controllers that littered the coffee table and sat beneath the giant, primary television monitor. One of them had been stickered with Pride rainbows. Vincent felt himself relax, just a little. He'd seen the rainbow flags in Wesley's room already, but the extra confirmation was always nice. There was at least one part of who Vincent was that Wes wouldn't be judging.

The carpet gave way to tile as the room turned hastily into a small dining area beside the walled-off kitchen. Papers and a few more potted plants had been stacked on the side of the wooden table, a giant doily spread under them like half a tablecloth. *Fuck everything, drink tea* had been embroidered sloppily along the edge.

Vincent loved it.

As he turned toward the kitchen, his attention caught on the sliding glass doors to the backyard. They reflected his hazy image where darkness swept down the hill beyond Wes's fence, before it finally turned into residential neighborhoods once more, but Vincent knew the landscape there by heart, from the rows of tombstones to the three stony mausoleums at the far edge to the little broken church where local teens came to vape and make out.

Such a different home from this one.

"You can sit if you want," Wes interrupted his thoughts. He leaned against the counter, trying to hold a bowl in the crook of one arm while pinning a ramen package with the other and opening one of its spice packets with his teeth.

"Here," Vincent said, stepping in to take the bowl.

Wes lifted a brow.

Vincent gave the bowl a sheepish look and set it on the counter beside the rest of Wesley's meal, which seemed to consist of the combined remains of three different bags of chips, the last brownie in a plastic grocery-store container, and something that might have been a salad beneath all the ranch dressing and croutons. His stomach rumbled.

"Is that how much you want to bite me?" Wesley joked.

The question went right to some primal part of Vincent, catching him deep in the back of his throat and tempting his fangs to slip out unbidden. He tried to ignore the ache that came with it. Maybe he had been right. Maybe this was too much.

Wesley seemed not to notice. "Oh, shit, vampires eat people food too, right?"

People food, not human food. Vincent's jaw hurt from clenching. "We're people, so yes?" It shouldn't have been a question, but the whole world made him feel like it was, as though he was suddenly *less than* just for having needs that others didn't. He cleared his throat. "Yeah we eat food."

That seemed to give Wesley a kind of uncomfortable, deliberating pause. Finally he smiled, only half as bright as before, but his words came a little softer, a little weightier. "Sorry, yeah. If you're hungry, I can get you something."

Vincent's anger melted back into a lump in his throat. "No, no I couldn't. That would be…" Rude? But he couldn't possibly get much ruder than creeping into someone's house to steal their blood. Multiple times. And then telling them you'd done so. Multiple times. And coming back when they offered seconds.

Get in, feed, get out, he reminded himself.

But already his body was leaning toward the front door, like the awkwardness of the whole situation might siphon him out of it entirely.

An emotion almost like panic crossed Wesley's face, but it was gone so fast it seemed a mirage. His shoulders bobbed, collarbones shifting beneath his t-shirt. "Yeah you probably don't want these noodles anyway, they're spicy as hell. I usually save half the red packet and put it in something else." His gaze bored into Vincent like he was drilling into Vincent's soul. "Unless you're up for a challenge?"

Vincent felt as though he was being set up, as though maybe this was *all* just a set up. But the way Wesley's lips twitched, his eyes narrowing and his neck bared as he turned his head to one side, standing here in this place that looked and smelled so gloriously of him, returned all the warmth and want that had urged Vincent back to this house in the first place. He was caving, he knew, the same way he'd caved to his cravings for Wesley's blood. The same way he was pretty sure if Wesley offered up another taste of himself, he'd cave to anything the man asked of him from here on out.

"I propose a wager." Wes tipped forward, just a little, his brows lifting deviously. "I bet that I can eat more spicy-as-hell ramen than you."

Vincent choked on a laugh. A spicy noodle-eating contest was not anywhere on his list of things he wanted to do with Wesley Smith Garcia. But the way Wes's eyebrows tugged together, his lips, a little fuller and rounder than Vincent's, puckering enough that Vincent swore his heart made a literal sound in his chest as it waved to his dick, he absolutely couldn't say no. He couldn't say yes yet either. "What are we betting? I don't—I didn't bring any cash."

"Cash is for cheapskates anyway. Let's say…" Wes shrugged. "Let's say that whoever wins gets to decide what we do after dinner?"

Vincent blinked, trying to dislodge the vision of all the things he could ask Wesley to do—*I want you to let me grip your hair as I suck on your neck, I want you to fight me just a little so your body presses into mine, I want you to run your hands over your skin and tug at your clothing and see how long I can hold myself back from biting you*—all things that had dwelt in his dreams the last few days, but which he would never, ever speak aloud as long as he lived. But he couldn't help the way his voice turned softer, almost broken. "Are there rules?"

"No rules." Wesley's throat bobbed, and he stared in a way that made Vincent feel like there was a fire hidden beneath the look. Then it vanished, the excitable neighborly Wesley returning so fast that Vincent swore the heat he'd seen had just been his imagination playing dirty tricks on him. Dirty, enticing tricks. "It's not legally binding or anything," Wes continued. "But if I win, I get to make you feel like you're a cowardly ass for at least a week if you don't agree to whatever I ask."

Whatever he asked. Vincent had to blink that back too. It came with another series of fantasies that Vincent could easily imagine this larger-than-life, up-for-anything Wesley uttering: *put your mouth here, say it like that, harder—*

Vincent coughed, forcing his gaze away from Wes and onto the dressing-flooded salad, then nope, somehow that was also too much imagery, and he shifted his attention all the way to his own haunting reflection in the darkened window. God, did he really look like that? So ragged and panicked. He had to get a hold of himself. Breathe. Think. Feed, and… well, not get out, not right away. The idea was as enticing as it was terrifying.

"Nothing dangerous for vampires, alright?" he asked.

"Dude, I just invited you into my house to drink my blood. If anyone is in danger here, it's me."

Vincent tried not to cringe. The idea that vampires were inherently more dangerous than humans just because they were stronger and faster and had fangs that could pass on their affliction was so rampant, even among humans like Wesley—humans who believed vampires deserved equal rights, or at least compassionate treatment—that the joke stung. "That doesn't prove you aren't a serial killer. Or a fetishist."

Wesley blanched a little. Definitely no fire there, then. Or perhaps he *was* secretly a vampire serial killer; Vincent was sure some of them were charming and good-looking and extraordinarily enthusiastic about their victims. They were also noticeably less likely to get caught or imprisoned. Murdering a vampire was technically still murder, at least in most states, but it was also far more commonly excused as self-defense, or the god-awful justification of *I panicked when I realized what they were*, like that hadn't also been used as a defense for the biased killings of fully human people in the past.

Still, Vincent didn't think he had to worry about that level of bigotry from Wesley.

He cringed as a thought hit him. "It can't be anything that would reveal I'm a vampire to the rest of the neighborhood, either." It was hard enough getting jobs as a pale, dirty pretend-human who refused to work during the day; he didn't need the sympathetic people who took pity on him to suddenly cave to the great opinions of society if he could no longer deny what he was. "You haven't told anyone else about me, right?"

"Absolutely not!" Wes grimaced. "Well, yes, I talked to my friend Kendall a bit, but she lives three hundred miles away and there's a twenty-three percent chance that she thinks I'm making the whole thing up."

This was such a terrible idea.

"Come on. It'll be fun." Wesley smiled, and he reached for Vincent, slowly, his palm flat like an offering.

Vincent let him, let Wesley pat his grungy jacket and squeeze his shoulder gently. He felt like putty inside. A half-melted chocolate puddle, transfixed by a single tender touch. It shamed him and burned like tears behind his eyes. This was, definitely, such a terrible idea. But he needed it, so desperately. "Fine." He didn't mean for it to sound like a growl, but that's how it came out, soft and drawn. "Hit me with your spiciest noodles."

7

Wes tried not to stumble over his own feet as he fled deeper into the kitchen. This had all been going so well; he'd lured Vincent inside, stopped him from running immediately back out, and had the brilliant idea to suggest this wager, which upon his win, he'd ask the vampire to come to Vitalis-Barron with him under the premise of a prank. Except then Vincent had called him a fetishist, and his voice had gone husky and breathless, and for some damned reason Wesley's body had decided the best response was to touch the vampire's shoulder. Wes was pretty sure those things hadn't happened in that order but at this point all he could quite remember was the weird chest-fluttering lightheadedness that had come over him, tightening his lungs and drawing up every unhelpful memory of Vincent's bite.

The vampire definitely had some kind of thrall over him. That was it. That was definitely also why this house-invader and serial assaulter seemed like a genuinely sweet and shy person. It didn't matter how Vincent appeared from the outside, his nightly actions were far worse than anything Wesley was doing. And turning him over to the mega pharmaceutical company currently killing its research patients was the first step in taking down that company and stopping those deaths.

A step that started with spicy ramen.

Wesley threw open the nearest cupboard door—not even the one he needed—just to put a shield between his face and Vincent. He shifted his mother's ancient collection of traveling mugs like there might be noodles hidden behind one of them, buying himself a few more moments to calm down. Except that Vincent, the same Vincent who had previously looked like he was one bad startle from flying out the door, somehow decided that was the perfect moment to creep up behind him.

"Oh," he said, his breath a hair too close to Wesley's neck for Wes to maintain any peace of mind. "That's a lot of travel mugs."

"Family tradition!" Wes grabbed two at random and darted around Vincent to set them on the counter. One had a fancy lattice of gilded vines on it, and the other displayed the worn-out image of a popular animated warrior-princess.

Vincent's left brow lifted ever so slightly at the sight of them. "You have a family tradition of eating ramen in travel mugs?"

"Only when it's extra spicy ramen," Wes bullshitted like his life depended on it and not just his sense of dignity and his fraying sexuality and ability to fuck over an evil pharmaceutical company. He flicked the kettle back on and dug through the cupboard—the right one this time—for another ramen packet. Their wrappers seemed extra-defiant tonight, and the squares of noodles wouldn't fit in the travel mugs until he snapped them in half with his fists.

He decided that struggling with the spice packets was too much catastrophe for one day and began opening them with the scissors when Vincent butted in.

"Do either of those have garlic in them?"

Wes froze. "You're serious?"

"I have an allergy." The center of Vincent's cheeks tinted red. It made him look… well, Wes didn't want to consider that. All the ways that Vincent could potentially flush had nothing to do with Wes. Unless one of them would get the vampire to come to Vitalis-Barron with him.

"Alright then, no garlic for Vinny the Vampire." He tugged the ramen wrapper back out of the trash and fingered down its ingredient list. "Garlic powder. It doesn't say which packet. No problem, we'll make our own hotness."

"We'll what?"

"Hotness." Wesley grinned. He flung himself full force into gutting the kitchen, forming an array of hot sauce and extra spicy salsa along the counter in various shades of red and green and brown. A final bottle peeked out from the shelf above the fridge, but Wes could barely tap it with his fingertips. He popped onto the nearest counter and reached across. Somehow Vincent ended up below him, his hand wrapping the bottle's base beneath Wesley's. As their skin brushed, Wes shivered.

He yanked back in a fluster. His foot slipped off the edge of the counter. For an instant, he thought he might be able to steady himself, hovering in the space between gravity and youthful immortality, but the world came crashing back in, and his body weight with it. As he fell, Vincent seemed to teleport, arm reaching above the fridge one moment, then scooping under Wes the next. He settled Wes onto the ground equally fast, leaving him swaying there with his heart pounding a thousand miles a minute.

Wes clutched the counter to steady himself. It was just the rush of the fall. Not the momentary feeling of Vincent's arms, the physical presence of him pressing into Wesley's space, his little sound of distress as Wes's mass settled onto him, before he'd immediately let go. Wes forced himself to smile, like getting gracefully caught by vampires was perfectly ordinary for him. "Nice save."

Vincent's gaze snapped to his neck, then moved down his chest. His throat bobbed. It seemed to be doing that a lot. "Thanks."

Wes accepted the hot sauce bottle from Vincent's without touching the vampire, and quickly motioned to the accumulation on the counter. "Help me check those for garlic?"

As Vincent sorted through the bottles, putting half to one side and half to the other, Wes continued scooting around the kitchen. He poured the water onto the ramen and shoveled down bites of salad, avoiding looking at Vincent as much as possible. One at a time, he helped the vampire dose both noodle-filled travel mugs with a fairly equal amount of every permitted hot substance.

He popped the final brownie out of its container and broke it, handing one half to Vincent. "Might as well eat it now while we can actually taste it."

Vincent nibbled on it experimentally. A little noise left him, more a hum than a moan, but it sounded just enough like something from Wesley's dreams to make him feel light and wrong all over again. This was not okay. He needed to be sane of mind and focused on taking down Vitalis-Barron, not *feeling things* about the very vampire who had been sneaking into his room to feed on him for weeks. Searching for the first possible distraction, he snatched a bottle out of the hot sauce line up at random and slathered his own brownie in it before shoveling the thing in his mouth in one go. The instant burn shot his senses back into place, but they couldn't quite overtake the memory of Vincent's little flash of restrained bliss.

And now the vampire was looking at him like he'd lost his mind.

"Never ever claim that the Smith Garcia household doesn't like it spicy," Wesley wheezed, trying not to cough.

Something unreadable broke over Vincent's face, a shambled mixture of pinched and flushed choking. It turned into a laugh as Vincent pressed his fist to his mouth and leaned against the kitchen wall. He looked somewhere off to the right as he muttered, "Yeah. Yeah you do."

For lack of anything intelligible to say through his sudden rush of brain mush, Wes cleared his throat. "Noodles?"

Vincent nodded. His expression returned to the distant and mildly panicked one he'd worn all night, but that moment of—of what? Joy?—clung to Wes's thoughts like a leech. Now he couldn't seem to stop staring at Vincent. This was bad. Shy kid Vincent was one thing, and weirdly enticing vampire Vincent was another, but this Vincent was both of those while also being easy to joke with and casually sweet.

And Wesley had to turn him in to Vitalis-Barron. However well they got along now, that was still the plan. That would keep being the plan, even if Wesley couldn't take his eyes off the vampire as he deliberated over the travel mugs, his lips a little pinched and his expression thoughtful. He chose the one with the warrior-princess cartoon.

"Astril was always my favorite team member, but Bellony had more fan merchandise, so she would do in a pinch," Vincent said, tapping the faded picture.

Wes's chest tugged itself into a knot. "Yeah, my mom used to say that, too."

Vincent opened his mouth and closed it again. He glanced toward the hall out of the kitchen, the one that wrapped back toward the stairs. "I remember your mom because she would bring us sopes on Labor Day. Or Memorial Day? One of those Monday holidays. She didn't even know us, but she did it."

Wesley gave a little laugh, small and wet. "She always loved shoving food at people. She was just like that."

Vincent nodded. He lifted his noodle mug like a toast. "Bottoms up?"

The return to topics unrelated to his mother should have released some of the tension building in Wes, but it still felt like a blister in his gut. He just had to keep pressing forward. Not think about her too hard. Not think about Vitalis-Barron either, not until he was at their doorstep tearing them down. So he grinned, lifting his own ramen. "On my count. Three. Two. One."

Around the third rushed bite Wesley Smith Garcia realized he had made a mistake: a very big, very spicy mistake that was currently burning its way through the roof of his mouth and turning his lips numb and forming a debilitating lump in his throat. He tried and failed not to cough on the lump, and that only shot the spiciness straight up the back of his nose. His eyes burned. He was fairly certain that holes were being scorched through his skull and into his brain, his vision peppering with black spots. His knees went weak.

He slammed his mug onto the counter and barreled for the fridge. The milk carton almost slipped from his grasp three times in a row before he managed to twist off the lid. He took a long swig directly from the carton and poured a little across the lower half of his face for good measure. His world went from inside-an-active-volcano level hot to merely smoldering, and his vision cleared, his breathing almost evening out. One hand still on the fridge to prop himself up, he turned his attention back to Vincent. He could let him take a single bite, then reassure him that the ramen wasn't worth the torment, and he was better off letting Wesley claim the victory by default.

But there was the vampire, mug tipped over his mouth as he drank the last of his hot sauce broth. He lowered it, panting in great sharp breaths, his cheeks bright red and his eyes wild. They barely seemed to focus on Wesley, locking and then slipping away and then locking again. "Did I... win?" he huffed.

"Fuck," was all Wes could say to that. He held out the milk.

Vincent took it gingerly, pouring a little into his mouth at a time as he slipped slowly down the wall.

"Fuck," Wes said again. If vampires burned up during the day, what if they burned up from hot sauce too? What if he'd just murdered Vincent Barnes. Murdered the vampire who might get him the truth about his mother's death. "Dude, are you okay?"

"Think so," Vincent wheezed. "Just—" He paused, guzzling more of the milk. "Need a minute."

Wesley slumped onto the ground across from him. His own mouth was still a raging inferno, but he couldn't bear to ask for the milk back. As Vincent seemed to shift through various stages of undeath, his legs loosened from where they tucked against his chest, slowly splaying between Wesley's. One of his feet tapped

Wesley's as it waggled back and forth. Duct tape crisscrossed the bottom.

Wesley's brow furrowed. That was taking the whole dumpster grunge to an unusual level, but to each his own, he figured. It wasn't his concern. He shouldn't have been concerned about this vampire who'd broken into his house to drink his blood in the first place. Except when he phrased it like that, his brain flashed up what it might be like for a vampire to consensually slip into his room and wake him with tiny nibbles as they tenderly pinned him down, their fingers tight in his hair, maybe their other hand slipping between his thighs—

Fuck, that was enough already. He couldn't bear any more hot sauce brain resetting.

Vincent hummed softly to himself and continued sipping at the milk. If he had looked a bit wrecked earlier, he was absolutely dismantled now, his hair unkempt, cheeks still brightly flushed, his usually thin lips a little swollen and puckered, as though he'd just come out of a rather long make-out session. Wesley detoured away from that train of thought before he could let it spiral and tried to focus on how they'd gotten to this point at all.

"Oh god." Wes popped back up. "I went to this little town in the mountains last year where one of those boutique hot sauce shops sold me what they claimed was the world's spiciest sauce. I stashed it in the cupboard when I came back for winter break and then forgot about it." Because his mother had vanished and never returned, and he'd had to throw her a funeral without knowing why. Without being able to prove why. He fumbled through the hot sauces, finding the little bottle sitting carelessly beside the others. "We used half of it."

"Fuck you." Vincent tipped his head back, his eyes numbly roaming the ceiling, but his lips were fixed in an almost goofy smile that made all of this kind of worth it.

Except Vincent had won.

Wes had been meant to win. This was going to be his way of getting Vincent to Vitalis-Barron and instead here was Vincent, half dazed on his floor and having earned himself control of a momentary piece of Wesley's life. He could do anything with that—and he was a vampire.

What would a vampire want from Wesley? His skin tingled at the thought. To chase him through the house before he bit him? To pin him on his stomach, helpless, neck crested to one side? To drain him until his vision blurred and he couldn't struggle anymore? Hopefully not that; it made him feel a little faint and the wrong kind of tense. Not that he was counting the others as the right kind of tense, even if they did put an exhilarating flutter in his stomach.

Vincent finished off the milk and dragged his feet back under him. He swayed, his nose pinching. His gaze jumped to Wesley's nearly full bowl of ramen on the counter. "Well, I guess I'm the hot ramen champion then."

"No contest." Wes stood, opening the trash compartment to shove the empty milk container into the recycling, packing it down when it tried to pop back up.

"I get to bite you still, right? That doesn't have to be my after-dinner choice, because you already agreed to it?"

Wes groaned. He considered trying to worm his way out of all he now owed Vincent, but he couldn't risk breaking the vampire's trust. And he maybe, kind of, almost wanted to be bitten. "No, you're right, that's only fair. You can bite me and one other thing."

"One other thing?" Vincent sounded almost loopy. The way he looked at Wesley for just a moment, Wes felt like a kind of prey.

A very good kind of prey. Wes's heart skipped over the rush of adrenaline that came with it, but he absolutely did not need that adrenaline, not when there were a hundred other ways to acquire it that didn't involve telling a vampire that the vampire could do *one other thing* to him. Oh god, he'd said that, hadn't he. No wonder Vincent was licking the edge of his puffy, reddened lips. "You can bite me," Wesley clarified, "and you can also pick whatever else you want us to do tonight. You know, hobbies, games, whatever."

None of which was going to include Vitalis-Barron.

Wesley's chest revolted at the letdown, but the only way to deal with that emotion was the same way he'd been dealing with everything else: full steam ahead, preferably while focused on at least three different non-Vitalis-Barron things at once.

"Got it," Vincent said.

Wes swore the vampire looked disappointed. He shivered, the feeling a lot less unpleasant than it should have been. "Why don't we…?" He trailed off, not sure where he'd intended the sentence to go.

Vincent, shy and awkward Vincent, picked it up easily, with something almost like a smile. "Let's go to the couch? I've only ever done this sitting down."

It sounded almost teasing. Who knew eating the world's spiciest ramen was such a vampiric confidence booster?

Wes shoved his thumbs into the loop of his jeans and shrugged, leading the way toward the living room. If Vincent could hear the pace of his heart right now… he didn't want to think about that. Or about the way his stupid, useless brain kept bringing up their last bite and how wonderful Vincent's mouth had felt on his neck. How this was going to be like that, except longer, and fully awake, and with Vincent sitting beside him. Or possibly straddling him. Oh fuck, there could be complications with straddling if this took too long, where too long meant almost any time at all with how his dick had decided it also wanted to be spicy today.

Wesley tried to avoid that option by lounging in his usual manner, one leg tucked crookedly under him and the other knee up as he propped his foot on the couch's armrest. It had a dip in it now. Maybe he should stop doing that so much.

Vincent eyed the couch and sat down like he was prepared for it to either dump him out or possibly turn him into a gamer. He tugged at his jacket, then pulled it off entirely.

Wesley watched him.

"Sorry," he muttered, pushing the hair out of his eyes and pulling a pillow into his lap. "I'm not used to being, you know, seen during this."

"Performance anxiety?"

Vincent's lips bunched. He kneaded his pillow with both hands.

"It's alright, I don't judge. I mean, you're the only vamp who's ever bitten me, so I don't really have expectations here. Am I just making this worse? I'm just making this worse. Shutting up now."

Vincent drew in a breath like he was preparing for war, and Wesley had to remind himself that this vampire drank blood from people on a regular basis without killing or turning them. He assumed. Maybe he should have clarified first.

But Vincent was already scooting until his thigh pressed against Wesley's. He leaned a little crookedly toward Wesley's neck, still gripping the pillow in one hand and the back of the couch in the other. Wes had just enough time to feel slighted that Vincent hadn't grabbed onto him instead, when Vincent's fangs pricked into his skin.

His neck erupted into burning.

His body instinctively jerked away from Vincent as he tumbled onto the floor. This time, he managed to press a hand to the wound before it began oozing. He gritted his teeth, the searing pain slowly fading.

Vincent stared at him in horror. "I'm so sorry—I've never—it normally doesn't—fuck," he stammered.

Laughter bubbled through Wesley, completely at odds with the stinging, each rack of his body making a little blood seep between his fingers when they slipped off the bite wound. But he couldn't help it. He'd been dreaming about this, yearning for it despite how often he told himself that desire was ridiculous, and this was what he got: pain in place of pleasure. And it was, technically, all his own damn fault.

Vincent's cheeks turned red against his pale face. "You're still bleeding. Do you need me to… to…"

Wesley kept laughing silently, his chest trembling and his head tipping backwards on the carpet. "Don't you dare touch me with that extra-hot mouth of yours!"

"My—" Vincent's blush doubled. And then he groaned, dropping his head into his hands. "The hot sauce."

"It still stings."

"I'm so sorry."

Wesley managed to pull himself together enough to sit up, his abs protesting as he kept accidently bursting back into a fresh round of chuckling. "You want a toothbrush or something? Maybe that would help?"

"I just drank more milk than is humanly possible. I don't think a rub of minty freshness will fix this." Vincent cringed. "I really am sorry."

Wesley waved him off with a hand flap and a grin. "It happens, dude, you're cool."

"Actually, it seems I'm hot." The very corner of Vincent's mouth quirked, and he bit the lip on that side, his exposed fang tucking into the still lightly swollen flesh. "You know, from the hot sauce."

Wesley's body protested that statement with a pinch in his gut and a rush in his head. Vincent was hot.

Oh god.

Vincent *was* hot.

It was a slightly off-brand hotness, with an odd mixture of dainty and rugged, a little tired around the eyes and unkempt in the hair, but beneath all that grunge, Wes swore there was something to Vincent that drew in the eye the more time you spent with him and turned the little subtle motions of his lips into something delicious. And those lips had just been on Wesley's neck, if only for a moment. That was it, that was still the cause of this nonsense. It was all rooted in the weirdly fantastic sensation of that first bloodsucking, now just mixing up his other feelings for Vincent. Other feelings, like how determined he was to get to the bottom of his mother's murder and how Vincent was nothing more than a means to that end. Even if he happened to be hot.

Vincent's brows tugged together and his distracting smile faded. "You're still bleeding a little." He stood, pillow clutched in his hands. He shuffled it between them once before seeming to realize he didn't need it and dropped it back onto the couch. "Do you have bandages?"

Wesley pulled his hand away from his neck to check and—yeah, definitely still bleeding, slow but steady. As he watched, a thin trickle pooled into the collar of his t-shirt. So much for keeping this one clean. "Downstairs bathroom, under the sink."

"Right." Vincent hopped over the back of the couch like it was nothing and headed across the foyer. He floundered for a moment around the room's eternally creaky floor panel before stepping over it entirely.

Wes's head spun just a little as he tried to follow, and he plopped himself back down on the couch. He patted at the wound to check it again. Somehow it was oozing more now. "Am I supposed to feel faint?"

"You're not bleeding that much." Vincent called from the bathroom. "But the fact that you've stopped applying pressure every ten seconds can't help."

Wes glared across the hall at its open door, the vampire moving around behind it. "How do you know I'm doing that?"

"I can smell your blood stronger every time you shift your hand. It's kind of frustrating actually. You should stop."

There was a hint of something desperate in Vincent's voice, and it shivered its way through Wesley. He pressed his fingers firmly to the wound just to spite the part of him that wanted to see what Vincent would do if he didn't. And because the more his head spun the worse he felt. "If you were drinking this blood, would I still be so lightheaded?"

"No, because as I said, your body's just being a dramatic goofball over the concept of it. You have plenty of blood still." Vincent sped back from the bathroom, a little blur that vaulted the back of the couch and settled at Wesley's side. The floor didn't creak at all this time. He opened the box of bandages, sifting through them as he explained, "Even if I did feed enough for that, it feels more like the kind of faint you might get while happily drunk or high. Except instead of drugs or alcohol, it's the venom in my fangs that takes away all the panic your brain is supposed to associate with it. It makes it feel nice, almost. Soft and cozy."

"How do you know? I thought you only snacked on people in their sleep?"

"It's not like I never got bit before I turned." Vincent carefully tore three little packages of gauze open, his eyes firmly fixed on his own fingers.

"Oh." It hit Wes a little more squarely then: this vampire who came sneaking into people's homes and stealing their blood hadn't merely been the human kid who lived in a house down the street once, but had matured into an adult like that, too, entirely human one day and then a vampire the next. Where in that timeline had he grown comfortable with assaulting people while they slept? What drove such a drastic shift to become something so monstrous? Wesley almost wanted to ask, but he knew the answer didn't matter. Vincent had been doing it. That was bad enough. "Wait, go back to the part where you have venom."

"It's not harmful. It's just a substance in my fangs that calms the, uh, the human." Vincent's nose wrinkled. "But it has an intoxicating effect, and it's

73

produced by my body to be injected, so it's still a kind of venom, I guess." He folded the gauze strips.

Wesley reached for them, but Vincent had already leaned in, twisting a bit to look at the side of Wes's neck. He seemed tenser the closer he came, his whole body poised and concentrated. Maybe it was all the blood. If he had been able to smell the difference between Wes holding the wound closed and letting it hemorrhage from all the way in the bathroom, then how much stronger was the scent here, his nose a foot away from where it seeped between Wes's fingers, his mouth so close to Wes's neck? How many times had Vincent's throat bobbed since he'd sat down?

But his focus didn't slip for a moment as he drew back Wesley's fingers, his hand gentle around Wes's blood stained-one, a little rougher and more calloused. He pressed the gauze to the wound, applying pressure as he fiddled free a bandage. His skin was warm where it brushed Wes's neck. Alive.

Wes had known he was. Vampires weren't actually as undead as they looked, with their own slightly darkened blood still flowing through them, and despite the myths of immortality they did still age and eventually die like other people, even if the wrinkles and aching joints never quite caught up with them. But it still felt wrong. Too human. Not that Wesley had anything against vampires in general, it just seemed that they shouldn't be so… so normal. A lump twisted in his gut. He untangled it with an awkward laugh that made Vincent squeak and realign his gauze. "So no garlic and no sunlight. But you don't turn into a bat, right?"

"I wish." Vincent sounded wistful.

Vincent, who had chosen to become a vampire. It didn't matter if he had been less monstrous once and his skin still felt like the skin of a person and the way he patted the bandage into place was more tender than most nurses. He had still chosen a life where he broke into people's homes nightly.

"The blood on your shirt is tormenting me a little. You might want to change it."

"Right, thanks. Kendall's usually the one who tells me to do my laundry. I can't smell for shit so if she didn't throw things at me in college I'd wear the same shirt for weeks." Wes grimaced. "I probably have the scent equivalent of *I'm a tasty meal* painted all over my shoulder again."

Vincent cringed, nodding slightly. "Pretty much."

Wesley gave his bandaged neck an experimental pat, which made Vincent snap his name with a glare. He wiggled his hand at the vampire and stood, carefully stripping off his shirt.

Vincent stared at him. His throat bobbed yet again, before he looked away so suddenly it seemed like he was trying to unsee whatever he'd just taken in.

Wesley glanced down at himself, quickly checking that there was nothing obvious he should have been embarrassed about. All normal. Maybe Vincent was a prude? Wes bunched the shirt in his hands once, then extended it over. "Oh here, do you want it? Because you couldn't feed on me. You're probably still hungry." The nicer he was, the more likely Vincent would come back.

It certainly got the vampire's attention back like a flash. "Are you asking me if I want to suck on your bloody t-shirt?"

Wes made a face. "It does sound gross when you phrase it like that." He pulled the shirt away and crossed to the foyer, instinctively stepping over the creaky spot in the flooring.

Behind him, Vincent shifted, then groaned. "No, wait, I never said I didn't want it!"

Wesley turned back. The vampire had draped himself over the couch, his lip pulled between his teeth and his eyebrows tight and a little pleading. Wes threw him the shirt. He snatched it easily out of the air, his expression agonizingly soft. "Thank you."

And there he was, being hot again. And adorable. With fangs. But those fangs had been in Wesley's neck before he'd given permission. Those fangs were going to trade him the proof he needed to take down Vitalis-Barron. And then, those fangs would be free again, once the pharmaceutical company was swarmed by police and its CEO on trial and its laboratories locked down. Free to keep biting more humans in the dark.

Wes's gaze darted back to Vincent, his mind conjuring all sorts of disastrous things, things like Vitalis-Barron's downfall and a particular vampire breaking into his room to thank him for it. He charged up the stairs before the ridiculous ideas could take over any more of his body.

Vincent

Vincent stared at the bloody shirt, trying to fathom how this awkward situation had happened, not once, but *twice*. Twice, with the same human. It had to be Wesley's fault. Wesley was a nuisance, he decided. A nuisance with delicious blood and a gorgeous body, a thick, sculpted chest with some grabbable looking pudge around his stomach and an adorably wild trail of dark hair creeping up from below his pant-line nearly to his navel. Even his tan-lines were cute.

Which was, all in all, a terrible development and Vincent knew it.

He held Wes's shirt to his mouth and breathed. It smelled just as much like the man whose scent surrounded him, delicious and dark, a little muskier and tangier than the blood itself. In short, it smelled like heaven.

As the urge to feed slowly grew in his gut, Vincent fought back a wave of mortification and let himself bundle the soaked fabric to stick it in his still burning mouth. He sucked. It wasn't anything like drinking from Wesley's neck, but it was still his blood, sweet and thick, and Vincent was ravenous despite the constant, searing throb that seemed to be inflicting him from lips to throat.

If only his parents could see him now.

Vincent had a silent chuckle over their imagined disgust and shifted a new slip of the shirt into his mouth. There was not nearly enough blood here. He'd have to wait until the spiciness settled and find a house to break into. Again.

"You still get to pick something for the night," Wes said, bouncing his way back down the stairs. "Just nothing that involves your mouth, please, I can't ruin any more shirts for you."

Vincent tried not to choke. If Wes would stop saying mildly sexual things at every turn, maybe he could stop picturing Wes doing sexual things just as often. But they seemed to be complete accidents, and Vincent was hesitant to put a stop to them, in part because he didn't want Wesley to feel self-conscious—if that was even a state the man was capable of—and because most of them were absolutely hilarious. And Vincent would be happily rerunning the visions they produced in private.

"What?" Wesley leaned against the back of the couch, looking just as delicious in his clean shirt as he had in the bloodied one, his skin a warm tan and a slight gleam to his full lower lip, like he'd licked it recently. "Did I ruin all your monstrously vampiric plans?"

"Absolutely all of them." He could not believe he was saying this, but somehow the words were coming out of his mouth anyway, spurred on by the shirt he was now wringing between his hands. "Frankly, all my pastimes involve my mouth. I should have my opposable thumb permit taken away."

Wes looked like he was about to say something, then promptly shut up. For the first time since Vincent had broken into his house—possibly for the first time since they'd met, over a decade and a half ago—Wesley looked away before Vincent did, almost flustered, and didn't respond.

That felt wrong. It felt like it was Vincent's job to be shier and smaller and more pathetic. He dropped Wes's shirt and snatched up the nearest of the five visible game controllers. "Actually, opposable thumbs practice would be good for me. For my wager reward, I want to play one of your video games."

That seemed to turn Wesley off and back on again. He blinked. Then his face lit up. "Yeah, dude, of course."

It had been a frantic impulsive decision but now that he was holding the controller, watching Wesley boot up the console, a little flutter of excitement formed in Vincent's chest. He hadn't realized how much he'd missed his own video games from his high school years. He wondered how long it had taken his parents to sell his console, or if they'd just thrown it into a dumpster with all the other things he hadn't been able to fit in his suitcase, tossing him out of their lives the way they'd probably been wanting to for years.

As Vincent flicked along Wesley's games list, pointing out some of his favorites—"Oh shit, did you ever play the old Dragon Eras? Those were the best. They're like my comfort plays now."—Vincent noticed a pattern toward the bottom: a collection of new vampire-related games. There had to be at least ten of them, excluding the first-person team shooter further up that had vampires in its list of general villains along with zombies, terrorists of uncomfortably specific nationality, and incredibly attractive assassins. Not a lot of points for realism.

Popular culture had never been great about accurately representing the vampiric community. A lot of people knew it, or at least admitted it was likely the case when pressed. That didn't stop the ideas the media presented from leaking into the social subconscious. It didn't stop the small subset of loud, angry anti-vampire bigots from feeding off those subconscious ruminations with vapid claims about the inherent danger of a group of people who were, sure, stronger and faster than others, but could also die from a mere half hour of direct sun exposure or a gram too much garlic. Vincent had grown up as a human in this world. Once upon a time he had been used to these sentiments, but even a callus could blister when placed under constant pressure.

He did his best not to sink into that misery—he knew just how trapped he would become if he did—and focused instead on the absurdity of the thing. Wesley Smith Garcia had managed to pack his catalog with over ten different vampire-focused games, most of them role-play heavy, which was more than Vincent had known existed in the mainstream. He tracked back through them with a cackle. "You *are* a fetishist."

Wesley looked a bit like he wanted to die. "I am not! I developed a perfectly healthy interest in vampires after I found out one of them had been biting me in my sleep."

Vincent flushed. The dates of purchase for the first couple he opened did seem to track with that. It gave Vincent an odd mix of feelings: he would rather have not been sexualized for his vampirism, but had Wesley considered that part of him sexually appealing, Vincent certainly wouldn't have said no. By the way the man was subtly scooting away from him, Vincent figured both those scenarios were out of the question. That was fine.

Disappointing, but fine. Understandable. Typical, even.

Vincent had grown accustomed to the idea that without the skill to seek out San Salud's underground vampire community he would never find a partner in his state. A momentary blip of desire for shared intimacy was easy to shove back down. He could quietly want Wesley without the man ever knowing or reciprocating, and they would both survive. Probably.

Vincent stopped scrolling at a virtual dating meets murder-mystery game that promised scantily clad, tragically hot vampires. The *monster-fucking* descriptor made him feel a little nauseous—not even in games where the vampires were meant to be sexy lovers instead of villains to kill were they viewed as anything less than malevolent—but with the logged number of hours played it was too intriguing to pass up. He lifted a brow at Wesley. "This one."

"I will throw your ass into the sun first."

"I won the bet. It's my choice. Besides, the sun doesn't come up for another…"

"You know what, Vinny?"

"Yes?"

"I think I kind of hate you." But Wes grinned, cradling his controller like he meant business. "Let's fall in love with some vampires."

At that moment, there was nothing Vincent wanted Wesley to do more.

It turned out that video games were just one more item for Vincent to add to his list of everything he enjoyed about Wesley. The man smelled good. He tasted good. He looked good. And he was positively glowing when he really got into a game. It didn't even seem to matter that this was a slutty-pics-first, plot-second style story with more drama than fighting and none of it easily effectible. Wesley still yelled at the romanceable characters for turning him down and strategized his way through every flirtation option and cheered when the vampire they'd been putting the most effort into stood up for their shared player character during an overly-dramatic bar fight. That outcome left both their character and the potential lover fleeing the police while half clothed. The whole time the vampire fought his natural instincts to feed from the player character's scraped chin and fuck them in a pushy, almost threatened kind of way that didn't seem quite consensual to Vincent.

"That's not realistic," Vincent reassured Wes. "The feeding instinct, a bit, but it's not like every time I smell blood I also have to have sex with the person."

"I know. I mean, I figured, since you haven't tried to, you know, bodice rip me or something."

Vincent choked, almost choosing the game's blatantly wrong dialogue option. "I did notice you have a shelf of those."

"They were my mom's. I've only read a couple of them. And most of those weren't bad, just saying." Wes's shoulders bounced like he couldn't care less what Vincent thought, but the defensiveness of his expression still won out. "And you know, some people think this kind of rough, pushy sex makes for a hot fantasy. And it's not like they want to be forced into sex in real life, or force anyone else; it's just the concept of it. It's hot to dream of being undone by some sexy growling fiend who just *has* to have you. There's nothing wrong with that."

He didn't look over for the next two game chapters. Vincent had almost brought the topic back up just to be sure Wesley didn't think he was judging him, but by the time they shut the console off, Wes was yawning so heavily he seemed to have forgotten everything but the concept of a bed. Vincent all but kicked himself out so the human would feel comfortable sleeping. As he stepped onto the front stoop, Wes stopped him.

"Since you didn't feed on me, do you still need blood?" His expression remained natural, but there was an edge of concern in his voice.

"I can go a night without it." Once the hunger bothered Vincent enough, he'd have to sneak back into someone's room, but he'd been feeding consistently since he found Wesley, so he figured he could last another day or two.

"Well, let me get your number then. For next time."

Next time. Vincent bit the edge of his lip as he typed it into Wes's contacts list, trying to ignore all the ways his heart wanted to make this out to be more than it was. So what if Wes had enjoyed the evening? It didn't mean that he wouldn't grow bored or annoyed with Vincent in a week or two.

"My phone's hit or miss, though. Something's wrong with my service, I think," Vincent added as he handed the phone back, because that was easier than explaining he didn't always have a place to charge it.

Wes nodded groggily. "Let's plan for something now then. Same time next night you're off?"

"That would be Tuesday."

"Same time Tuesday, then."

Vincent swore he sounded just a little disappointed.

∾↝

Their night left a flutter in Vincent's chest all the way back to the cemetery.

After the warmth and glow of Wesley's little house, everywhere else seemed stiff and empty, but Vincent held tightly to his contentment. It reemerged on and off the rest of the night, bringing with it the memory of Wesley's grin and the way being with him, in his home, in his life, had felt so light and comfortable by the end. It was more than attraction—more than a crush, even. Being with Wes had reminded Vincent of what it was like to have a life. To have friends. To have the safety just to relax and enjoy the moment.

Vincent had missed that so much more than he had realized.

But he tried not to let it distract him. This friendship with Wesley was momentary. The man had already proved that his life was a spontaneous array of excitement and nonsense, and he'd lose interest in Vincent eventually, move on to werewolves or fae or something even more rare or just outright mythological. Whenever that happened, Vincent still needed to have necks to bite, constant shelter from the sun, and some kind of job to keep him fed and clothed. Even if those necks weren't as handsome as Wesley's or the shelter as cozy.

At least his job situation was looking up.

His newest one was a consistent, if unusual, intelligence gathering gig for a mildly intimidating white man with slicked-back salt and pepper hair, squint lines around his eyes, and a ridiculous number of trench coats. Vincent decided he was probably San Salud's worst-marketed freelance detective. He certainly played up the private eye act whenever he wasn't quoting one-liners from movies or comparing gaming statistics with his loud and intensely animated assistant.

The work he assigned Vincent included tracking when specific people came or left a place and recording what kinds of visitors they received or how often they conducted suspicious activities, like hiding behind hoods or carrying umbrellas during clear weather. Considering how interesting it sounded, it involved a lot of "sit in the micro-cemetery on Peach Street and write up a description of anyone who enters the red door on building #3607 between the hours of 9:00pm and 5:30am," which his employer, Matthew Babcock, treated like a series of bizarre mini-quests. They often took up the entire night and grew boring faster than blood cooled in the winter.

This was probably why Babcock had been willing to hire a raggedy odd-ball with no address and no references who only took cash. Also the fact that he wasn't paying much, all things considered. But it was enough reliable income for Vincent to feel comfortable making a few well-deserved purchases. He picked through the thrift store after that night's work for his own long coat with a hood large enough to hide him from the sun and splurged on a sandwich at a rundown café with plugs for phone charging.

That was the highlight of his day, sitting in a back booth with his phone and texting as he nibbled at his meal. His mouth still stung mildly from the spicy ramen, but the lingering pain of his time with Wesley was well worth it to watch the man's messages appear in sporadic bursts.

Vincent3510
Wait am I supposed to set my name to something cool on this?

LordOfTheWin
You can use the nickname function.
Or you can be boring, I guess.

LordOfTheWin
Your call.

Vincent3510
Okay hold on.

NotABoringName
How about this?
Wait wait I'm changing it.

HotMouth
Tada!

This is better.

LordOfTheWin

Dude I just choked on my breakfast.

(I love it.)

HotMouth

Please don't die.

LordOfTheWin

Not without you here to exsanguinate me ;)

HotMouth

No!

Also that's disgusting. I would never feed off a corpse.

LordOfTheWin

How is it any different from drinking blood from a bag?

The bag is just dead flesh.

HotMouth

A dead PERSON.

Worse it would be a dead you.

LordOfTheWin

Aw how cute, you care.

HotMouth

Why wouldn't I?

Wesley's icon vanished from the app for a bit after that. It returned when Vincent was heading home twenty minutes later, along with a video of an extra hot chicken wings contest featuring a gaggle of celebrities and the message *next time*. Vincent huddled beneath his hood on the shady back of the bus, one eye always on the sun's progress, and sent back an erotic vampire webcomic. Wes returned a set of swearing emojis, then went quiet for a noticeably long time for someone who'd admitted that he had no job and no scheduled commitments.

Vincent absentmindedly counted the cemeteries they passed as he waited for a response. The city tried to fashion all of them after the older ones San Salud had acquired in its early years as a sanatorium town, but Vincent had spent enough time in them to spot the differences between the truly aged graves and the ones made to look old for the sake of tourism. *Most cemeteries in one city* was a hell of a slogan during the summer Ghost and Ghouls Festival and the last week of October, but the rest of the time it just seemed a bit depressing. When Vincent had been a kid, San Salud had also hit the charts for vampires, but the city must not have been thrilled about that particular connection because the last five years the vampiric population had taken a sharp decline.

A pair of large men eyed Vincent from three rows up, and he sank a bit more in his seat, trying to look bored instead of tired and scared. They had finally decided to ignore him when his phone buzzed.

LordOfTheWin
Is holy water actually Like That.

HotMouth
Deadly?

LordOfTheWin
I was going to say an aphrodisiac but sure.

HotMouth
Wait what?
Is that in the horny vampire comic I sent???

LordOfTheWin
It was a joke. You know jokes?
Yes fine it was in the comic shut up.
Still not a fetishist.

HotMouth

Still doubting that tbh. But the answer is no and no. Not deadly and not an aphrodisiac. Probably, anyway. I don't think any vampires have actually tried it for that purpose.

Don't quote me on this, but I think the original myth was born out of the intolerance of religious figures who were trying to keep vampires out of their congregations when vampirism was first on the rise in the middle ages?

But then the intolerance turned into straight up murdering and vampires went into hiding for so long that everyone returned to thinking we were myths and making up wild shit about us.

That's all kind of stuck around even with our untimely resurgence in the mid-1900s.

Sorry that was like a whole novel.

LordOfTheWin

You did a lot of research into this?

HotMouth

I was thinking of majoring in something related to history or maybe anthropology and one of the classes I took that first semester touched on it.

In retrospect, they were still pretty terrible about the whole idea of vampires. Treated them like a fun specialty topic and not living

people who have to still deal with this stuff
daily.

LordOfTheWin

That sucks.

You ARE kind of special though, just saying.

LordOfTheWin

;) ;) ;)

But not as special as werewolves.

Do you know any of THEM?

You're not really mortal rivals like in that one
mafia show, right?

HotMouth

That seems wildly inaccurate, but I also don't
know any werewolves personally so I can't ask.

I think they mostly live up north.

They like the cold.

LordOfTheWin

I'd think vamps would also like it up there. Less
sun.

HotMouth

The farther north you go the more sun you get
in the summer. Makes it impossible to do

much for months of the year. I have enough seasonal depression already, thank you.

HotMouth

Besides, I've always lived here.

LordOfTheWin

And I'm here.

Which makes this the best place to live.

Statistically proven.

HotMouth

Ha ha.

They went on like that all the way back to Vincent's crash pad, until his phone died again a few hours later, its five-year-old battery protesting up to the very last moment. It took him another hour to fall asleep, the soft aches and pains of second-hand sun exposure tensing his muscles and tingling in his nerves until he craved Wesley's couch almost as much as the man's blood. But it was worth it.

So worth it, that the next day he did it all over again, staying later at the café with two sandwiches instead of one and texting with Wesley until the sun was high overhead. No matter how much he ate, he couldn't stop his blood thirst from curling through his gut and tugging at his attention, making his focus jump to exposed necks and wrists and thighs when anyone came a bit too close to him. That night he finally snuck his way into a house three streets over from Wesley's and scooted onto the bed of a middle-aged woman who smelled about as good as bland oatmeal. He sunk his fangs in with a pinch of venom that would usually send a human into a blissful slumber. Instead, the woman wailed and jerked, reaching for her neck.

Vincent scrambled away, certain he'd woken her up. She drifted right back into a disruptive sleep, rubbing at her oozing wound like it was a bee sting. Or a hot sauce burn.

Vincent's heartbeat sped to a rattling rhythm that made his head light and his lungs clamp up, but he forced himself to press a bundle of tissues to the fang marks until the woman stopped bleeding, and creep back out her balcony door before sliding into a complete panic.

What the fuck had that spicy ramen done to him? How was he supposed to eat if he couldn't bite anyone? The steadiness of this current job had cushioned out his wallet some, but it was nowhere near enough to buy a blood bag off a black-market vendor—assuming he could find the San Salud vendors in the first place—and the human blood banks all had protections perfectly designed to catch a single, desperate vampire in the act.

Until whatever spiciness lingering in his venom glands faded, Vincent Barnes the vampire was fucked.

9

Wesley was having one hell of a week, that was for sure. Between updating Kendall on his vampire situation so often his friend was developing an unhealthy obsession and rearranging his sleeping habits in order to message Vincent as much as possible, he was starting to feel like a puppet on a string. But the more Vincent trusted him, the easier it would be to lure the vampire to Vitalis-Barron. To find proof of his mom's death. To take down the sack-of-shit pharmaceutical company who was hurting—killing, even—not only humans but also vampires, so that nothing like what happened to his mom could happen to anyone else.

That was still the end goal.

As Wes headed out of his room, his legs carried him past the stairs, further down the hall. His chest tightened and his gut roiled like it might launch him straight at Vitalis-Barron's doorstep. He barely felt the cold of the master bedroom's handle, blinking at the creak of the hinges as he pushed open his mother's unused room.

He stood in the doorway, her things made into haunting silhouettes by the dim light of the streetlamp outside: her shelf of historical romance novels cluttered with dragon plushies and figurines from cartoon shows; the queen-sized bed she had let Wes crawl into for years after his father left, never once suggesting that he was too old to sit and read with her; the stacks of board games she'd bought and never used, too many nights and weekends spent on overtime at the hospital as she fought to pay off this house for Wesley, to give him the generational wealth she'd never known.

And Vitalis-Barron had carelessly thrown out her life with not so much as a date for those who loved her to mark her death. People died in medical research; Wes had looked up all the statistics with such tunnel vision that he'd been shaking and stewing over it for a mess of uncounted hours. They died because they were already dying and the new procedure didn't work and they died because of rare and horrible side effects and accidents. And maybe—maybe—Wes could have accepted that, if Vitalis-Barron hadn't covered it up. Hadn't pulled her into it with the kind of stealth that screamed of dubious legality. They'd taken this determined, kindhearted, nerdy woman with claims of help, knowing fully well that she might never come out again, and been willing to cover it up when she hadn't.

For that, they deserved to burn.

This wasn't about vampires. It wasn't about Vincent. It was about justice. Until Wesley found proof of his mother's death, and saw the people involved taken down, it couldn't be about anything else. All the video games, the bets with Kendall, the messages with Vincent, were just a distraction to keep him from detonating or breaking down before he could get into Vitalis-Barron's research lab and find his proof. And once he did…

Then Vincent would be free again. There was no crime they could pin on a vampire for having been lured into an illegal laboratory. When the lab was shut down, they'd have to let him go.

The ding of Wes's phone dragged him out of his thoughts, leaving him a little jittery and a lot nauseous, but more determined than he'd been in days. He browsed his heap of unread messages and notifications as he ambled down the stairs. With a fresh email from the pharmaceutical company's research department sitting in his inbox and Kendall on his back with such a constant string of "If you like the vampire so much then just apply for a job elsewhere" that he hadn't picked up a call from her in two days, he decided to try something new. He flopped onto the couch, tossed one leg over the arm, and began typing away on his phone.

Dear Taylor,

I'm still very interested in the patient recruitment position! I have a prospect for my signing recruitment, but I was curious if you could connect me to a current employee for some tips. I want this to go well so I can get started with you all soon!

Best,
Wesley Smith

Was that too many exclamation points? Too pushy? Too weak? Wesley closed his eyes and hit send. By the evening, he had a reply.

Wesley,

Taylor forwarded me your email. I've been on their research subject recruitment team almost since it began, focusing entirely on bringing in vampire subjects. I'm happy to give you tips.

So you've spotted a vampire you think would be right for our research program? What are they like? Have you made contact? How are you going about this?

Regards,

Matthew Babcock
Subject Recruitment Specialist
"Always up for the hunt."

Wesley had to admit that the man's signoff quote made him a little uncomfortable, though he was probably just referencing a popular deployment line from War Call. The game *was* currently one of the most played first-person shooters in the world—Babcock's inclusion of it could have nothing to do with vampires being an enemy in its massive lineup. Either way, Wes had already known that these people weren't that morally commendable going in. He was here to ruin their company and destroy their jobs, after all.

Matthew,

Thanks for reaching out! First contact has been made. He's actually been breaking into my house for weeks now to feed on me while I sleep! (So ironic, but I'm making the best of it.) I think I've managed to convince him we're friends now though; I got him to game with me on Thursday. But I doubt he trusts me enough to walk straight into the lab. He's pretty skittish. What are your recommendations here?

Wesley

Wesley erased and retyped *convince him we're friends* a few times, biting the inside of his cheek so hard he could taste his own blood in his mouth. That made him finally commit. Matthew responded almost immediately.

Wesley,

What a creep! I wouldn't have the balls to fake niceties to a vamp after they've been violating me like that; I'm impressed. He sounds like a good target, though. I can't vouch for all of Vitalis-Barron's recruiters but I only go in for the vampires that need to be off the streets in the first place. Lucky for us, that's a never-ending list these days.

You probably don't want to get physical with him, since it's your first time and you're alone. Vampires are a combination of stronger, faster, and more agile than people, so unless you know exactly where yours fits on that spectrum, it'll be hard to take him in a direct confrontation. For now, I suggest something more indirect. Can you find out where he keeps his blood bags and slip something in one?

Matthew

P.S. You game? What's your poison?

A knot in Wesley's gut unwound. At least Babcock wasn't trying to forcibly volunteer the vampires who were harmlessly living their lives, just those like Vincent, breaking into homes, committing assault, or other violence probably. It still didn't make it right; Vitalis-Barron wasn't the law, and Babcock wasn't a jury. But Wes did feel a little better working with him for the moment. He almost wanted to say so, but he wasn't sure how to write *thank god you're not one of those people who thinks all vampires are evil* without sounding entirely too on the nose. And he was intending to leave the man without a job at best, so it felt slightly hypocritical.

Wes moved on to the relevant information: strength, speed, agility. From what he'd seen of Vincent, Wesley was pretty sure his vampiric abilities were on the fast and furious end of things. But that certainly didn't mean Wes felt comfortable battling him with pure strength either. The more he lingered on that thought, the more pieces of it appealed, the idea of him trying to wrestle Vincent off, only to lose. Only to be bitten, Vincent's body pressing him down and his mouth moving along Wesley's neck and—fuck it all the vampire was a home-invader and serial assaulter whose demise he was supposed to be setting up. He could not be thinking like this. At least not until after he was done making his preparations.

Matthew,

No blood bags. He feeds straight from humans.

I thought vamps were immune to poison and viruses and all that kind of stuff?

Yeah, I go for a mix. Just finished an Over the Edge: Skyline play-through last month, and I've probably logged about a thousand hours on Ancients Return, but I'll take a good puzzle or sim too. Can never go wrong with War Call though! "You were dead the moment I got here."

Wes

He debated the inclusion of *War Call* and the kill line he'd added in after it. He didn't particularly want to game with this man, but if the connection could tip Babcock into putting in more effort on his behalf then he'd happily take advantage of it.

Not when we make the drugs especially for the vamps. I have something that will knock him out for a solid hour or two.

He's that feral then, is he? Be careful with him. In my experience, they can be very good actors and display genuine-appearing sweet sides when they think they can get something out of you, but when a human gets turned by force or accident, it's usually one of them to blame. You push them a little too hard and they'll go from kind to deadly in an instant.

So long as you're cautious though, you should be able to handle this one. You sound like you've been doing great so far. And as a fellow War Call fan, you're in the right place joining subject recruitment ;) All the best of us play.

Let me think on what to do about your bloodsucker. I'll get you some more ideas tomorrow.

Matthew

While Wes's *War Call* reference had certainly worked as intended, he wasn't entirely comfortable having his enjoyment of the game equated to the real life equivalent of hunting vampires, even if they were only luring in the morally dubious ones. That unease was eclipsed by the fear Babcock's earlier statements induced, though. Wes hadn't been able to justify the difference between the vampire he'd caught trespassing onto his bed and sinking fangs into his neck with the one who laughed and joked and blushed in his living room. But here was the explanation he should have realized all along. Of course Vincent was being cute and sweet and funny now that he'd been offered a willing neck on a platter. How long would that last, if he kept being unable to feed from Wesley? At what point would he decide that just taking what he wanted was better than humoring the weird little human who'd let him through the front door?

Wesley shuddered, caught half by the terror of the imagined situation and half by the way he pictured Vincent's fangs gleaming in the darkness, his hands gripping into Wes's flesh, his voice thick with need as he demanded—

That was a very different situation after all. But it was a much less painful one to focus on, and after the bout of emotions he'd already been through, he needed something to take his mind off all the things he couldn't change yet. Despite how wrapped up in those things Vincent was, he was still an easy distraction.

And he was supposed to be there soon.

As Wesley flipped over to Vincent's messages, his stomach knotted. He stared at his phone, trying to read them in any other way than what it very clearly said.

HotMouth

Hey, sorry to bail, but I still have spicy fangs apparently.

I promise we'll get your fetishist dreams sated soon.

Wes?

Just let me know you're not waiting up on me.

Wes would quit staring, any day now. Any day, his chest would stop with the subtle burning working its way up his esophagus. It wasn't that he worried over

Vincent; not after the way they'd met. He was only concerned that if Vincent stayed away now, he would never get the vampire to Vitalis-Barron. That was all.

HotMouth

Okay, I see you're on so I'll just assume you got this?

LordOfTheWin

Are you okay?

Sorry I was having a moment.

You can come anyway, of course. I'm more than a sexy neck.

He regretted the message the moment it sent. Maybe Vincent staying away was actually better for him. If he distracted himself with Vincent tonight, it would be another evening of laughing at his awkward jokes and basking in the little twitches of his lips and thinking way too much about how his mouth would feel on different parts of Wesley's body, all while ignoring who the vampire was beneath the act and the betrayal Wes had planned for him. Through all his agonizing, he barely realized how long it took Vincent to respond.

HotMouth

You have a neck though, which could be a problem for me right now.

Not that I'm about to attack people at random or anything. I just might have trouble sitting next to you for long periods of time.

LordOfTheWin

Usually when someone says they'll have trouble sitting next to me, they want to jump me in a very different way, so at least you're being original about it.

HotMouth

XD

Vincent's icon went its offline gray with his final emoji haunting the bottom of the chat. He wasn't coming. And he was starving, so starving that he couldn't just sit with Wesley and play video games. The kind of starving that reminded Wesley of the vampiric portrayals in those very games, the salivating lunging monsters who would drain their victims dry without a second thought, or else stop their feeding at the very last moment, just as they realized they were killing someone they loved.

He'd paused the vampire dating sim game on one such scene when he'd been playing before dinner, and it popped back up as he tapped a button on his controller. The vampire's long nails dug into the player character's arm so hard that blood welled beneath the painted points. Their fangs were bared and their eyes red with something that seemed halfway between hunger and lust. The player would live through it, of course. They would live to be fucked and bitten again, perhaps kick their vampire lover around a bit with their newly acquired martial arts skill in between. Maybe they'd even be equals for a moment. But then the vampire would swoop back in, hungry.

Wesley quit the game and, in a spontaneous rush, he deleted it too. The moment the file was gone, he sulkily maneuvered back through his past purchases and re-downloaded it. But he couldn't bring himself to play again.

It didn't matter how much he found himself cackling at Vincent's jokes or grinning at his phone every time a new message appeared. Vincent was still the vampire who'd broken into his house. Maybe they weren't all like the media portrayals, but this particular one shared some qualities with the bloodsuckers in his video games. He was still willing to go to great lengths for blood, still a predator, still a certain kind of monster. Wes just happened to like this kind of monster, was the problem. He liked Vincent.

And if he didn't get the bloodsucker to Vitalis-Barron soon he was in danger of liking Vincent a little too much.

Wes squinted at his phone screen in the darkness. He barely shook as he began to type.

Matthew Babcock,

Actually, scratch that. If I can get a blood bag from you, I'm pretty sure he'll drink it.

Wesley

10

VINCENT

By his seventh day without blood, Vincent Barnes was starving.

It was the kind of starving that superseded his hunger for traditional food, making a black hole in his gut that felt hollow no matter how many peanut butter sandwiches and baggies of nuts he forced into it. It ate through him like an infection, turning his skin pale and papery as a ghost and making his shaggy hair brittle and dry, matting it into tangles that he didn't have the focus to work through. He couldn't reach a deep sleep due to the incessant tug in his stomach and the dryness of his mouth no matter how much water he drank. Bags sunk under his eyes and the whites were shot through with a grimy, black substance that had started leaking a little out the edges when he closed them for too long.

He hadn't looked half this bad on Monday evening when he'd shown up for work—a simple job of watching a cotton-candy haired artist who drew caricatures outside the more popular downtown bars on weekend nights—but Mr. Babcock had still eyed him like he was about to collapse at a moment's notice. Or burst into flame. Vincent had concealed his vampirism from the man as much as possible, taking as many jobs with sunlit hours as he could confidently survive and nodding along when Babcock's assistant made an insulting vampire joke about their fellow night owls.

"There's more than a few around here that are probably night bats," she'd said. "Not even the nice kind, but the gross little rabid balls that end up everywhere you don't want them. But at least most real bats have the decency to eat the mosquitos instead of being the mosquito."

Babcock had hmm'ed in response but hadn't contradicted her.

Vincent wanted to walk out on them both. But he'd offered up his notes and taken his cash. As he'd turned the corner, he'd caught a final jest from Babcock's assistant.

"I get it," she replied with a harsh laugh. "Two rabid bats, one stone. A double kill."

Vincent had tugged up his hood and kept his head down despite the sky still being mostly black against the streaks of pink.

But now it was Wednesday morning, and if he had to go to work like this he was pretty sure Babcock would at the least send him to a hospital, and at most make him stand in the sun just to prove something. He'd have to call in sick. That would give him enough time to try biting someone again tonight. His attempt on Sunday had gone about as well as the first, but by now the numbness and tingling in his fangs had almost vanished. No more hot mouth.

Very little HotMouth too, since he'd had to keep his phone off to conserve its power the last few days. Every time he held down the button, he gritted his teeth, hoping it would decide it had just enough battery left to return to him. When the little animated bat on his lock screen appeared, he breathed out, only to cringe at the 13% on the corner dropping to 12%. His notifications popped in: three memes, a blurry photo of Wesley's bedhead, and a small essay regarding the nature of one particularly annoying lesbian named Kendall, all from Wesley.

The most recent message Wesley had sent lodged in his chest, and he had to reread it, once, then twice. A little bit of liquid pooled in the corner of his eye. He wiped at it before realizing it was not the weird dark stuff leaking from his bloodstream, but a tear.

LordOfTheWin

Dude, you still having problems with biting?

I got you a blood bag. Don't ask how just worship me.

(That was a joke, you don't have to worship me. I do have a bag of blood for you though. Hope you like AB positive.)

Vinny, you okay?

I can come to you if you need me to. I'll leave it on your doorstep. No sexy necks in sight.

I'm not saying I'm scared for you but dude if you could answer me I'd feel a lot better right now.

Vincent?

I'm basically pleading for a response at this point.

Beneath that he sent a picture of a bag of blood set on a fancy plate with condiments smeared elegantly beneath and garnish sprinkled on top like it was a dish at some expensive restaurant instead of swiped from a blood bank. Vincent sniffled, pressing a hand to his nose. This was so much. It was too much. No one should have been going to these great of lengths for him, pathetic, mildly useless vampire that he was. And yet here was Wesley, having found or bought or stolen a blood bag, for Vincent.

Vincent tried to think of another time someone, anyone, had put in that much effort when he'd been sick or depressed or desperate. His parents? Absolutely not.

His sisters? If it didn't cost them time or money, maybe. Friends? He'd never had any he considered close enough to share the extent of his troubles. But he hadn't even told Wesley just how badly he was doing, and this man he'd met through the shoddiest of circumstances and who'd been nothing but kind to him had still gone through all this trouble. And he smelled good.

Goddamn him.

HotMouth

Sorry, phone was off.

You're amazing though.

He erased *I think I'm in love* and *you're my god now* before finally settling on *I owe you one* just in time for Wesley to reply:

HotMouth

I owe you one.

LordOfTheWin

Thank fuck I was about to call the national guard.

Can you come here or should I go to you?

HotMouth

I'm not too far away, I can come. Be there in five.

LordOfTheWin

You'd better be. I set a timer and everything.

Wesley hadn't been joking.

When Vincent stumbled up the street, hunched forward with his hood pulled low against the sun, Wes already stood in his front yard with his phone ticking away, bouncing on the balls of his feet. He shouted and sprinted out to Vincent, wrapping an arm under his and helping him toward the safety of the dark house, its blinds lowered and curtains loosened.

Each step they took together, Vincent could smell Wes's musk like an intoxicant, could smell his blood beneath it. His mouth went even drier as his fangs slipped free. He tried to pull them back, to swallow down his hunger and clench against the urge to bury his face into the scent, jaws open and teeth bared. But as they moved into the shade of the porch and the direct sunlight receded from Vincent's mind, his whole world tightened to Wesley. The sound of his panting breath. The bead of sweat dripping down his neck. The bounce of his curls over such fragile skin. The pump of his blood, fast from the quickened beating of his heart.

Vincent lunged.

He slammed Wesley into the wall hard enough to thud. The shorter man resisted, and Vincent's hands instinctively pinned his wrists, hip digging into Wes's pelvis to hold him in place and one of his own legs tangling with one of Wesley's to keep him from kicking out. Wesley made a noise that might have been Vincent's name, but all Vincent got was the vibration of it, the low, taut sound rolling through Vincent like a physical ache. He shoved his head against Wesley's jaw, forcing the man's chin up and to the side to expose his neck; he could already feel the venom sliding down his fangs. Wesley went still, a tremble running through him.

There was a reason Vincent wasn't supposed to do this. There was a really, really good reason, it was just so muddled by every cell of his body telling him that he should, that he needed this, that he was literally going to die without it. Without Wesley.

Wesley.

Oh fuck, Wesley.

Vincent's instincts continued to flare, but his horror cut through them, turning his limbs to putty. A sob choked out of him as he slid down Wesley's body. Wes caught him, half pulling him up, half dragging him toward the living room. But his neck was still too close, his blood still so hot and—

Vincent sprang away from him, stumbling the rest of the way to the couch where he collapsed, head tipped back and eyes closed. "I'm sorry," he gasped. "I'm so sorry."

He could feel the bob of Wesley's throat from across the room, the little blip in his heartbeat. "You had warned me, so it's my bad, really. Do you need me to leave? I can give you space."

"No, I—I'm in control now, I swear."

The scent of Wesley—of his blood pounding through him—grew stronger again, testing Vincent's statement as the man approached. Wes looked nervous but almost eager, like a person on their first skydive, an adrenaline junky pushing his luck. As he flicked on the living room lamp, his brow tightened, his mouth falling open. "Ah fuck."

He stopped in front of Vincent. His thick brows were tight, his full lips a little wrinkled, and the colorful beads of his wrapping bracelet shifted as he tucked back a loose curl. Hesitantly, he reached out his fingers after, as if without touching Vincent, he couldn't be quite sure he was still alive. Strong fingers, stockier than Vincent's and just as handsome as the rest of the man.

Vincent's gaze snapped to the underside of Wes's palm, his fangs still pressing obnoxiously against his lips. But he could restrain himself. He would restrain himself. After everything Wesley was doing for him it was the absolute least Vincent could offer in return.

Wesley's fingers brushed Vincent's cheek and Vincent's heart caught in his chest. Then the touch was gone, withdrawn along with the rest of Wesley.

"The blood's in the fridge, hold on," he said, his gate a little lopsided as he moved through the dining area and turned out of sight.

Vincent relaxed, the edges of his hunger fading without Wesley there to antagonize him. His gaze wandered. The blue recliner had a fresh pile of laundry, and new mail had been added to the stack on the table, but otherwise the house hadn't changed an inch. Beyond the generous offer of blood and the joy of seeing Wesley again, it was a relief just to be here, in this cozy space of four walls and few expectations.

"I still don't understand why you wouldn't just pin someone down. You're strong enough," Wes called from the kitchen, "Your bite might hurt them for a bit, but they'd get over it."

Vincent couldn't tell if the man's tone was off, or if his perception was just tainted by the violent disgust that hit him at the mere suggestion. "Wesley." It came out a little rough, a little weak. "I won't hurt people like that."

Wes reappeared around the corner with a medical bag of dark red liquid in his hands. "But you're already breaking into their homes and taking their blood."

"I know. And I hate that. I hate that I have to *do* that." Vincent took the bag with a little nod, feeling far too nonchalant about it but not knowing how to say a proper *thank you* without making it a whole scene.

He stared at the bag. His hunger fought with an entirely different twisting in his gut. Some human had produced this, bled this. Some other human was probably meant to receive it, to help save their life. Nowhere along the way had anyone wanted it in the mouth of a vampire. But here he was, starving and going to drink it anyway.

He cringed.

"But why do you do it, then?" Wes crossed his arms. "Why do you think you *have* to?"

"I don't know how you got this, but…" With how very human Wes was, maybe he just had to walk up in the direct sunlight and ask. "I haven't been able to afford bagged blood before. Since returning to San Salud, I haven't even managed to find the dealers in the first place. The black-market blood community is around here somewhere, I'm sure—most vampires don't like feeding straight from humans if they don't have one who's specifically theirs, so that's where they get a lot of their blood from—but I don't know where to look, not without revealing what I am. And I can't just grab random people off the street like *hey, I'm a vampire, I'm looking for blood* and not expect most of them to call the cops on me."

"So you just bite them in the dark instead?" Wes shot back, but it felt less like a barb and more like a void, hollow and needy.

This had hurt him.

Oh god, this had hurt him; Vincent's intrusion, however he acted. Of course it had, and Vincent felt like shit for assuming otherwise. He lowered his face, a little tremble running through his shoulders. "I'm so sorry that I did that to you—to anyone."

"But you did! You fucking did man, and—" He seemed to cut himself short, like he was battling something internal, his face pinched and his jaw tight. A shaky sigh left him, and Vincent wasn't sure he'd ever seen someone look so determined and so defeated at the same time. "I just need to know why. Why do you think that's okay?"

"It isn't okay," Vincent said, and he meant it, felt it, deep down in his bones. "I've been stealing blood from sleeping humans because it's not forcing anyone else to suffer in my place. If I do it right, then they don't even know I was ever there. And that doesn't make it okay. But that's why I can only force myself to do it when it doesn't mean holding someone down or burning them with my bite. Because if my existence starts hurting anyone but myself, then maybe I don't deserve to exist at all." The last words caught in his throat, and he could barely lift his gaze back to Wesley's after.

Wes watched him with a twisted expression, tight and emotional and entirely unreadable. "Or, maybe," he replied, voice as low and tense as the look on his face, "*fuck that.* You have a right to live the same good, happy life as every other damn person." He clamped his mouth shut at the end and looked away, towards the sheer curtains on the dining room windows and the obscured lines of the cemetery beyond.

Vincent wanted to believe him. It sounded nice. And it sounded selfish. But Wes—Wes who'd done so much for him, after being hurt so much by him—had affirmed it. Vincent's chest swelled like something was trying to burst out from beneath his ribs. He didn't know what to do with that. Instead, he let himself sink back into his hunger, turning his attention to the bag in his hands.

"I…" Wesley started, not meeting his gaze. He rubbed a hand against his neck. "Maybe you should…"

As he fumbled for words, Vincent began to drink from the bag. His fangs punctured the plastic easily. The first rush of blood that hit his mouth was the best thing he could have imagined. It didn't matter that it tasted a little bitter, a chemical edge to it from the plastic, nor that it was cold and thin with none of the sweet, dark flavor of Wesley's blood. His body needed it so desperately that it could have been months old, scraped off the concrete, and Vincent would have still guzzled it without a word.

"Ah," Wes ended.

Vincent stalled to glance at him properly, but he shook his head.

"Drink your blood."

Vincent did. He forced himself to slow as the bag neared halfway empty. If his venom glands still hadn't cleared of the hot sauce effect, he'd need to portion out the rest. Whatever Wes said, he refused to bite someone if it hurt them, and there was no way he'd ask Wesley to go through the effort of finding him a second bag of blood. He pulled his fangs free of the plastic and licked. As he drew his head up, the blood immediately sprung from the holes.

"Fuck." He impulsively squeezed harder, shooting the liquid at his face in a spray before he had the sense to pinch the holes closed. "I forgot plastic doesn't heal."

Wesley laughed, and the sound almost sounded like himself again. "Dork."

"That's cruel! I'm half dead; my brain is mush. Cut me some slack."

Wes only grinned. "Hey, I'm just happy not to be the one covered in blood this time."

Vincent paused from licking the side of the bag to glare at him. "Be useful and get me something to put this in already."

"Fine, fine."

"Thank you!" Vincent shouted after him.

Wesley banged around in the kitchen for a minute, returning with a container and a lid and a couple of paper towels.

Vincent stood to set his bag casually into it with the fang holes facing up. He rearranged it a couple times before managing to fit it so it didn't start leaking again and accepted the paper towel for his face, turning it a bright scarlet as he cleaned the blood off his cheek and the crook of his chin. When Wesley didn't take the container back to the fridge, he blinked. "Do you want me to…?" He didn't quite know what he was asking. What odd notions of vampirism was Wesley trying to abide by now?

"You're going to drink the rest of it, right?" Wes asked, sounding just a little flatter than normal.

"I feel okay, I thought maybe I'd save it." Feeling *okay* might have been an overstatement, but he did feel quite a bit better, a little faint and weak still but the ferocity of his hunger had subsided and he didn't have the overwhelming urge to sink his teeth into Wesley. Just the regular urge, the one that came with a nice array of other desires, ones that pulled his gaze over the warm tan of Wesley's skin and along his full lips and broad jaw and down to his sturdy wrists, perfect not only for nibbling but for running a thumb along in gentle circles as he was pinned in place—if the man wanted that. Vincent found his desires now involved slamming Wes into walls for reasons that had nothing to do with starvation and everything to do with the fact that the sound he'd made as Vincent had grabbed him had left something throbbing and a little undone inside Vincent. But he was fully capable of resisting *those* urges.

Wesley's jaw pulsed. His eyes kept drifting between the bag and Vincent.

"I mean, if you don't mind a half-drunk blood bag in your fridge," Vincent added.

"You're sure? You still look a bit ghostly." He pushed the container towards Vincent, then seemed to think better of it, pulling it to his chest instead.

"I think I'm sure." Vincent rolled his tongue through his mouth. As the final traces of blood vanished, it left a weird aftertaste clinging to his gums, but there was something better about this than the way it had been feeling for the week prior. "That might have fixed the hot mouth problem, actually." He extended his fangs, wiggling his fingernail and tongue between them and the surrounding teeth. The subtle burning that had resonated from them since the spicy ramen incident was gone. "May'e tha hos sauce was jus' caugh in ma fangs'racks?"

"Your fang sacks?"

Vincent stopped fiddling long enough to speak clearly again. "Tracks! My fangs' venom tracks. God, Wes." But he was laughing, and the flabbergasted yet thoroughly amused smile on Wes's face warmed his chest.

"It's not my fault you're playing with your fangs."

Vincent gave him a parody of a scowl. "Don't you know it's rude to mock a vampire's equipment?"

"Oh, come on, they're adorable. So small and sharp."

"You can stop teasing me now, I get it," Vincent grumbled lightheartedly. But when he looked closer at Wesley, the man didn't seem to be teasing at all.

"No, I mean it. They're cute." Wes appeared almost flustered, the softest hint of red on his cheeks. He didn't meet Vincent's eyes, wrapping his arms around the container of blood like he was trying to hug himself. If Vincent hadn't known better, he'd have thought Wes was serious. Serious that he found Vincent's fangs cute. Cute, not like a pet or a kid, but like a blush and a touch to the cheek.

But he couldn't have. He was just being Wesley, cracking innuendos at all the wrong times and skipping from one goof to the next. Only that wasn't right either.

Since Vincent had arrived today, Wesley had been softer, gentler, almost… almost…

Vincent swayed. The world spun around him. He held out a hand for the couch.

"You okay there, Vinny?"

He wasn't imagining the fear in Wesley's voice, was he?

"Maybe you should sit."

Vincent did, but his vision still whirled and his mind sloshed like he'd drank a bottle of whiskey on an empty stomach. "I don't feel—don't feel so good."

"Would more blood help?" Wesley sounded distant and a little wrong. He blurred in and out as he moved, squatting down beside Vincent.

"Maybe," Vincent muttered. When he reached for the container, it was somehow still out of his grasp. He felt the ceiling fly away. Or maybe that was the side of his head? He reached out again. "Fuck. Wes." But as he said it, he hit a pillow, everything going sideways.

Wesley's hands wrapping around him, touched him, his voice echoing oddly off to one side. "Vinny, I'm here. I've got you."

"I-I don't want to…" *I don't want to die*, he'd meant to say, *I just met you, things just started to get better*. He was finally feeling like he had a place in the world, in someone's life. And now his body was numb and his mind was being dragged off by a dark, monstrous thing.

A vampire maybe. He grabbed Wesley's hand, trying to hold it, but his fingers were failing. Everything was failing. "Please," he managed.

"I'm here," Wesley repeated, holding him right back. "I've got you. I've got you, Vincent."

Wesley. If Vincent was going to die in someone's arms, at least he had Wesley.

11

WESLEY

His vampire lay unconscious on the couch, and it was all Wes could do to keep breathing.

His lungs felt tight. His chest hurt. His knees wobbled. A panic attack. He was having a panic attack. He'd suffered from a couple during college, and a couple more after his mother's death, but it had been months since he'd had to actually work through one. No matter how much his body didn't want to function at the moment though, somehow he had to force it.

Because everything else was already *so* not going as planned.

Wes had been fully prepared to drug a hot, playful vampire, one who was acting sweet to get what he wanted and committing serial assault in his spare time. What he'd *not* been prepared for was to learn that his hot, playful vampire was genuinely as sweet—if not sweeter—than Wes had assumed and thought his only options in life were to find the least harmful way to steal blood or else let himself die. Yet Wesley had stood there and watched him drink the drugged blood and said nothing.

Because this still wasn't about Vincent. It was about taking down Vitalis-Barron so they couldn't kill anyone else, vampire or human alike. It was hurting one kind, wonderful vampire for a moment to fix a problem that had been plaguing many more of them for who knew how long; years probably, considering when the vampiric population in San Salud had first begun to decline.

Wesley focused on that, focused on it with each shallow, lightheaded breath that seemed to burn behind his eyes as his legs threatened to give way.

If enough good people saw the way Vitalis-Barron had treated their vampiric research subjects, maybe laws in California could be passed to give vampires the same rights as human patients in such settings. It probably wouldn't be a Supreme Court ruling or a constitutional amendment yet but, with how the government tried to treat them as a separate entity, not covered by *we the people* simply because none of the people who'd written those words had been explicitly vampires, it would still be something. It could do genuine good for the vampiric community.

It would be worth it, in the long run, no matter what sacrifices were made getting there or how awful

Wesley's stomach felt or the way the world still seemed to be collapsing in on him.

Also, Vincent had drunk half the drugged blood. Which meant that whatever Wesley did now, it was unlikely he'd ever be trusted again. He'd lose Vincent no matter what. Selfish as that thought was, it stuck with him.

The vampire looked so rough, still too ghostly with his hair matted and shadows under his eyes, but now he made tiny, mangled sounds, his eyes rapidly moving behind his lids.

He would be okay though. He had to be okay. The researchers would want him alive, and they'd keep him that way as long as possible, leaving plenty of time for their lab's atrocities to be uncovered and the vampires in it released. And besides, he'd only drunk half the bag.

He'd only drunk half the bag.

What did that mean? Half the amount of time asleep? Half the deepness of the sleep?

Wesley wanted to throw up. And stick his head in the freezer. And maybe undo all of this, all the way back to where he'd let this beautiful, kindhearted vampire into his life, and find some actually monstrous bloodsucker to trade for the proof that would burn Vitalis-Barron's research facilities down.

"But if my existence starts hurting anyone but myself, then maybe I don't deserve to exist at all."

Damn him. Damn Vincent Barnes for being this good and damn himself, fucking Wesley Smith Garcia, for being this much of a shit to him.

But maybe he could do Vincent one better. If he could get inside Vitalis-Barron, he'd be trusted. He'd just have to find their research records. Wherever they cataloged and disposed of the humans that died during their studies would most likely be in the same place as the vampiric ones, hidden away so no one who hadn't already sold their morals to the company would find it. Then, on his way out, he'd bring Vincent with him. An hour at most, that was all he needed, then Vincent would be free again. An hour, in exchange for a better future for vampires across the city.

It was only half a plan. But it was the soundest one he had.

Wes pressed his forehead to Vincent's chest, his breath still ragged as he wrapped his fingers through the vampire's limp ones, hands shaking and fluttering. "I'm going to get you out of this," he whispered, sealing the feeling in words. "I wager my life that you're going to keep yours."

But in order to save Vincent, Wes had to give him to Vitalis-Barron first.

He stood, wobbling as he turned around once, then again. The car. He'd have to get Vincent into the car.

Right now though, just staying on two feet seemed like an impossible task. He needed backup.

Wesley almost dropped his phone as he dragged it out of his back pocket, quickly flicking away the messages from Vincent before he could fixate too long on the *I owe you one.* Vincent absolutely didn't owe Wes in any way, at all. He flicked to his favorite contacts. His thumb hovered over his mother's number. If only he could call her. Could hear her bubbly Mexican accent and constant use of mangled movie quotes, and get her opinion on this. Would she want to be avenged if it meant someone else got hurt in the process?

He moved down one line and pressed Kendall's number.

She answered on the second ring, a little low but questioning. "Hey dude, I'm at work."

"Can you not be at work for like, ten minutes, por favor?" The Spanish slipped out as if it were his mother he was talking to after all, mangled a little by the American pronunciation he could never quite get rid of.

Wesley forgave Kendall for all her pushing and teasing as she instantly replied, "Yeah, of course. Heading for the bathroom now." After a series of shuffling and a muted, "Sorry Matt, the toilet is calling me!" the soundscape changed from distant office drabble to the whirl of a background fan. "It's a private stall, what's up."

"I drugged the vampire but now he's on my couch. I know this isn't what I implied I'd be signing up for but I guess I'm secretly a vampire hunter now." For one day. And then he'd move on to researching them.

"So you need to get him to that pharmaceutical company?"

"Si—yes."

"Wesley." She took the kind of breath that came before a lecture. "This vampire is a person."

"I know, but I'm doing this." His voice cracked. He could feel his knees caving. "I need to do this. Please, I can't explain now, but you have to trust me." If only he trusted himself at the moment.

There was a long pause, followed by a sigh, before Kendall replied, "Alright. How can I help?"

"Just talk to me? Or let me talk to you, I don't know."

"Wesley Smith Garcia, I bet you ten bucks you can't carry that fucked up vampire from your couch to your car."

"Deal."

Wesley got to work. With the speaker turned on, he slid his phone back into his pocket and stooped over Vincent. He tried to ignore the tight pain on the vampire's face. His breathing seemed too shallow, and he whimpered slightly as Wesley fit an arm under his back and another under his legs. Despite the extra inches he had on Wesley, Vincent seemed to weigh about as much as a toothpick—a gangly toothpick with awkward legs and a neck that flopped back at an uncomfortable-looking angle. Wesley tried to reposition his hold on the vampire with a grunt. The shift brought Vincent's head toward his, and the vampire curled into his embrace almost instinctively, slotting his face against Wesley's neck.

Wes froze.

No fangs pricked his skin, just Vincent's soft exhales. They seemed steadier now, his whimpering lessened. It was such a tender change, Vincent tucking himself against Wesley like he was seeking protection. Wes's gut twisted into a series of knots so tight he thought they'd never come out.

"I bet you, Kendall," He huffed, carrying Vincent across the hall and out the little side door to the garage, "that I'm going to win those ten bucks."

"Did I say ten?" Kendall coughed. "I meant five."

"Fucker." Wes had to shift Vincent even further against his shoulder to finagle the passenger door of his mom's old silver minivan open. "Okay he's in. Aw, shit, seat belt. There."

"And a blanket?"

"A what? Why?"

"For the sun. He's a vampire, Wes. It's almost noon. I don't know what the hell you're on about here, but you're not murdering him."

"Fuck, right, you're right." Wesley's insides descended into a bout of nausea to go with their twisting. He could have killed Vincent, here, in the car, with his own stupidity.

Wesley stole a blanket straight out of the dryer and tossed it over Vincent like a shroud, tucking the ends onto the seat's headrest to keep them in place. The sight of the vampire strapped in and so buried in fabric that Wesley couldn't even see his chest rise made everything worse somehow.

"I'm getting in the car," Wes stated.

"I wager five dollars that you're just standing next to it."

He absolutely was. "You can prove nothing."

The minivan's alarm went off as he closed the driver door. He lost thirty seconds to cursing and Kendall's shouting as he fought to turn it off, and another thirty seconds searching for the garage door opener, before finally backing out onto the street so fast he had to slam the brakes to keep from hitting his neighbor's ancient RV. Vincent's head wobbled beneath the blanket. Wesley grimaced.

He took off slower, cruising down the street at just above the normal ten-miles-over-the-speed-limit that the city abided by. His neighborhood of little old houses blurred by, with their painted stucco exteriors, tight stoops, and disgruntled lawns. Glimpses of the cemetery appeared between them until he pulled onto the larger suburban road, heading through the gentle hills toward the distant skyline of the inner-city and the gleam of the lake beyond it.

More cemeteries popped up along the way—San Salud was famous for them. San Salud: St. Health. A bad translation on a bad translation. The city had sprung out of a series of sanatoriums, both the rich-catering, long term care facilities for terminal tuberculosis patients and the 'madhouses' notorious for locking in anyone with no funds and no loving family, rumored to have been using them as lab rats for their more experimental treatments. If Wesley's mother was any sign, Vitalis-Barron's big new branding and distribution across the country hadn't stopped it from doing that. Which was why *he* had to do *this*.

His gaze leaped to Vincent's blanketed form and back to the road.

He had to do this.

"Talk to me, Wes." Kendall's voice through his phone speakers made him jump.

"I'm getting on the freeway. Vitalis-Barron's central headquarters are across the city, against the lake, so it's less direct but I think it'll be faster than trying to fight the inner-city traffic."

Kendall didn't need to know any of that, and it was clear by her hum that she also didn't care. "Wes, not to beat a dead horse—or an undead bat, I don't know—but are you sure you want to do this?"

"Yes!" But despite all his rationalizing, everything in him said no, no he was not sure at all. He wiped something wet off his face and clenched his hand around the wheel. "I don't know."

"I know you, Wes. You're an impulsive gambler, and you're very good at taking shitty risks now in the hopes that it'll turn out well in the long run. It's a terrifying sort of optimism, and it can be kind of great until it starts putting people in danger and blinding you to the consequences."

"That sounds like a lot of judgment for someone who claims to be my friend."

"I am your friend. I'm still here, aren't I?" Kendall sighed, so deep and long that it scraped at Wesley's soul. "I love you, Wesley. I don't know why you think this is the one and only job for you, but have you ever considered that maybe what you're doing right now is an incredibly fucked up thing and it's not worth whatever you think you're going to get out of it?"

"Yeah, I've considered it a lot, thanks," he grumbled, because a low mutter was all he seemed capable of giving without releasing the tornado-sized ache that was growing in his chest. He could tell her all the good this one horrible act would accomplish. He could make her understand. If only he understood it all himself. "You know, I think I need my attention for the road. I'll call you when I'm done."

"Wes, please—"

But he was already shuffling his phone out of his pocket, drifting into the next lane as he did it, and flicking the call off. The moment the screen went back to the home page, Wes slammed his fists against the wheel. He'd hung up on Kendall so many times before— it was basically tradition at this point—but this time it felt different. It felt shitty. The quiet left an empty spot where she should have called back, or messaged at least, a hollow silence that let Vincent's little unconscious sounds of panic and pain echo around the minivan.

Wes flicked on the car radio and forced himself to keep driving. Even the chatter of the host's talk on health smoothies couldn't distract him from the way Vincent was growing slowly more restless, his half-dose of Babcock's drug wearing down in his system too fast. Wesley sped up.

As he made his way around the central mass of the city, Vitalis-Barron's main complex began to loom off to his other side, the massive compound starting in warehouses and industrial factories that wrapped toward the lake, where the main laboratories lay behind high, barbed walls, overlooking the city from a hill. San Salud's first sanatorium had stood there, once, back when the entire downtown was a single street, before the vineyards all sprung up to the west and the boats filled in their shimmering lake, when the whole region of California was just tiny towns and Hollywood hadn't even named itself yet. The city had come so far from those days, yet something dark still lurked at its core. Something that killed people. People like Wesley's mom.

Like Vincent.

Wesley's chest ached as though it were being torn open, and he gritted his teeth, staring at the road ahead of him. Staring so hard that his exit whipped past. The freeway curved toward the lake, tightening to two lanes as it wrapped itself between the touristy boardwalk shops and the downtown skyscrapers. Wes cursed, slowing to accommodate.

Beside him, Vincent groaned. A real, solid groan, halfway to being awake. No, this was too soon. If Wes could just turn around, he could still make it to the research labs in time. He could still do this. He could—

"Wes?" Vincent's tiny mutter sent a tremor through him, tightening his throat so hard he could barely breathe through it.

"Yeah. I'm here," he whispered.

Vincent's hand slipped out from under the blanket, fumbling around to find Wesley's arm. "You can't—you can't take me to a hospital," he said, words still a little slurred. "No insurance."

"Oh," was all Wesley could manage. Vincent thought Wes was *helping* him. But of course he would. Why else would Wesley have loaded his unconscious body into a car, after playing video games with him, laughing with him, messaging with him like it was his job, finding blood for him, caring about him? Why would it occur to someone as genuine and good hearted as Vincent that all of that had just been a scam?

Particularly, when not all of it was.

Wesley inhaled, and it sounded, stupidly, like a sob. "No hospitals." No research labs, either. No proof of his mother's death. Nothing to bring Vitalis-Barron to its bastardly knees. But Vincent... Vincent was going to be okay. "You're awake? You're feeling better?"

Vincent gave a little sound almost like a laugh, but with no humor and all relief. "Like something chewed up my organs. But I'm alive. I think."

Wesley's arms shook. Vincent had to be feeling it through his grip. He had to be sensing the stutter in Wesley's heart, the lump beneath his throat. He had to know. His voice trembled a little as he asked, "What do you think did that?"

"I'm not sure." Vincent went quiet as Wes turned them back onto the freeway, heading the other direction, toward the Vitalis-Barron complex once more. "Not eating so long, then the sun, then feeding that fast?"

Wes watched the exit he'd missed last time. He tracked their path toward it, beside it, and passed. Then it was behind them, taking its dark and deadly future with its dark and deadly history with it. And he had absolutely no idea what he was going to do about that.

"Can we go back…" Vincent muttered, trailing off for so long in the middle that Wesley thought he'd finished, "to your house?"

"Back home, got it."

Vincent squeezed his arm and pulled his hand under the blanket. "Don't worry, if I pass out." He already sounded halfway there. "Brain's still mushy."

"You sleep if you need it. I'll be here." The words made Wesley's mouth dry, sounding wrong, miserable. Lies. But he was pretty sure Vincent couldn't tell, because he was pretty sure Vincent was already asleep.

∼✷∽

Wesley managed to wake Vincent again just long enough to help him to the couch, settling him down where he'd first passed out nearly an hour ago. He tucked a pillow beneath the vampire's head and laid the blanket from the car ride over him.

"I'm going to shower," he said.

Vincent curled into the cushions with a hum. Same couch, same vampire, same state of consciousness, same asshole staring down at him with weak knees and shaking hands. But now Vincent looked so different: soft and loose, a bit of color back in his pale skin and the tension gone from his forehead. In the little gap between his lips, Wes could make out one fang.

His phone chimed, and he pulled it out on instinct, expecting a message from Kendall. Instead he found a check in email from Matthew Babcock. It ended with an encouragement and a picture attached of a half-conscious vampire looking nearly as pained as Vincent had earlier, their cotton-candy colored hair fallen into their eyes and a cut across their cheek. Wes swore they'd drawn a cartoon of him outside a bar the month after his mother died. It had been the only time he'd smiled all week.

> Soon you'll be recruiting with the best of us, or as War Call puts it, you'll run them up the white flag and down the other side!
>
> Matthew

Wesley shoved his phone back into his pocket and stalked to the fridge. He yanked out the blood bag, needing desperately to get it somewhere that Vincent wouldn't accidently find it—or drink it—ever again, but as his vision tunneled and his feet moved, he found himself carrying it up the stairs and into the bathroom with him. He stripped out of his clothes and turned on the shower. By the time he'd come mostly to his senses, he was sitting in the empty tub, staring at the blood. A little voice in his head taunted him to drink it; if he suffered too, wouldn't that make up for all the shit he'd put Vincent through, all that he'd failed his mother in life and in death, all the ways he couldn't live up to being a real adult like Kendall with a job and a retirement fund, all the lives that were going to keep being ruined every day Vitalis-Barron's research labs ran?

"But if my existence starts hurting anyone but myself, then maybe I don't deserve to exist at all."

Wes wrapped his hands furiously around the bag of blood, shooting the crimson life source across his feet and down the drain. He breathed hard after, as though he'd climbed over a mountain and come down the other side. His whole body felt like it, worn through, torn up, chest broken and heart bleeding.

The shower's water slowly washed away the blood. He sat and watched it, sobbing until his eyes burned, until he was pretty sure the only time he'd let himself sob this much had been the night after his mother's funeral. He leaned his head against the tile and stared at the drain, hair matted down around his face and water still pouring across his cheek. Everything he'd done to bring himself—to bring Vincent—to this point seemed like a brand on his soul. He would not forget it.

Because there was no way in heaven or hell or anything in between that Wesley Smith Garcia was ever letting Vitalis-Barron get their hands on his vampire.

12

VINCENT

The house was quiet when Vincent woke. The digital clock on the old cable box showed 8:15pm. He groaned. Babcock would be expecting him on the job soon. But Vincent lay there for a few minutes longer, soaking in the smell of the couch—Wesley's scent, along with the faint lingering of something a little more floral—and tracking the way the shadows from the streetlights fell across the coffee table.

Wes had left a note on it.

> *Gone to bed.*
> *PS: I tried to move your bag of blood while looking through the fridge and I accidently dumped it, sorry! You can have some of mine whenever you need it though, hot mouth or not. You deserve to live.*

Vincent stared at the writing for so long that he swore under his breath when he glanced at the clock again. He couldn't quite remember what had transpired after his first wave of dizziness, but he knew deep in his bones that Wesley had tried to help him, could still feel the way Wes's hand had gripped his, his soft voice never leaving. The idea of walking out after all that, without so much as the ability to say thank you, felt wrong.

But the longer he stood there, brain still a little mushy and muscles sore, the faster he was going to have to run to make his bus. His phone had long since died, but he tore off the edge of Wes's note to scribble on.

Thanks! Gotta work. Phone dead. TTYL.

It seemed so blunt and bland, nothing to demonstrate his gratitude. Nothing to show that he understood the burden he'd been placing on Wesley and would take responsibility for it. Nothing to prove that he would pay Wesley back. He flipped the paper over.

I owe you a million.

He squeezed in a little heart and then a scribble of his name, the way he would for his sisters when they'd bothered to tuck him a hot-pocket after their parents had decided that *"if you can't eat at the table then you're not hungry enough to eat at all,"* and he didn't pause to wonder if maybe it was too much or too childish or too—fuck—romantic until he was already standing at the bus stop watching it pull in.

Vincent sat at the window, watching the flashes of suburban neighborhoods and cemeteries turn to run-down apartments with the gravestones still squashed between them in the form of awkward alleys and gated courtyards. The occupants who lingered on the streets after dark in this neglected part of the city looked just haggard and hopeless enough to seem to belong in graves instead of tucked around them. If Vincent had been any less shy when he'd first arrived back in San Salud, he'd probably be there with them instead of the city's outskirts. Maybe then, he'd have had connections to other vampires, other ways of getting blood. But then he'd never have met Wesley.

No matter how hard he tried to focus on the scenery, his mind kept slipping back to Wes. He really did owe the man so much—more than he could ever repay—yet the longer he lingered over that, the more he began to linger on other things. Things like the promise to feed whenever he needed it and the sound he'd made when Vincent had pinned him to the wall and the way he'd gone loose under Vincent's grip, like he'd wanted it. Craved it. The way Wesley had devoured every sexy comic Vincent recommended and started sending others back, ones of lower quality from the deepest depths of the web but with happy, stable couples. Like maybe he was trying to say something.

The bus had nearly moved on by the time Vincent realized it was his stop. He shouted an apology and shot out of the closing doors. As he sped across the pavement, he collided with a tattooed man smoking at the corner.

"Hey, hey!" The man grabbed him.

Vincent startled.

He let go immediately, displaying his palms. "Pull your fangs in," he hissed, "Before someone else sees."

Vincent flushed. He covered his mouth as he retracted them. He hadn't even realized they'd been out in the first place, but thinking of biting Wesley, of dragging his fangs over Wesley's lower lip and sucking the wound closed as he gasped... those thoughts must have slipped them free. Were trying to slip them free now. Fuck. He tipped his head to the stranger and muttered a soft, "Thanks."

The man just lifted his joint and turned back to the road.

It was kind of him. Maybe he was a vampire himself; he looked the part, dark clothes, tattoos, an odd almost sickly tinge to his olive skin. Or maybe he was just another person who understood having a need for something that most others didn't.

Vincent jogged down the street and veered into the next alley. The plaque on the second door was so worn that only the D and G were visible and two of the metal bars on the little window were broken, but the bolt inside had looked new enough when Vincent had been in last. It wasn't Babcock's actual business address; he was pretty sure the man would laugh him off if he asked to visit there. This was just the place he or his assistant would show up to meet their informants and pass off their nightly pay.

But tonight, the light was off.

Vincent hesitated. A familiar tang filled the back of his nose. He knocked softly. When no one answered, he pressed his palm to the knob. It turned for him.

As he cracked the door open, the scent hit him properly: a slightly rank version of the lush, thick blood that flowed through a human's veins, drawing his fangs out and stirring the still not-quite-sated hunger in his gut. It pooled across the floor, the puddle a monochromatic outline in Vincent's vampiric night vision. His feet carried him inside, one step, then another.

"Is someone hurt?" God, he did not want to find a body in here. Especially if that body belonged to one of his employers.

But there was no corpse, just a puddle that ended before it reached the far wall.

"Mr. Babcock?" Vincent called warily.

Behind him, the door swung closed.

He turned, catching a flashlight beam to the face with a grimace.

"You thought you could wear our humanity like a skin to be shed, a wolf among the sheep," Babcock said. It sounded like a line from a game or a movie, but his tone held none of the lighthearted humor with which Vincent would have quoted it. "Thought we wouldn't notice that you're the kind of vamp who bleeds this city dry."

Beside him, his assistant vocally sneered.

"I—I'm not—I wasn't—" Vincent squinted against the blinding beam, holding out his hands, palms up like the man on the street corner. "I've done everything you've asked without problems. I can do my job." But that meant nothing to them. Vincent didn't have to see their expressions to know it; he could feel it in the way they talked at him rather than to him, like every other person who'd dropped him at the first sight of what he was.

"You're a parasite," Babcock's assistant snapped. "A parasite just waiting to make more little squirming, hungry parasites."

Babcock lifted a hand to silence her, but when he spoke it was with equal distaste. "If you come with us quietly, you won't get hurt." Something flashed in his grip, still mostly concealed by his long coat—a weapon?

A shudder went down Vincent's spine. So long as he didn't get shot he could probably take them in a fight, but if he hit back and they reported the incident, he was the one who'd be blamed for it. Finding work was hard enough without the police looking for him.

"You don't belong in this city." Babcock took a step forward. "We have a better place for you."

That was another set of familiar quotes, ones with their own specific meaning. In them, the *better place* was not one with the soothing safety of a home like Wesley's, but a camp, a cage, or a grave. They would have to drag Vincent there if they wanted him to go. By the looks of them they were more than willing.

His heart pounded. The windows had bars and the doors to his left and right only led to dead-end rooms. Babcock and his assistant stood in front of the only way out, and even that was closed. As Babcock continued drawing free his weapon, a terrible burning tingled along Vincent's exposed skin, prickling and scorching. He raised his arms instinctively to cover his face. His limbs felt weak, sluggish. He stumbled, his knees threatening to buckle. His boot slipped in the puddle of blood.

As he steadied himself, he caught sight of the weapon: long, thick, and silver. Not literal silver—that had never bothered Vincent—but a silver that burned. He had encountered nothing like it before, and by the way his skin felt even this far from its exposed metal, he would have been happy to never do so again.

The window rattled suddenly as someone banged on it from outside, and all three of them jumped.

A shout came through the entrance, "Hey, you got a lighter in there?"

Babcock turned just as the door flung open, blocking the silver weapon from Vincent's line of sight. Its effects dimmed instantly. Vincent seized his chance.

He tore past the startled Babcock and his assistant, stumbled straight into the person outside. The man grabbed him by the shoulders, wheeling him onward. Vincent recognized him from the street corner.

"Go," the stranger mouthed and winked.

Vincent obeyed. He sprinted down the alleyway, only glancing back long enough to be sure that Babcock and his assistant weren't heckling his timely savior before turning onto the main street and dashing into the night. With his speed, his legs carried him outside the pair's reach in seconds. He turned north on Wine Street and west on 34th and caught the bus back toward the suburbs.

Only then did his limbs begin to shake.

He leaned against his knees, cupping his forehead in his hands. All he wanted was to show right back up at

Wesley's, to curl on his couch with him in the safety of his cozy little house and nibble on his neck and make him laugh and pretend that this hadn't just happened, that he hadn't lost the best job he'd had in months and been attacked—attacked—with some terrifying burning metal. But he couldn't do that, couldn't put that pressure on Wesley after all the man had already done for him.

He couldn't make himself more of a burden.

So when he got off at their neighborhood's stop, dead phone in one pocket and all his ragged emotions bundled in the other, instead of knocking on Wesley's door, Vincent slipped around to the backyard. He settled against the wall beside the tarped exercise bike and plugged his charger into the external outlet. His phone chimed as it woke up, and he frantically muted it, glancing at Wesley's window on the second story. His room remained as dark as the rest of the house.

HotMouth

Hey, phone's charging now, just letting you know.

Thank you again for everything. I'll make it all up to you, I promise.

Work's going to be funky for a bit so just let me know when you're free next.

As his final message sent, a dim illumination reflected off the edge of Wes's windowpane—a phone screen, Vincent realized. Wesley's icon brightened. It felt just a bit stalkerish to watch, but Vincent figured this was a step up from breaking and entering. And there was no way he could handle sitting in anyone else's backyard to charge his phone in his current emotional state, risking someone calling the cops on him or worse. He needed this: being here with Wesley's fences on all sides and the comfort of the house at his back. He needed, just for a moment, to feel safe.

LordOfTheWin

I've been a shit to Kendall lately so I should probably reserve tomorrow night for her.
What about Friday?

HotMouth

Friday it is :)

Vincent tucked his phone against his chest. Friday then. It left an odd flutter in his stomach, a combination of excitement and dread. He wanted this—wanted to be around Wesley, to bask in his kindness and try to repay him for it. But at the same time, he knew himself and the patterns his life took on. He didn't want to drag Wes into that. And he didn't want to be kicked to the curb again when Wesley finally realized just how much Vincent wasn't worth his effort.

13

WESLEY

Wesley was half awake, caught between detachment and misery. He'd fallen into bed post-emotional breakdown with the intention of napping to clear his head, but he'd managed to sleep for over eight hours and still had not removed the numbness from his mind or the ache from his chest. With his own hands, he'd come so close to placing Vincent in inconceivable danger and backing out had left Vitalis-Barron still standing. It was still standing, still killing, still putting mothers in unmarked graves and forcing their children to bury empty coffins, and Wes was doing fuck all about that, at the moment.

Because he'd chosen Vincent.

Wesley had no regrets about that, but he still had a whole lot of other feelings, ones he couldn't bear to deal with yet. He was supposed to be coming *out* of an emotional breakdown, not falling back into one.

Still, he stared at Vincent's final message for longer than he should have before flipping over to his DMs with Kendall.

LordOfTheWin

I'm an ass and you were right. Of course I couldn't go through with it. Sorry I hung up on you. You're a good friend and you deserve better. I owe you like a hundred bucks now I think, and my Thursday evening is yours.

KendallCanoodles

To be fair, I was 98% sure you'd see the company's front gates and realize you were the world's hugest morally gray idiot. But you still suck and you'd better not do that again, or else I'll fly down there for one hell of an intervention.

There will be round kicks.

LordOfTheWin

If there's a next time, you have permission to round kick my ass to the moon.

But hopefully there won't be a next time for any of this.

Also you're half right, I backed out at the freeway exit. Didn't even get to the gate.

Also(x2) I'm so sorry, I'm a shit, please forgive me.

KendallCanoodles

Play capture the flag mode with me and maybe I'll consider it.

LordOfTheWin

No wait I take back everything nice I ever said to you.

Jk, 4pm good?

You are a blessing and I adore you btw.

I know you've been dealing with all my shit lately but I swear I'll fly up there and serve you on hands and knees if you want.

KendallCanoodles

Not the kind of kinky I'm personally into but you do you, fam ;)

Though if you help me by picking up a custom cosplay staff I want to order for Leoni's birthday, that would be incredible. Apparently there's a metal worker in San Salud who makes all kinds of incredible shit like it, but you have to actually show up at his house to examine and collect the thing because he's weird about mailing and doesn't do returns.

LordOfTheWin

Done deal.

KendallCanoodles

Hope he's not a serial killer, just saying.

Oh and can we make gaming 7pm instead? I have a late meeting and I'll be starved after.

LordOfTheWin

Corporate sellout

KendallCanoodles

Jobless prankster

So you finally going to tell that vamp you're into him?

LordOfTheWin

First, I think I need at least twelve hours to process things. Second, I don't know if he's gay. And third, I'm not into him, so one and two don't even matter.

KendallCanoodles

You're a river in Egypt.

I bet you back your hundred bucks that you won't ask him on a date.

LordOfTheWin

I'm going to bed now.

As he typed it, he slipped *out* of bed instead, but it was the sentiment that mattered.

KendallCanoodles
Is that code for my pingly is tingly and I have to find the lotion.

LordOfTheWin
Scratch that I'm going to bed FOREVER.

KendallCanoodles
;))))

Wesley returned her message with angry purple imp-faces, which started a ten-minute series of obnoxious emojis and gifs, until Kendall finally stated that Leoni was "incoming" and her icon went gray. It seemed like everyone was getting tingly in their pingly but Wesley. He thought of Vincent and swallowed.

Kendall was wrong. Wes wasn't in denial, just a whole lot of guilt, which he was aggressively trying to ignore. He had a healthy admiration for Vincent to top it off. Vincent was just—he was so—damn him, he was a perfect mix of adorable and dangerous and sexy, and Wesley was already emotionally three inches inside the vampire and wanted very much to be physically three inches inside him too. But he was never going to tell

Kendall that, because he and Vincent were never going to go there. If they did, he'd have to tell the vampire just how much of an asshole he'd been and whatever Vincent may or may not have felt towards him would vanish in a puff of smoke, making the whole ordeal a gratuitous tragedy.

Wesley shoved on his mother's oldest, fluffiest bathrobe that he'd stolen from her in high school and shuffled his way groggily through the dark, down to the couch. He booted up the vampire dating sim on instinct. Or, maybe it wasn't instinct, exactly. Maybe it was the tingly his pingly was sorely missing right now. And maybe, if he focused on that enough, he could finally make the pain in his heart subside.

∿

They were messaging again—he and Vincent—like nothing had happened. Of course they were, when Vincent didn't actually know what *had* happened. And what it had almost led to. His ignorance lulled away Wesley's guilt; he seemed so happy, so unhurt by it all. But every time Wesley would fully settle into their upbeat back and forth, Matthew Babcock would check in.

Wes kept putting him off with vague replies that the vampire hadn't come around again and he was still interested in the job but he needed to find a new target to lure in. He couldn't make himself shut down the conversation entirely. It was still his best bet in proving his mother's death and taking down Vitalis-Barron. Even if he couldn't use Vincent to get the job, maybe he *could* find some other vampire instead. There were thousands of them in San Salud after all. Not all of them could be decent people. If there were genuinely asshole humans, there had to also be genuinely asshole vampires; Wesley would just take more care in judging them next time.

Since Vincent had explained his feeding situation, Wes had started on a bit of research. Searching for certified blood banks that served vampires came up with nothing but frantic news stories of vamps stealing from human-designated ones. Less-certified charitable organizations working through legal loopholes revealed a few more options. All were located in large cities, and all run by humans. They had cute little logos, and cute little front-page anecdotes about how vampirism had touched the lives of the humans who worked and donated to them, and every third article about them had a major focus on how few humans actually wanted one in their neighborhood, and the ones who did were only happy so long as the charities worked strictly with their own local vampires and didn't draw in any new ones. The opinions of the vampires themselves didn't seem to factor into this.

And there were none in San Salud. Not anymore, anyway. There had been a vampire-accepting day shelter, a trio of mobile religious-run blood banks for vampires, and for a few years in the 90s a little place had presented itself as a safe location for humans to get bitten, but that seemed more geared toward human intoxication than actual vampire feeding. The other two had done alright for themselves, funds waning and waxing over time, but seven and a half years ago they both changed hands, and it was reported that the vampires slowly stopped showing up, until their underuse prompted their closure.

That sounded strange to Wesley. While vampirism in San Salud had started decreasing around that time, there were clearly still those who couldn't afford black market blood. On impulse, Wesley looked up the owner of the blandly named company that had purchased them, and his gut twisted, his vision narrowing around the edges. Vitalis-Barron. No wonder the vampires had avoided it. That was probably about the time they'd kicked their vampire research into high gear.

And they were still at it, expanding from just vampires to humans as well. The knot in Wesley's stomach twisted tighter, seeming to grow a gravity of its own that threatened to pull him inward. He didn't have time to succumb to it though; Vincent would be here in an hour. There had to be something to preoccupy him until then.

Something that would make Vincent happy.

∽⌁

Wesley waited in the foyer for Vincent to arrive. He leaned against the wall with his phone as they sent back and forth an overall useless yet entirely wonderful series of texts that consisted of Vincent ascribing stories to random things in the neighbor's yards he passed, giving special attention to his old house. Wes replied to every message with a bad joke. He half expected Vincent to be rolling his eyes on arrival, but as Wes opened the door, he found the vampire with one hand raised to knock, staring at his own phone with the widest lopsided smile Wes had ever seen on him.

Vincent dropped his hand. The expression dimmed, but it seemed to cling to the corners of him, pressing into his eyes and loosening his shoulders. "Hey," he said.

"Hey," Wesley replied. He just stood there then, his gaze dragging across Vincent's face and down his usual grunged-up coat and back again, before he managed to jerk himself back into focus. Grinning, he motioned inside. "Hope you're hungry."

"I'm always—" Vincent began, but the rest of the sentence died in his throat. He stared across the living room at the dining table with its simple arrangement of plates.

"It's just dinner. And *not* spicy this time. Also no garlic in yours, I made sure." Wesley laughed, and it sounded a bit like his soul escaping his body. "I'm not claiming it's even good either, my usual cooking skills are about the level of putting peanut butter on crackers, so doctored mac and cheese from the box is already a step up." He didn't know how else to say *dear god, please, please like this or I might die* any better, so he shut up and watched Vincent make his way over.

The vampire touched one of the spoons like they were made of silver, if the metal were actually as dangerous as the myths, then examined the little place card with the fanged emoji-head beside his bowl. He brushed his fingers over it with the same almost terrified reverence. "It's…"

"Let's eat already, it's probably getting cold." Wesley's heart hammered, propelling him forward. "Actually, I can microwave it? I'll microwave it." He grabbed both bowls, but Vincent snatched his own right back, hands sliding around Wesley's.

"I like it cold," he whispered. His cheeks reddened. "I mean, it's a nice change of pace from the typical hot kind. Who wants hot mac-n-cheese all the time, anyway?"

Still holding his own dish, Wesley sat down awkwardly. This was too much like a date he hadn't actually invited Vincent on. And for the life of him, he couldn't tell if every little flustered, soft reaction from the vampire was a desire for that to have been Wes's intention or a fear of it, and Wes absolutely couldn't ask now. He shoveled food into his mouth instead. It wasn't too cold, and it wasn't too bad either. He'd have to make this more often.

Vincent hummed as he swallowed his first bite. "That's kind of delicious."

"Only kind of?"

"It's your first try. I have to leave you room for improvement."

"Fuck off, you know I'm already perfect." Wes had meant it as a joke, but Vincent seemed actively trying not to look at him now.

"Well, I wouldn't go that far. Incredible, maybe," the vampire muttered, a little flushed.

Incredible, maybe. An incredible *asshole*, absolutely. Wes guzzled half his water, trying to calm the buzz of guilt and nerves in the back of his head.

Vincent was still just eating, awkwardly avoiding Wes's gaze as he dragged his spoon downward against his tongue at the end of every bite. With the hint of red still lingering in his cheeks, the subtle gliding of his lips over the metal made Wes short circuit everywhere but his nether-regions. He wasn't allowed to be feeling this *now*, not while he still withheld the truth from Vincent.

He attempted to distract himself by cartwheeling to the first new topic he could think of. "So you know my friend Kendall?"

Vincent looked at him finally. "The annoying lesbian you're in love with?"

"Yeah, that one." Wes drank the rest of his water like it might save him. "She wants your chat app username. I think she's planning on interrogating you through DMs. She can be like that. With my friends. Friends who are vampires, anyway."

"You have many of those? Vampires, I mean." Vincent's lips had a little quirk to them.

"Oh, loads. This neck has *been* places." What was even coming out of his mouth anymore? Wes wasn't entirely sure. It still sounded English, at least. Once he started babbling at Vincent in Spanish it was time to launch himself into the sun.

Vincent poked his spoon towards Wes like a sword. "You've been cheating on me! I knew it. I bet he has bigger fangs, huh? More intoxicating venom?"

Never, Wesley wanted to say, *there's no one I could ever crave the way I crave you,* but he detoured right around that to a shambling laugh and a, "Please, you assume they're a dude? I'll have you know that I'm happy to get my blood sucked by vampires of *any* gender. Or all vampires, of all genders! Bite me up, baby."

The joyful expression didn't drop from Vincent's face, but his brow tightened and he grew a little more serious. "Wait are we—what are we talking about here?"

This was it, Wes was done for. This had all been a mistake: the dinner, Vincent, his existence, queerness as a general concept. If he had ever been a truly practicing Catholic, maybe he could have confessed it all back. He let his spoon clatter into his bowl and dropped his head into his hands. "Fuck if I know," he groaned. "I am perfectly happy with just one vampire, I should probably clarify that now."

Vincent hummed softly in the silence. He scraped the bottom of his bowl a few more times before asking, so gentle it almost hurt, "You are bisexual, then? Sorry if that's a weird conclusion to draw, it just seemed like, from your joke…"

At least Vincent hadn't taken it too seriously. Wesley breathed in, then out, and forced himself to shovel down more food, twitching his lips into something like a smile. "Yeah, I'm bi."

With the serious nod of an assassin about to commit to a murder, Vincent said, "Hi bi, I'm gay."

That undid Wesley so fully that he choked on his last bite of mac and cheese. "Don't you fucking dare."

Vincent lifted his spoon threateningly. "Do not cite the deep jokes at me, son, I was there when they were written!"

"Damn you." Wesley shook his head and stumbled out of his seat. "How much garlic do you take before you go into anaphylaxis because I think—" he gasped, coughing through something stuck in his throat as tears welled in the corners of his eyes, "I think there's a dad in you that needs to be freed."

"No, no that's for werewolves and grandmothers, and you do it with a knife, like in Little Red Riding Hood." Vincent grabbed Wes's arm, cackling as he pulled him back.

The pressure of his hands lit something inside Wesley, so overwhelmingly hot and light that he stumbled into Vincent. Their brushing chests and knocking hips sent sparks trembling beneath Wesley's skin as the vampire guided him back into his chair.

He collapsed there, still half coughing, half crying, and all laughing. "You know if you explain the reference it doesn't count anymore."

"If I don't explain the reference people might not get it." Vincent snorted, but his lips still quirked at the corners. He pulled back and reclaimed his seat. The withdrawal of his touch left Wes tingling hot and cold in his wake.

They were just staring at each other now, Wesley realized, two sloppy smiles and empty bowls. Vincent looked away first. Then he took the edges of his chair and scooted it toward Wes. He leaned one elbow against the table. A few tangles of his hair fell across his forehead and he pushed them back. Wesley's eyes tracked the motion, then slid down, across Vincent's eyebrows, over the curve of his cheekbones, to his mouth. Two little fangs pressed against his upper lip, their delicate tips appearing as he breathed.

Wesley ached, from his core to his groin, every available piece of him straining for things he knew he couldn't—shouldn't—have. He had betrayed Vincent. He had almost brought him to a place that had been the death of people before and of vampires most of all. He wasn't allowed to want this, not the thought of Vincent's mouth on his neck or Vincent's hands in his hair or any of the feelings that came with it, not the ones in his dick and definitely not the ones in his heart.

Wes had to tell him.

Then, if Vincent still wanted his blood, he could have it. He could bleed it out of Wes into a mug and drink it that way, if denying Wes the feeling of his mouth and fangs would make it better. He could drain it from him until his heart stopped if that was justice enough. But he deserved to know. Yet, as he leaned toward Wes, brows tight and lips parted, Wesley's resolve died instantly. Panic replaced it.

He stood up, scooting his chair back in the process. "I wager that you've never crashed a party before. Or stolen a boat. Or eaten loaded French fries on the top of that big skyscraper on Fourth and Sapphire." He didn't know how Vincent had reacted because he couldn't look, already turning to jog toward the coat that currently lived on his stair banister. "Come on, the night's young, we're young, we should do something."

He didn't hear Vincent stand, or the sound of him approaching, but suddenly he was beside Wesley, both arms wrapped around himself as he shrugged. "I haven't done… Well, I haven't done *much*. So yeah, I'm down."

Wesley shimmied into his jacket with a grin. "Dude, we're going to do so fucking much tonight it'll give you a concussion."

"Can I please at least be conscious at the end?" Vincent winced as he said it.

Wesley laughed and clapped him on the back. "I wager you one terrible ballad that I can drink more Lake Monster shots at the Fishnettery than you."

"What's the Fishnettery?"

"Vinny." Wesley paused just long enough to blink at him. "Vinny, you're killing me. You were raised in this

173

city and you're gay and you don't know the Fishnettery?"

This time Vincent's flinch was a more palpable thing, his expression going tight.

Wesley backpedaled. "Sorry. I know not everyone gets to have the um, the queer experience?"

That just seemed to put something bitter in Vincent's mouth, and he bit the corner of his lip before letting it out again. "That's not the only kind of queer experience, you know."

"No. No, I know. Fuck, I'm sorry. I just—" How could he already be making so many different kinds of messes in one evening when it was only half past seven. "Maybe I should phrase this better. Vincent Barnes, do you want to go to a very gay, weird ass micro-brewery crab-shack combo, get covered in glitter, and down alcohol that tastes a bit like three layers of food coloring and leaves your tongue a weird purple for a week? My treat."

"Yeah, that…" Vincent's expression softened. "That sounds kind of fun, actually."

"Brilliant." Wesley exhaled in relief and threw the front door open. Distraction, here they came. "First stop, shots. Second stop, everywhere else."

∽↝

Wesley lost the Lake Monster shot contest by a whopping five shots.

"You just really don't know when to stop putting stuff in your mouth," he said as Vincent slammed the last one down.

The vampire had looked at him so strangely then, fangs puckering gently at his lips and his throat bobbing. Their only salvation had been the incredibly hot, dark-haired man with dangling earrings and a leather jacket who'd tried to flirt with Wesley at that exact moment. Wesley had managed to chat a name and a drink out of him—Andres and an old fashioned—before he'd taken a second look at Vincent and the corners of his eyes had tightened.

He growled a quick, "If I'd known his blood was claimed, I wouldn't have wasted my time," and vanished back into the crowd.

"Oh god, he was a vampire," Vincent hissed, leaning so close his mouth brushed Wesley's ear, sending a shiver down Wes's entire spine and some places Kendall would have made jokes about.

"Fuck." Wes laughed shakily. "I think you just saved my life."

Vincent grinned at him. "I had an anterior motivation."

"Ulterior motive."

"Same difference."

They emerged covered in a little less glitter than Wesley had promised—a smear across Wes's cheek and a fluff of it in Vincent's hair—but with tongues so eggplant purple that Vincent groaned about it getting into his fangs. Wesley sang his loser's ballad in an unhinged, off-key voice that was ten times worse than his natural one. He kept it up all the way to the boardwalk of shimmering lights and laughing people, until he spotted a wedding reception in an elegantly remodeled warehouse that looked out at the water.

"I bet you can't crash this party so hard that someone kicks us out," he said.

Vincent swayed just a little. "Bet *you* can't! Wait—no, Wes, I don't actually—Wes!"

Wesley won that wager in exactly four minutes and ten seconds, shirtless, with a microphone. "Just be happy I didn't get arrested this time."

"Wes! How many times have you done that?"

Wesley only cackled and pulled Vincent along.

He wagered a celebrity impression that Vincent couldn't get one of the slightly-too-early-for-Halloween tourists to take a selfie with him. After he lost, Vincent wagered a fake fact about the moon that he could skip more stones across the smooth, dark lake than Wes, and won. Vincent seemed to be doing an awful lot of the winning in their friendship. With anyone else Wes might have been jealous, but the way it lit up Vincent's face and made him look as if, for one shiny moment, he almost believed himself worthy, and that was far better than any victory.

Wesley bought them an extra-large hot apple cider called *the sleeping devil* from a food truck parked outside a cemetery-themed tourist-trap bar after Vincent spent three full minutes trying to drunkenly calculate whether the price of two small drinks would be more than one large one. They walked by a series of gated marinas, passing the drink back and forth and cursing every time they found it was still scalding. Vincent pointed at the distant boat parties and bet that Wesley couldn't guess what they were up to. After each consecutively more outrageous story, Vincent nodded and conceded the win.

"Hey, hey, I wager you my most tasty blood that we can't have our own boat party," Wesley whispered, leaning in like it was a secret. He'd been doing that a lot since their first stop; making everything a secret, as though this entire night were an inside joke between the two of them and not a one-way street of him trying to get his lips as close to Vincent's skin as possible.

Vincent laughed, and he turned his head to whisper back, his face so near to Wesley's neck that Wes could feel the warmth of his breath in the chilly October air. "How are we going to get a boat?"

"We'll steal it. Just for a bit." Wes grinned. He swept toward one of the little bobbing dock ramps that stuck out into the lake, pulling up his hood as he went. When he reached the locked gate that separated them from the boats, he gave it a little rattle and looked up. "Can you climb?"

He couldn't quite see Vincent's expression beneath the vampire's oversized cowl, but his half-gloved fingers wrapped back and forth around the cider cup and he sounded a little wary. "The fence, yeah. But isn't this illegal?"

"How many homes have you broken into, Vinny?" Wesley nudged him in the shoulder and then took a few steps back. With as little fumbling as he could manage, he lunged at the fence. He grunted his way up and over it, the metal cold against his bare hands and his muscles screaming. A rush of excitement hit him at the top, and he landed with a smirk, turning back to loop one arm casually through the bars of the gate.

"That's not fair," Vincent grumbled. But he pressed the cider into Wes's hand and scowled at the top of the fence.

Wesley lost track of his movement in the darkness, watching the vampire crouch on the dock one moment, then balance on the top of the gate the next. His coat fluttered around him as he dropped down the other side, arms outstretched and knees pulled in. Wes could see the bat comparison; majestic and shadowy and so graceful he seemed to be flying. It took Wes's breath away. He fought to regain his senses as Vincent casually took back the cider.

"So, a boat then?" Vincent asked.

"A boat!" Wes clambered down the dock, glancing into one then the next before randomly picking a white speedboat with pink and purple stripes. He all but fell off the edge trying to climb in, the gentle rocking of the dock turning to a slightly different rhythm as he jumped to the little vessel's deck. He tottered and flopped into the cushioned bench beside the driver's seat.

Vincent laughed, joining him at a much more reasonable pace for someone carrying a steaming drink. He scooted close until their thighs touched, then their shoulders, snuggling down like a wolf in a den. Behind them, the back of the bench rose high enough to block out the boardwalk and before them stretched the lake, a few glimmering lights on its dark surface. It felt like a world all their own.

This seclusion hit Wes in a blow, both stronger and somehow different from the privacy of his own home. It made him want to slip his arm through Vincent's and lean his head on the vampire's shoulder and whisper all the desires that had been aching within him—the craving for Vincent's mouth on his neck and his hands dragging down the front of Wesley's pants, but something more than that too. For the promise of just this, again: to sit in the dark, shoulder to shoulder and hip to hip, passing back and forth their drink in silence and simply existing together.

It was a yearning that should have been less sexual, a step back from the lust of his initial urges, but it wasn't. Instead it was magnifying, turning those desires brighter and bolder. And he wanted it, more of it, now and tomorrow and the day after, and the fact that he'd almost taken this away from them to get into Vitalis-Barron turned his stomach.

Telling Vincent what he'd done would break this as certainly as delivering him to the lab would have. But maybe he didn't have to say anything? In the end, nothing bad had come out of his assholery. He'd learned his lesson. He could be better to Vincent now without telling him how badly he'd fucked up—without ruining everything they had together—couldn't he?

It sounded like the dialogue option in a dating sim that made everything blow up later in the story, but the other option, the one where he destroyed this moment forever, sounded far worse. Certain imminent destruction or a possible future one? That wasn't such a hard choice after all.

"You should really just bite me already." It sounded a little less like he was offering his body up on a platter and a little more like a bad advertisement for a health product.

Vincent drew back just enough for it to feel like miles without actually shifting their legs apart. In the dark his face was a silhouette, his voice soft and almost pathetically tender. "You don't have to do this for me, you know."

"No!" Wes didn't mean to shout but it came out that way, all of his emotions tumbling together. He added, calmer, "I want to. I promised you could back when we first met." Even if he'd had other reasons at the time, and now all that remained was his craving for Vincent's mouth on his skin and his desire to give the vampire something as important and personal as he could, to start making up for everything he couldn't risk telling him.

"This means a lot to me." Vincent sounded almost breathless as he said it. He shifted further away again— way too fucking far—so he could turn toward Wesley. "I'll be gentle. I don't have to touch you, outside my fangs. And if you're more comfortable with your wrist or your inner-arm instead, those work too; I only go for the neck because it's faster. But maybe you want it over faster, I get that too. Or if you want to—"

"Vincent, shut up." Wesley laughed, grabbing for him in the dark and finding the front of his coat, pulling him closer with a fist of it. "I said I fucking *want* you to bite me. We've practically done this twice already. More, if you count the times I was sleeping. You don't have to coddle me through it."

"Alright." Two of Vincent's fingers rose to brush the edge of Wes's hand where it still held his coat. "Just tell me how you want it and I will."

Tell me how you want it.

Part of Wesley screamed to hide, or run, or at least tuck his desires away. He could just give Vincent his neck and be happy with that. Not be the cringe-inducing weirdo who not only *liked* to be bitten but liked to be pinned down and roughed up too. But part of Wes was also still a bit buzzed and outside his head the world had turned to an odd kind of static.

"You know what you did when you were starving?" he whispered. "I want you to bite me like that."

"Oh." A little tremble went through Vincent, strong enough for Wes to feel it in the grip he somehow still had on the vampire's coat, the grip he couldn't seem to let go of as though letting go might mean Vincent would poof into a bat and fly away. The tremble turned to a soft laugh, then Vincent was cackling, leaning forward and gasping through it.

Wesley finally did let go of him then, pulling back a little horrified. "Fuck, sorry, that was—"

"Oh, Wes," Vincent finally muttered, and the affection in his voice froze Wesley in place.

He wanted to bail right out the side of the boat, and he wanted to grab Vincent by the face and kiss him like he was the one feeding, and he fucking *wanted* Vincent, wanted to fuck him and be fucked by him, wanted him so much he could feel it in his bones.

Vincent was still just sitting there, saying Wes's name with affection, yes, but no more or less than he might have a good friend who'd done something a bit stupid.

"Don't pretend you didn't know," Wes grumbled.

"Well, yeah, it's pretty obvious that's the sort of thing you're into," Vincent laughed again, this time harsher. "I just thought, I don't know, that you wouldn't want it from me? I'm kind of pathetic, as vampires go. I don't make for a dramatic, mysterious predator. I'm like the grimy sewer variety of a vampire that you shoo off your lawn with a broom."

"I think you're underselling yourself there. You make a pretty dramatic and mysterious silhouette in the window." Wes swallowed. "You're not weirded out that this is almost like a... a fetish?"

"No." Vincent's voice was a hollow squeak and it gave Wes the suspicion that maybe he was lying.

But Wes was still just a little too tipsy and a little too happy that Vincent had actually agreed to it. He had agreed to it, hadn't he? In a friendly way, a non-reciprocal fetishistic *this isn't about you* way, just two queer men agreeing to let the other person have his own sort of fun without it being a thing, right?

But the longer Vincent stayed silent, the more Wesley wondered if he'd misread everything, up to and including Vincent's desire to feed off him in the first place.

"If you *are* weirded out—"

This time it was Wes's turn to be interrupted, and it came not with a laugh, but a growl. "Be quiet, prey."

Wesley swallowed, accidently making a noise in the process, something tight and small and *wanting*.

"Was that alright?" Vincent asked, but he still sounded just a little rough, a little like he would enjoy pinning Wesley down and making him shut up.

Wesley whispered back, "Yes."

And Vincent leapt at him.

It turned out the distance Vincent had pulled back was good for that, good for throwing Wesley onto the cushioned bench with such a perfect mixture of force and tenderness that despite the sheer rush of adrenaline that shot through him there was no fear, only excitement and need. Wesley wiggled slightly, not sure how much to push back. Enough, apparently, because Vincent made a deep almost bestial sound and grabbed Wesley's wrists deftly in one hand, pressing them over his head as he shoved Wes back down. He loomed over Wes, a shadow against the sky. For a moment, he didn't move, like he was sizing Wesley up, taking him in maybe, making his heart stammer and his desire strain. With his free hand, Vincent brushed a fingertip along Wesley's temple, tracing his hairline with a nail the way Wes was pretty sure one of the vampires in the dating sim had done. But he was also pretty sure Vincent hadn't been present for that chapter. Wesley shuddered, and it was all thrill that coursed through him as Vincent slid his fingers into Wes's hair, pulling his head back and pressing his chin to the side.

It should have been terrifying; it should have felt too vulnerable, Wes's entire life pounding through veins, so exposed that a vampire could drain it away without a second thought. But this wasn't just any vampire: it was Vincent. And being vulnerable for Vincent wasn't frightening. It was freeing.

Wes relaxed beneath his hold, loosening his shoulder from his neck and sighing in a small, soft sound. He expected teeth—a pinch, then a moment of bliss—but what he got was Vincent's nose brushing his cheekbone, and his ear lobe, his breath intoxicatingly hot along Wesley's jaw and down the side of his neck. Lips followed, a little too light to be a kiss, working their way to his pulse. Vincent hovered there so long that Wes whimpered, and that scared him more than anything else they'd done in this boat. He was pretty sure if Vincent held him in suspense for too long he was going to start begging, and he really, really didn't want to jump there yet.

"Vincent," he whispered, breathless and aching.

"Shush," Vincent whispered back, mouth brushing against Wes's skin.

Wes missed the moment his fangs sank in, it felt like a tiny, affectionate nip and then his body was pulsing and a moan slipped from his lips.

Just a kind of venom, he tried to remind himself, just hormones hitting his nervous system and lighting fireworks in his brain. But where Vincent's halfway bites had left him with a wanting, like the first touch of a high that slipped away too fast, this built with a fiery bliss. It was almost sexual, almost orgasmic. By the way his dick ached for contact and his mouth for Vincent's fingers to slide like an innuendo against his tongue, *almost sexual* was a blatant lie. This, now, with Vincent, knowing how much he wanted Vincent in all the traditional erotic ways on top of his bizarre, vampiric prey desire—this was more sexual for him than anything erotic he'd done with partners in the past.

If only Vincent had actually wanted him that way.

14

VINCENT

Vincent wanted Wesley.

Just being near Wesley, having the man whisper into his ear and laugh at his jokes and tease him with the fondest, fullest smile all night had turned his yearning into a force that could rival the momentum of the earth around the sun. And like the earth, he felt as though he'd been orbiting Wesley, basking in his light but always just a hair out of reach. Until Wesley, ridiculous and wonderful Wesley, had said, *"I want you to bite me like that."*

And Vincent had caught fire.

This was just a very specific craving Wesley happened to have. It wasn't about Vincent himself, nor was it an offer for anything more than a bite with a lightly predatory flare. Even if it was a bit sexual for Wesley, it certainly wasn't about finding *Vincent* sexy. It couldn't be.

Wesley moaned when Vincent's teeth sunk through his skin, and he pressed himself against Vincent like an instinct, the bulge of his dick so hard where it rubbed Vincent's hip that Vincent's own erection ached. They were still just friends. Friends who happened to be a human with a bite kink and a vampire so in tune to that human's scent that it engulfed him like its own kind of intoxication. But all that knowledge seemed launched into the void suddenly.

Vincent grabbed firmer onto Wesley's hair, stroking the man's wrists and pressing down on him with his body as he fed in gentle, extended nipping and sucking like a series of tiny, aggressive teeth kisses that trailed along Wesley's pulse. Wes's fingers curled around Vincent's and fluttered there, like he didn't know whether to hold on. It was such a singular sweet gesture in the midst of their almost violent thrill that it made Vincent ache in two different places at once.

He didn't just want this. He wanted this and more.

As he finished feeding, Vincent gently pulled Wesley up. He wrapped an arm around Wes's back and he dragged his tongue up the side of his neck to heal the little bite wounds over, savoring the last hints of blood and the scent of Wes's skin. Wes relaxed against the back of the bench, but he seemed tight and alive beneath the outward languidness. It had to be the same tension that was still bundled up in Vincent. It had to be.

The man leaned toward him.

Vincent acted on impulse and the lingering effects of too many shots: he tried to kiss Wesley Smith Garcia. Except, as it turned out, impulse and alcohol had equal potential to create and destroy. Instead of meeting Wes's lips with his own, he found the man's nose with the tip of a fang.

Wes jerked back, cursing. "Ah fuck, was that you? Ah—" And he sneezed.

Vincent bolted to his feet. "Sorry, god, I'm sorry! Are you bleeding, should I—"

"Shit, no, you're good," Wesley said, standing, but as he did so, he sneezed again, bonking his head into Vincent's chin.

Vincent lurched. The back of his knees hit the edge of the speedboat. On any other night, in any state of sobriety, he could see himself catching his balance, laughing as he praised his vampiric agility. But this night must have included one too many drinks or one too many shocks or hopes or other debilitating emotions, because this night he toppled uselessly backwards, and the chilly lake slammed into him.

Water rushed over his head and leached into his coat. The heavy fabric felt like a sea monster wrapping around him, pulling him down. A mix of panic and mortification shot like ice through his veins, but he fought against it, forcing himself to stay calm.

Accidentally stumbling headfirst into the freezing lake was no more horrific than failing to kiss Wesley. Particularly if Wesley had realized Vincent was trying to kiss him and avoided it on purpose.

Oh god, maybe he was better off drowning here.

Wes was still on the boat, though. Vincent had to face him, one way or another. He pushed through the bitter cold of the October night water, kicking his legs and pumping his arms toward the haze of dim light between the undersides of the boats. He broke the surface with a gasp, treading water to keep afloat. "Wes?"

"Fuck." It sounded just a little like Wesley had been crying. He'd torn free one of the boat's bench cushions and was halfway through tugging out a life jacket, but he dropped it and slammed himself against the railing, gripping the side with both hands. "You're okay?"

"Yeah, just cold and wet. And also in the water. Kind of sucks." Vincent's teeth chattered. His fangs felt like they'd retracted so far back into his skull that they would never come out again, and if he ever needed to get rid of any other erections fast, now he knew the cure.

"Ah shit, that's going to make what I'm about to do incredibly stupid, isn't it?" Wesley stared at the water for a moment before shrugging. "Bottoms up or something." He stepped onto the boat's rail and vaulted over the side. Tucking in his arms and legs, Wes splashed like a cannonball into the lake close enough to dowse Vincent with a wave of the icy water.

Vincent sputtered as he reemerged. "What the fuck, dude!"

"I don't know, it felt like the right response?" Wes wiped his face, squinting in Vincent's direction as he swam. A choppy laugh spilled out of him. He hollered, throwing both his arms out and plunging backward like the world's worst breaststroke. As he came back up, he shook his head like a dog, flinging droplets away from his head. "You weren't joking, this is freezing!"

Vincent swiped him with a splash. "You could have given me your jacket but now it's wet, you ass!" Through his shivers, he found his smile creeping back into place. This man—this ridiculous, wonderful, nonsensical man who thought the best reaction to his awkward, bumbling vampire friend falling in the water was to jump in himself—this man was perfect. Wesley Smith Garcia was perfect, and looking at him made Vincent's heart stop, and turned even the freezing cold water brighter and warmer.

Wes wiped back his hair, tucking the short, drenched waves behind his ears, and grinned almost sheepishly. "Shit, you're right. Next time you fall into a lake, I'll take off my clothes before I join you."

It didn't sound like flirting; it sounded like every other weirdly suggestive joke Wes had blindly stumbled into, his expression still casual and friendly. Vincent opened his mouth, and closed it again, kicking his legs a little harder. He regressed to splashing Wes a second time.

Wes lifted his hands. "I get it! I get it!" He laughed. "It's really fucking cold, dude, do you want to…?" He motioned vaguely toward the little public beach that butted the boardwalk between their gated marina and the next.

"Please," Vincent all but whined.

They were both doing more shaking than laughing by the time they pulled themselves back onto dry land, and Wes had begun muttering about his great multitude of life regrets. He pulled his phone out and Vincent cursed, digging around in his pockets for his own. Dead, as he'd suspected, but he wasn't sure if it had been that way before the water or not. Wesley's still worked just fine.

"Completely waterproof." He waved it at Vincent, showing off the loading app for a taxi service as he did. "I broke like five different phones over freshman year of college and now Kendall buys me a heavy-duty case for every birthday." His hands shook as he typed, and he bounced on his heels. His lips looked a bit blue.

Vincent grabbed his arm. "There's heaters outside that little pub across the street."

Wes only grunted, letting Vincent lead him to a nearly-empty patio, the last pair of customers paying their bill. Their waitress gave him and Wes a skeptical look but Vincent smiled awkwardly and made a show of shrugging. The woman just sighed.

"Car will be here in seven minutes," Wes muttered. He crossed his arms, exhaling a shaky breath.

Vincent pressed his shoulder against Wes's. He felt noticeably colder—the difference between human and vampiric homeostasis probably. The city was so quiet now that it left Vincent's gaze always wandering back to Wesley and he had to keep pulling it away to stop himself from overly focusing on the bunch of the man's gorgeous lips and the bob of his throat, the way the specks of rainwater still caught in his dark eyelashes shone and the perfect line of his sturdy jaw. He forced his attention elsewhere, finally fixing it on the building to their left. A glass box of fliers had been mounted against its near wall, the largest one at its center advertising a new Vitalis-Barron Pharmaceuticals research opportunity. *Payment in gift-card or cash*, it claimed in bold lettering above the two words *vampires wanted*!

It was probably good money—better than what Vincent made off his random odd jobs—but their express desire to conduct research on vampires when the company had produced nothing to help them in all the years of its growth and progress had always turned his stomach a little. So rarely did anyone ever want vampires for anything. When they did, it was never for the vampire's benefit.

Well, perhaps not *never*. In Wesley's case, they were both benefiting equally off the human's enjoyment of being bitten. Whether or not that had been Wes's intention, Vincent found he wasn't actually sure. His chest tightened. Fuck, this *had* started as Wes wanting an adrenaline kick. Maybe that was still all Vincent was to him? He didn't want to believe so, not after all the other amazing things Wesley had done for him, but now that he'd considered it, the doubt caught hold of him like it had claws.

"Hey, Wes?" He asked.

"Huh?" Wesley glanced up. Vincent swore his gaze lingered somewhere between Vincent's chin and his nose, as though looking for his fangs.

"You know all my jokes about fetishes and stuff— that's all it is, just me trying to be funny." He cleared his throat. "I mean, that *is* what it is right? You're not…"

Wesley looked paler than normal, his tanned skin a bit ghostly. Panic tightened around his eyes. When he spoke, it was a little harsh and a little empty all at once. "Not what?"

"You're not *only* hanging out with me because I can bite you?" Vincent felt his own fear growing, and he stared across the street as he spoke. "It's fine if that's your kink or whatever—I thought it was great, too—it was *really* great, actually. I didn't know biting someone could be like that. But um, I guess what I mean is, I'm more than *just* a set of fangs, and I—" *I like you, Wesley Smith Garcia, and I need to know you see me as a person, even if you don't like me back.* He wanted to say that, he wanted so badly just to be out with it, but it caught in his throat, a tight, terrifying bundle that seemed so wrong for this moment, both of them sopping and shivering and scared.

Before he could find the courage, Wesley took over for him. "No! No, Vinny, I…" He trailed off, wiping a trembling hand through his hair. His gaze slid to that glass box with the Vitalis-Barron flier, and he looked like he was going to throw up. His phone beeped. "That's the car."

Sure enough, a black sedan with a taxi sign in the window pulled around the corner.

Vincent's heart pounded as it approached. He trusted Wesley, believed that if he said Vincent's fears were wrong, then they were—but this didn't feel over. It felt like they had tried to unravel something and only tangled it further. But the driver pulling up in front of them was already eyeing their wet clothes like she might just keep going if they didn't pile in fast enough, and there was no way Vincent was continuing this conversation in some random stranger's car.

Wesley opened the door, his grin not quite filling out his face the way it usually did as he confirmed with the driver. A little further down the street, a small, laughing group of people spilled out of the only other open building. As they turned toward Vincent, his body went a whole new kind of cold. He nudged Wesley inside the car, but before he could follow, the lady at the front of the group locked eyes with him.

Mr. Babcock's assistant.

She stared at him as he fled into the car and slammed the door closed. Vincent didn't exhale until they'd turned down the street and out of her view. No one chased after him, no aggressive blacked-out cars suddenly pulling out on their tail like they might in a movie. Of course not. Babcock and his assistant were cruel bigots, but they had just been taking advantage of the fact that their employee was a vampire. They wouldn't hunt him down so long as he stayed out of their way. He was safe now.

His tension remained, though, transferring from thoughts of Babcock's assistant to the shivering mess beside him. He turned the backseat heater on full blast.

Wesley closed his eyes and leaned his head on Vincent's shoulder.

Vincent's chest warmed, but he caught a glance from their driver and looked pointedly out the window after. They were just friends; no one had any right to judge them for their physical contact. But Vincent wanted more than friendship. He wanted to be coming home from a date, Wesley's head on his shoulder because they were going to climb into bed together later and wake up tangled in each other's limbs the next morning. There were people in this city who would judge them for that; he had known them, grown up with them, felt their conviction like sand trapped under his nails and a constant eternal buzz in his ears, even when they hadn't known it was *him* they were judging.

At least his parents never had the chance to kick him out for his sexuality. If he came out openly now, they would probably never find out.

For all his fears, there were also plenty of people in San Salud who wouldn't judge him and Wesley just for the simple pleasures of existing. Maybe the odd looks had nothing to do with their genders and everything to do with their state of dress. Any taxi driver with a passenger who shivered as much as Wesley had every reason to keep glancing back, if only to check that they were still conscious. Vincent couldn't help it if he assumed the worst, but neither did he want to live his life trapped dwelling on the worst either.

The driver gave them a final worried look as they stopped in front of Wesley's house, but when Wes straightened himself up and thanked her, she seemed a little more relaxed. She didn't drive away until they were inside.

Vincent still felt instantly better with the door closed and the walls of the house blocking out the rest of the world. What was it like to be Wes, to know that no matter what he faced he would always have this place to come back to, a safe space to be himself without fear of judgment or aggression? Wes didn't even realize how good he had things.

A little bundle of resentment flared deep in Vincent's gut. He stamped it down. Wesley had paid for everything throughout the night, had offered up his blood and his food and his friendship without question. It was so much more than Vincent could ever dream of repaying him. He deserved this home and all the safety that came with it.

Wes groaned his way to the stairs. "I can take the master shower so you don't have to wait."

Vincent wavered. Blood, food, friendship, and now this too. "You're sure? I can always just head out—"

"Like fuck you will." Wesley scowled. "You're not going anywhere until you shower."

Vincent's heart stammered and his lips twitched. He followed Wesley up the steps. "Alright, then, I'm not going anywhere. I guess I should probably stay to make sure you live through the night, anyways. Not because I care about you, or anything. I just want to get to eat you again in the future."

Wes stopped so suddenly at the top of the stairs that when he turned he was looking down at Vincent for once. He tipped his chin with a smirk that Vincent wanted desperately to wipe off the man's face with his lips and fangs and tongue. "Addicted to me already, huh?"

Vincent growled and pressed up the last step, forcing Wesley into the wall with one hand on his shoulder and the other on his elbow. "You're my *prey* now. I can thirst for you as much as I like." He was ninety percent sure he was quoting either the vampire dating sim or a screenshot of a comic Wes had sent him, but at the moment all his memories were being replaced by the way Wes's throat bobbed and his breath stuttered just a bit, his light shivering only adding to the effect.

Then Wes snorted and pulled out of Vincent's grip in a playful shove. "Oh, fuck off, I have to shower." But he looked back on his way to the bedroom, his lips quirking. "You have to save some of those predatory instincts for tomorrow, you know."

"You asked for them!" Vincent shouted after him, laughing.

"And I will absolutely have them, you be-fanged dork!" Wes returned with towels and two fresh sets of pajama clothes—looser ones for Vincent's taller, ganglier body—and vanished into his mom's old room. He left the door ajar behind him. Vincent waited for the sound of the master shower turning on before locking himself in Wesley's bathroom.

Wesley's approximately ten thousand different bath and body supplies lined the shower rack. An irrational number smelled faintly like Wes's skin and hair, but somehow they took away from the overall Wesley aroma of the house instead of adding to it. After the whole night with him, Vincent had almost grown accustomed to the human's natural scent. That should have made it less wonderful, but instead the familiarity turned it from a temptation at the front of his mind to a soft, happy thrill in the back.

Standing in Wes's shower now, Vincent could imagine the man was here with him, giving rambling explanations of each product, laughing as they bumped each other in the small space, Wesley's fingers fiddling with Vincent's hair, working their way down Vincent's body. Vincent cringed as the thought brought to mind all the things he wished he had said or done at dinner, or on the boat, or waiting for the cab, or even the first moment Wesley had opened the door that night.

He leaned on the wall of the shower and let the hot water soak over him. It felt like he'd come too far, skipped too many right times to tell Wes he liked him. Like he had doomed himself into this, maybe.

But that didn't mean he couldn't enjoy the thoughts of Wesley's body beneath him and Wes's hard dick pressing against his hip, without the man ever having to know. He sunk a little lower against the tile, replaying that memory of the boat in excruciating detail as he rode out the pleasure he'd so desperately wanted then. It wasn't as good as it would have been *with* Wesley. But damn was it still good.

15

Wesley

When the hot water ran out, Wesley assumed he must have taken longer in the shower than Vincent by at least fifty, possibly sixty years—a time he hoped Vincent would blame on the chill and not the fact that one thought of the vampire's bite had set his body right off again. He'd laid beneath the stream, his head tipped back and one leg propped up, and taken all the time he'd desperately wanted Vincent to take with him, easing out his pleasure for so long that the sudden shift from hot to cold had been enough to make him come all on its own. But when he turned the water off he was met with cursing from across the house and something that sounded an awful lot like a particularly awkward vampire falling out of a shower.

"Vinny?" he shouted, wrapping the towel around him as he climbed out. With his body temperature no longer in the Antarctic regions and his brain a haze of tired and post-orgasmic, he felt a bit like he was sleepwalking.

"Fuck!" Vincent shouted back. "I'm okay."

Wesley felt himself grin. He ruffled his clean hair into something that loosely resembled his usual part and shoved on his clothes, yawning as he made his way downstairs to flop on the couch and mindlessly scroll through his phone. He ended up on one of the vampire comics he'd been reading that morning—more a comedic series of skits about a trio of nonhuman roommates than a real story with anything romantic or sexual about it, but the vampire roommate had a few one offs with human dates that seemed a bit too close to what he'd experienced with Vincent to be coming from anything other than personal experience.

Not that he and Vincent were dating. Platonic kink exploration was a thing, right? That's what Vincent had called it: not a fetish but a kink. It made sense, though he was fairly certain there were also aspects to it that weren't as sexual as kinks. Unless there were kinks that weren't necessarily sexual? He would have to look that up.

Wesley had barely input the words into his search bar when Vincent came thumping down the stairs. He shot up, turning his phone off like he might be judged for it, despite Vincent having already agreed to partake in his kink and admitted to enjoying it just as much as he did after. But all his embarrassment vanished as his eyes locked on the vampire and his chest tried to escape his ribcage.

Vincent looked different, impossibly, minutely different, like every little piece of him had been rearranged just slightly. He rubbed a hand-towel over his wet hair, bundling the ends to squeeze the water into it. The dark strands were clean and combed through, shining a little in the electric lights, and where they'd just begun to dry they seemed almost silky. The blue of his eyes looked brighter in comparison. The slightly grimy shadowing and light fuzz of stubble that Wes had always taken as a part of his overall grungy look were gone, leaving his face to its own natural, harsh contours. His feet were bare for the first time Wesley had ever seen and his nails looked like he'd found a manicurist hiding somewhere in Wes's bathroom. He even seemed to hold himself a little looser, his weight relaxed onto one hip. The edge of his borrowed shirt rode up, revealing a thin waist, and his arms—arms Wes had never seen before— were well defined around their gangly joints.

Vincent paused, the hand towel still in his hair. "What?"

"N-nothing." Fuck he really needed to pull it together. "You just clean up well." He laughed, but it sounded wrong in his ears. God, his dick was doing things it didn't have a right to after all the shit it had already pulled tonight. "I swear your skin is like an entirely different shade of pale."

This new shade was clean and crisp and lovely and came with a bright pink flush in the cheeks. Vincent muttered, "It's been a while since I took a shower like that."

"It's a good look on you!" Wes tried to reassure him.

But it seemed like some invisible damage had been done.

Vincent looked away and back again. As he lowered the towel from his hair, Wes caught sight of a series of short scars along the inside of his left arm. His brain stalled on them, leaving him to stare a moment longer than he should have as he tried to place their meaning. Oh. Oh, *fuck.*

"If my existence starts hurting anyone but myself, then maybe I don't deserve to exist at all."

Wes wanted to be angry, angry at the entire world for ever making Vincent feel this way, and angry at himself for laughing at Vincent as a child and fucking with him as an adult and for not being able to convince him of just how much he deserved to exist in any and every way possible. But all Wes could feel now was horror.

"I should go," Vincent said.

No, he shouldn't. Wes didn't want him to. He wanted Vincent to stay and be safe and happy and know that there was someone who cared about him, as a weird shy kid or a vampire or anything else he was or ever would be.

Except Wesley had just cared so little for him that he'd nearly delivered him to Vitalis-Barron. In his rage and recklessness, he'd valued the company's downfall more than the life of a vampire who was good and kind and deserved so much better than to be an unwitting sacrifice. If Wes had trusted Vincent, perhaps they could have worked together on this, but now that was not even an option, because the moment Vincent knew, he'd never trust Wesley enough to rely on him for anything again. And that knowledge was still skipping around in Wes's head, making everything else too hard to put into words.

So instead he squeaked something like, "We've got time, it's cool."

Vincent's brow tightened. He crossed his arm over his chest. "You're tired."

"I'm not—" Wes's body chose that very moment to yawn. "Not that tired," he finished.

Vincent edged toward his damp clothes piled beside the foot of the stairs, his prior relaxation vanishing with every tiny step.

"Tomorrow night?" Wes pleaded. "We can game then, or eat, or go on another adventure, or you can bite me, or you can *not* bite me, whatever you want. Or it can be Sunday. Or Monday. My schedule's basically just you." He didn't know what else to say, how else to say all the things inside him. Instead, he settled on, "Please?"

Vincent's shoulders slowly loosened, the edge of one side of his mouth quirking. "I have to see if my phone works." He swallowed. "But Sunday? How about Sunday."

"Yeah, totally." Wesley felt the fear in his chest release in a flutter of butterflies and exhaustion. "I'll see you Sunday."

∿

"So it's a date?"

"It's not a date!" Wes curled his toes over the side of the couch's armrest, shooting a scowl toward the little video of Kendall at the edge of his second screen. "We're just friends."

"Friends with benefits."

"Not those kinds of benefits!" He lifted his controller a bit to the left as he directed his mage to form a defensive shield on that side. *War Call* had been Kendall's first choice but right now that game reminded him too much of Babcock. "To your right, there's a—"

"Got it." Kendall's character glowed shortly before releasing a blast at the veiny, dragon-like monster charging her through one of the gaps in the labyrinthine coliseum. "He agreed to put his mouth on your skin."

"That's how vampire bites *work*."

"You said he called it a kink!" Kendall shouted at him, then whooped as her target dropped dead. "Take that, you motherfucker. God, I love this spell."

Wes rolled his eyes. "Kinks can be non-sexually intimate, I looked it up. There's like, whole tiny communities of people who are into certain kinky shit just for the emotional return."

"So you're literally giving him a piece of your body, he's at least emotionally invested in sustaining your kink, and he's agreed to continue this on a regular basis. Pretty sure that's dating."

"Also pretty sure that if he wanted to date, he would have said something by now. He's had every opportunity." Wesley vaulted his character onto the next monster's back as he said it, shoving his sword through the back of the creature's skull. It only lost a quarter of its health, which seemed a bit unreasonable considering he was spearing it through the brain. Maybe it had four brains. That, at least, would make more sense than whatever he had or didn't have with Vincent.

"Have *you* said anything during all these opportunities?"

"Fuck no. I already had to tell him about the whole kink business. There's no way I'm pushing things."

"You really like him." They were soft words, and when Wesley glanced at Kendall's version of the screen, her character had stopped moving. Her brows were tight in a tender way that made Wesley want to duck behind the couch for cover.

"Yes, I get it, you're happy I have a crush again finally. The world is back in order." He didn't mean to sound so snippy, but the way she was acting stripped down something inside him, making him feel raw. He launched a detonating spell at the newest two enemy monsters,

Kendall's character continued standing still as she stared at him through the feed.

"You going to help me here or not?" Wes snapped.

"No, Wes…" She set her controller down.

Wesley was pretty sure this was the first time she'd ever done that by choice in their entire five-year friendship and it terrified him; terrified him just enough that he couldn't think of a way to redirect the conversation.

"I have seen you blow up so many potential relationships by throwing yourself into them full force until they fizzle out or combust, then spring forward after like nothing happened."

"This is not the comfort you think it is, Kendall." Wes grit his teeth, scowling as he tried to take down one of the monsters on his own while out maneuvering the other.

"No, hear me out." Kendall looked at him like she was trying to cast a spell through their video chat. "You've never cared enough for the people you've dated to… to gentle your edges for them, I guess. And maybe that's okay in a lot of ways because if someone doesn't actually want you for all of who you are, then going too far with them just hurts you both. But you're scared of Vincent seeing the whole you. Because you *like* him and you're afraid of ruining things with him."

"It's not that," Wesley protested, barely dodging a volley of acid breath in the game. Somewhere behind him, Kendall's character had died but she didn't seem to care. "It's just that I think Vincent has been hurt before. I know he has; *I* hurt him. I don't want to accidentally hurt him again. I don't want to ruin this." He put the last words together slowly, his brain fitting them piece by piece beside Kendall's assertion and finding an exact match. His hands drifting towards his lap, fingers stalled over the controls. On the screen, one of the monsters drove its horns through his character's torso, and a *round lost* notification appeared. It didn't seem terribly important suddenly. Nothing seemed terribly important, except Vincent and the way the thought of him fleeing now made Wesley's chest feel like his game character's, ravaged and bleeding. "Fuck."

"It's okay," Kendall said gently.

"Fuck," Wesley repeated. His eyes stung. He launched his controller into the pile on the floor. "Well, what the hell do I do about it?"

"I don't know." Kendall ran a hand through the short spikes of her hair as she leaned back, nearly out of view of her camera. "But you've got to tell him. It's hard. I know it's hard. God, it took me three months to ask out Leoni! And then three months after that she had to ask me whether or not we were dating. Relationships are a fucking minefield and if there were right answers then someone would have written them in a book and gotten really rich by now."

"Pretty sure there's lots of rich people with books on dating."

"Yeah but they're all straight and white and mostly wrong, so they don't count."

Wesley sighed, flopping his head against the top of the couch. "What if Vincent and I just keep doing the thing we're doing now and I don't say anything and it stays like this until we die? That's an option, too, right?"

"Would you be happy with that?" She sounded serious, but her voice took on a teasing twist as she continued, "I mean, if your pingly—"

"No!" Wesley howled over her. "I will not be having any more sex talks from you, woman!"

"You've been saying that for the last five years, but you haven't complained to HR yet, have you."

"No, but I am hanging up! And unfriending! And stealing your future children and all your left socks!"

Kendall held her camera to her face, so close that her eyes went a little bugged. "I love you Wesley, but you're an asshole."

Wesley smiled at her, all teeth and unbridled affection. "I hate you Kendall, but you're wonderful."

And he hung up.

∿

Kendall was right. Sunday night passed in a blissful mess of laughter and video games and snacks, with a bite at the end that lasted for an intoxicating twenty minutes of Vincent's hands in Wes's hair and his right leg casually slipping up and down Wesley's, leaving Wes to jerk off in his bedroom after, then the shower, then his bedroom again, like he was sixteen and had nothing better to do. And still Wesley couldn't bring himself to admit to Vincent that he wanted more. One last not-a-date, then maybe he'd be willing to tempt this fate.

Not Tuesday though, when he and Vincent walked the neighborhood reminiscing over their childhoods and sneaking into their old elementary school's playground to sit on the swings and laugh about the trials of growing up. Not Thursday either, when they brought back burritos from Wesley's favorite Mexican takeout and watched all three of the old Squid Attack movies until Wesley fell asleep on the couch and woke up to a note of thanks signed with a little heart before Vincent's name and a *PS: Tonight?* after it.

Tonight—Friday. A perfectly good night to finally say either of the things that had been haunting him all week, hopefully not in the same sentence. *I would very politely like to touch your dick* and *I almost betrayed you to get vengeance on the pharmaceutical company that built this city* didn't go together very well.

First, Wesley needed to deal with the pharmaceutical company in question.

Over the week he'd applied for all three of their research lab's other job openings under different versions of his name, and even started looking, rather fruitlessly, for ways to break in. The more dead ends he hit the more he found himself emailing with Matthew Babcock. There had to be a vampire out there somewhere who was biting unwilling victims for the fun of it. Just one single vampire Wesley could feel comfortable handing over to Vitalis-Barron. The stereotypes came from somewhere, after all.

Wesley,

Sorry to hear about your mishap, but I hope this news will cheer you up.

My assistant has been looking into a vampire who lives in your general area. Based on his appearance, he probably resides in one of the nearby cemeteries. My previous altercations with him have shown that he's a coward, easily cornered, and seems to rely more on instinct than smarts. We last spotted him luring a drunk, possibly drugged human into a car over the weekend. Chances are high that's his typical feeding tactic.

If this seems like a catch you can handle, let me know. My assistant is moving to a full post soon and if you can get a recruitment signed by then I'm happy to take you on. Another War Call geek is always welcome with me.

Matthew Babcock

A shudder ran across Wes's shoulders. This was good. He tried to convince his body of that, to calm the tightness in his chest and the tangle in his gut. Another vampire lived in his area, this one willing to take advantage of drunk humans, possibly even drug them. That was an asshole move, a level even Vincent, with no resources and no way around taking the blood he needed, would never have resorted to. This was good.

He could find this vampire, use them to get into Vitalis-Barron, and tell Vincent how he felt and what he'd done only after he had proof that he had contributed to taking down the company that was putting people like Vincent through so much pain. This was good. He could do this.

Things were looking up for Wesley.

16

VINCENT

Vincent's life was falling apart.

He had one good thing left: Wesley. Wesley was amazing. Feeding off Wesley was amazing. Being near Wesley, in the glow of his cozy house with him, was amazing. Wanting more from Wesley and being pretty sure the man wasn't interested in that was less amazing, but still, the fantasies Vincent indulged in before falling asleep in the mornings were pretty damned good. Outside of Wesley, Vincent's already pathetic and mediocre existence had turned into a shit-show.

Suddenly everyone seemed to know he was a vampire.

The local suburban newspaper, who was usually happy to give out one or two runs to people who needed a bit of extra cash, had told him to take his fangs and scat. The new soup kitchen he'd eaten at most Monday nights since it opened had quietly turned him away at the door. Even the clothing donation box the church three streets down left out for an hour or two after sunset was mysteriously moved inside at the first sign of dusk.

It had taken him most of the week to finally run into the source of it all: a flier with a sketched version of him and a warning underneath. *Highly dangerous vampire. If seen, contact below.* All the phone number slips had been torn off it already. It sent a chill down Vincent's spine.

He wanted to tell Wesley. More and more, he wanted to lay his head on the man's lap and complain about all the pain and fear that hounded him from every corner, even if Wesley himself could do nothing about it. But Wesley *couldn't* do anything about it. And the more Vincent made it seem like it was Wes's problem to fix, the more likely it was that Wes would decide the effort wasn't worth what he was getting out of their strange friendship.

The last cash in Vincent's wallet dwindled into a handful of ones, then pocket change, and he still couldn't find a way to make it back. A human in his position had options, even if they were all bad ones— street corners to beg on, if nothing else, but most people didn't give money to anyone after dark, anyone who wouldn't stand in the light for it. If he was going to spend an hour writhing as his body tried to burn away the sun's toxins in order to beg five dollars off someone, he'd go apply to the Vitalis-Barron research laboratory first.

'Vampires wanted.'

He shuddered.

Even the local library branch had been set up to dissuade vampires, with hours that always started after sunrise and ended before sunset and high windows that acted as skylights over most tables in the small building. There was a single chair squashed in the nonfiction section where from nine to ten thirty the light was just dim enough that Vincent could curl up there with a visored beanie he'd taken from Wes's laundry room, plug his phone in, and spend some time messaging Wesley.

That was his one spot of good luck so far: his cell hadn't been slain by the lake after all. Though the amount that he and Wesley were continuing to text seemed to be giving it a much slower and more agonizing death. Vincent snorted at Wes's most recent meme, a popular multi-panel one from a TV show Vincent had never seen. Wesley had scribbled in vampire fangs and rewritten some of the dialogue with his favorite brand of cliché predator-prey language.

The sandy-haired man beside him huffed to himself. He'd been there when Vincent arrived, already set up next to the only chair that was vampire-safe this time of day and had been awkwardly pretending Vincent didn't exist since their initial greeting. He had a laptop open in front of him, a dozen different fandom stickers peeling off the back, but for the hour since Vincent had sat down he'd been jotting notes in a physical notebook while chewing the eraser off the end of his pencil.

It chose that moment to give in, the pink nub tumbling across the table in front of Vincent. As the man grabbed for it with a hasty apology, his gaze drifted over Vincent's phone screen. He did a double-take.

When he opened his mouth, Vincent was prepared to flee headfirst out the library entrance despite the aches and shakes it would inevitably cause, but what he said was so odd that Vincent could only stare at him.

"Is that popular right now?"

"Is what popular?" Vincent asked.

"Sorry, how rude of me. I mean the meme format with the vampire connotations. I'm working on an article on the new trend where young people present themselves as vampires."

Vincent wasn't sure how he felt about the idea of people wearing the media flair of his life like a costume they could take off whenever it became inconvenient. "Um, no, I don't think so? My friend and I just play a vampire RPG game together. The meme is a reference."

"Right." The man turned back to this laptop, rubbing his hands down his face. He looked like he was in physical pain and there was something very much like a piece of eraser stuck between two of his teeth.

Vincent glanced at his phone, then back at the man. "Are you okay?"

"I'm writing a fluff piece that's sole reason for existence is to let an older generation complain that their kids are depraved and foolish and ruining the best things about society, so not really." He shrugged, then sighed. "There's actually some very interesting social introspection to be done about the cycle behind the framing of vampirism in media and the ways that it builds into culture and cultural knowledge, particularly starting with the youth. But no one wants to pay money for that. Though you probably don't want to give away your free time for it either." He shook his head. "I'm sorry. Please, go back to your memeing."

The societal progression of media to culture and back actually sounded rather interesting to Vincent, but the man had already begun scribbling again. Vincent held his phone at a more private tilt as he messaged Wesley a series of laughing emojis and a short description of the conversation he'd just had.

LordOfTheWin

So you mean like, how video games affected what I thought of vamps before I met you?

HotMouth

Yeah, but more than that. It's like

Like how you bought a bunch of those vampire games to try to learn from them.

How the dating sim ones made you want me to bite you more, but then I bit you and you realized that the thing from the game was a vague stereotype of the bite, but that you could still bring the things you enjoyed from the game into the real version to enhance it further. It becomes a kind of recurring loop, where your interactions with media feed into real life, then real life feeds back into media, in order to create something more complex than either on their own, sometimes for better and sometimes for worse.

But when people engage with kindness and empathy as their foundation, I think those interactions are mostly positive ones.

LordOfTheWin

Okay, that's super cool.

But now I'm just thinking of your teeth. On my neck. Tonight.

Bros For Biting TM

Vincent lifted his shoulders a little higher as he sunk into his chair, like that might hide his blush.

HotMouth

That's never catching on you know.

LordOfTheWin

Blood Exchange Program, but Sexy This Time.

HotMouth

N. O.

LordOfTheWin

Queer Men's Biting Club.

HotMouth

That's definitely already a thing, it just doesn't mean what you think it means.

LordOfTheWin

What, like I've never bitten any men before?

I've bitten many a man in my day, I'll have you know.

Three entire men, actually! And two women, and one person who was only kind of a woman. (Her words; she was exactly the right amount of whatever genders she was, but we had totally different tastes in ice cream cake so it would never have worked out.)

HotMouth

Two questions.

One:

Is the biting here an analogy?

And two:

If you ever want to bite me *just say the word.* But he couldn't bring himself to type it, not to Wesley, not sitting in a library, not when there were so many ways that could go so wrong. Even if he had, Vincent was fairly certain Wes wouldn't get it. The man made weird sexual references like it was a second language and seemed to assume that anyone else flirting was just doing the same. It was the only thing about Wes that frustrated Vincent, mostly because he wanted to *legitimately* flirt with Wesley, instead of doing... whatever this was.

HotMouth

And two, I think I'm going to have to report you to the vampiric imposteration council.

LordOfTheWin

Imposteration isn't a word!

And that wasn't a question.

Also if you must know, it's only kind of an analogy. Congrats on the inside scoop to my sex life. You are now ranked beside Kendall on the list of people who could successfully blackmail me.

Vincent wanted to laugh, and to cry, and to point out that he already knew on a pretty intimate level what exact phrases and grips would make Wes's pants tent fastest, so that had probably already qualified him. Instead he sent an evil smirking imp emoji and a gif of a little creepy looking man rubbing his hands together ominously.

LordOfTheWin
Okay I spilled my beans where are yours.

HotMouth
In my pants.

LordOfTheWin
Oh look who's getting good at this!

HotMouth
Being real here, they kind of are? I never dated in high school for the kind of obvious reason of being utterly terrified of human contact, and I only went to college for a semester before I got turned. Most people don't want to date a vampire.

LordOfTheWin

Most people should absolutely want to date a Vincent though.

HotMouth

I'm blushing.

LordOfTheWin

I'm serious, dude. You're thoughtful and funny and when you actually shower you look like some dark avenging knight who happens to also trip over his own shoes when he forgets they're by the stairs. You would be a catch for any guy.

Any guy but Wesley, apparently. But Vincent's cheeks were burning up now and the journalist across from him kept deliberately avoiding looking his way.

HotMouth

That's kind of sweet, actually.

He added a peach emoji at the end out of panic, then immediately pressed onward with the first question he could think of.

HotMouth

You've been living your bisexual bliss for a while now then?

That was the weirdest way for me to state that fuck.

What I meant was, you've been out for a while?

LordOfTheWin

Yeah my bisexual bliss has been in everyone's face for as long and loud as humanly possible.

That tracked with the rest of Wesley; Vincent couldn't imagine a scenario where he hadn't been this loud and proud about who he was in all facets of his life, even if it hurt him to do it.

HotMouth

Personal question, but, did your parents support you?

LordOfTheWin

Dad's wishy-washy on things but he's mostly fucked off anyway so he doesn't count.

Hold on essay incoming.

So it wasn't perfect at first, with mom. I was fourteen when I told her.

She grew up Catholic, and there's a lot of queer Catholics don't get me wrong, but there's also a lot of pressure and bias and distrust and some outright hatred there, you feel me?

HotMouth

Yeah I feel you.

(Shit am I not supposed to be interrupting?)

(Please carry on the essay.)

LordOfTheWin

You can interrupt! It's a soap box not a TED Talk.

Anyway after mom divorced my dad, (which was before I came out), she faced a lot of nastiness herself, so she'd already kind of opted out of the judgment side of all that. She always said that she'd known her divorce was the right choice, and that she didn't want to ever make anyone feel the way she'd been made to feel over it, especially not me.

HotMouth

Bless your mom.

Vincent meant it; she sounded like she'd been an amazing parent. But it was the kind of amazing that formed something dark and green inside him. He sunk a little deeper into his seat, trying not to glare as he kept reading.

LordOfTheWin

For real!

Growing up we'd visit her whole Catholic family in Texas over the big holidays, but they took it pretty badly that first year. Mom realized it was hurting me to be around them, and she let me stay home instead. Pretty sure my abuela told her she was betraying her familial ideals or whatever by not forcing me to come, but she never gave me grief for it.

By the end of high school she was the mom at pride giving out free hugs.

As hard as Vincent tried to dissuade it, his jealousy sat in his chest so heavy and thick that it made him almost mad at Wesley. Wes had gotten the kind of mom Vincent always dreamed his might turn into, and a life in the kind of home where he'd felt safe to be himself. Meanwhile, Vincent had seen his family harden before his eyes, turning their house to a place where he was too terrified to even show his support for the queer community, much less come out. A place that didn't feel like a home at all. He had to peel his emotions apart glob by envious glob to reach the real anger and fear buried beneath. Maybe if he had been like Wesley, sufficient and confident and engaging and all the other things that would have made his parents proud, maybe then he would have been the kind of son who *could* convince them that his sexuality was something worth loving.

But he didn't know how to express that yet, not without it combusting into a breakdown. He had to reply soon, though, or else Wesley would notice something was off.

HotMouth

I've never been to pride.

LordOfTheWin

Dude, you'll have to come with us next year.

There's a group of queer guys I hung with through high school. We all got brunch first at the Fishnettery last year.

It was great, I'm sure they'd love you.

Until they learn I'm a vampire?

HotMouth

If you can make the city hold the parade at night, I'll be there.

Wesley didn't respond right away, and when his messages finally started coming through, they were slower.

LordOfTheWin
Shit, I didn't think, I'm sorry.
That's rough.
It really sucks being a vampire, doesn't it?

Despite all the time they'd spent together, this conclusion seemed to be hitting Wes anew. It irked Vincent that the man needed this much prompting to notice the struggles that plagued vampires on a regular basis. There would keep being more pieces of Vincent's life that Wes didn't quite comprehend or barriers he didn't consider until he had them pointed out to him. And Vincent worried that every time it happened, it would feel like this. Their friendship would be worth it, but, god, it really, *really* sucked being a vampire.

He didn't think he could push that in Wesley's face without wearing the man down in the process, so he pared his emotions into something he figured would be more tolerable.

HotMouth
Yeah, sometimes it does.

Vincent tugged down his beanie cap and double checked the time. He'd already stayed in the seat ten minutes longer than he should have. He couldn't quite feel the sun-induced pain coming on yet, but the delay was what made it deadly, never knowing whether to push through or hunker down until it was too late.

HotMouth
Hey, I have to run, sun's gonna get me.

LordOfTheWin
Don't burn up! You're already hot enough!

That made his lips quirk, even if the expression felt forced and tired. He paused as he passed the journalist, trying for something that looked a little less like he was simultaneously pining over his only friend and battling a closet's worth of internal turmoil. "Good luck on the article."

The man mirrored his half-hearted smile. "Thanks. Don't get bit by any vamps out there!"

He was probably just referencing Vincent's meme; he sounded teasing, if a bit strained. But Vincent still couldn't get the bad taste out of his mouth. At least being bitten by vampires was one thing he *didn't* have to worry about.

As he passed the reception desk, the librarian scowled at him. It might have been over anything—his clothing, the general griminess that was building back up after his shower at Wes's house last week, his choice to sit in a house of books and look at nothing but his phone, or maybe she was just having a bad day—but the way she tucked a familiar-looking flier below her desk as he passed made his stomach twist. He pulled his hood up, shoving his hands into his pockets, and hurried. As he approached the door, it opened before him.

Matthew Babcock stood in it, his hair slicked back and his trench coat flaring.

Vincent had known; he'd known that the fliers and their fear mongering had to be Babcock's doing. But seeing it confirmed still rattled him, stalling him in place a moment too long. Babcock's mouth twisted into a smile. He grabbed at Vincent's clothing, latching on so hard that Vincent stumbled as he tried to yank away. A button snapped off and somewhere near his shoulder the fabric ripped, but Babcock's fist came free.

Vincent ran.

WESLEY

Wesley,

I slipped a tracker into our bloodsucker's pocket a couple hours ago. We can catch him as soon as he bunkers down. It looks like he's smart enough to keep on the move so far, probably trying to bide his time until the sun sets, but by then he should have the aches and shakes so badly he'll be an easy grab.

I'll let you know when we close in.

Matthew

Wesley unbuckled his seatbelt and closed Babcock's email with a cringe. He thought of Vincent's final text of the morning, the casual words taking on a little more threat with the reminder of just how serious the sun's effects could be on a vampire.

Sun's gonna get me.

Wes's facetious reply felt inconsiderate now. He'd have to ask if Vincent was alright with him cracking jokes about the tougher parts of being a vampire. He knew from experience just how necessary it could be to make light of something painful—and just how horrible it could feel when the person doing so wasn't someone who had to experience that pain in the first place.

He told Babcock he'd try to be there for the catch before shifting over to Kendall's email, where she'd forwarded him instructions from the smith she'd hired to make Leoni's birthday present. Wes was still following them around the side of the man's house toward his work shed when Babcock's acknowledgment appeared in a peppy little notification along the top of the screen.

This was good; this was progress, wasn't it? A new vampire, a new chance to take down Vitalis-Barron. Except Vincent would be coming over around sunset. If the capture happened before that, then Wesley would have to cancel on him—another lie by omission that he didn't want to add to all the things he'd kept secret—and if he was called away during their not-date, he'd have to explain why he was leaving. He doubted *mysterious vampire hunting outing* was a reason Vincent would accept without question. Or without bailing on their friendship entirely.

Which left Wes with one thing he desperately wanted to do before any of that went down: the one thing he'd been dreading all week.

His mind was still anxiously circling around the idea as he greeted the smith. "Hey, um, I'm Wes," he managed, slipping back to his usual charisma with a smile. "My friend had a custom staff she wanted me to pick up from you?"

"Right, Wes, come in." The man waved him inside.

He presented the staff on a long velvet cushion. Wes snapped a few pictures before carefully examining it. While he knew little about cosplay and even less about metalwork, he was pretty sure the elegant piece of polished wood with its partially inlaid metal sculpture of an elaborate blooming tree was somewhere between incredible workmanship and divine intervention. He paid the remaining cost for Kendall—it only felt right after everything she had done for him lately.

As he waited for the smith to package the staff up, his gaze roamed the rest of the man's collection: metal projects in various stages of completion, from weapons to jewelry to things that looked like they belonged as part of a dungeon, if that dungeon involved a fair amount of velvet and all the victim's groaning and begging was sensual. A pair of little golden vampire fang cuffs sat among them, each with a tiny plastic harness to strap them to the vamp's blunter canines.

He imagined Vincent wearing the little sheaths, drooling and whimpering but unable to feed until Wesley let him take them off. The picture kindled just enough of a spark for him to understand why it appealed to some, but the idea of being bitten *less* during sex went counter to his own cravings. If he were the one with fangs, then perhaps…

The smith caught him staring, and his lips quirked on one side. "I don't judge the kinks, I just make the toys."

"For vampires?"

The man lifted one brow. "You have a problem with that?"

"No, no, I—" Fuck, what was he allowed to say to a stranger without Vincent's permission? "There's this vampire I've been with recently, and I'm realizing there's a lot I didn't know about them. Not just in terms of kinky shit, but in general. It's been kind of eye-opening."

"Ah, I see." His expression softened. "It took me a while to sort through all the facts from the myths myself. But you'll get there if you work at it. Vamps aren't much different from us when you really get to know them. Not so scary or mysterious, just people with needs and strengths and limitations like everyone else. And just like everyone else, you can treat them best if you understand those things."

Wesley's mind went to the conversation he'd had with Vincent earlier, to every half-right piece of media lore that had shaped his idea of vampires. Vincent was a flash of fangs in the night and a beautiful, growling predator that sent shivers down Wesley's spine, but far more than that he was a gay man who couldn't go to Pride because no one had thought to make it accessible to someone who couldn't stand for hours in the direct sunlight, or perhaps someone hadn't wanted it to be accessible in the first place and nobody had bothered to fight against that.

It sucks to be a vampire, doesn't it?

Wesley cringed, his own ignorance already coming back to haunt him. And he still had so much left to learn. As daunting as it was, he felt no dread, only resolve. If this was how he could help Vincent, then he would cringe at his own ignorance a thousand times over. He turned back to the smith. "What do you know about the effect of the sun on vamps?"

"Sun-poisoning." He slid the final wrapping into place around Leoni's gift and tucked it into the box. "It produces some kind of toxic chemical in the vampire's skin that's then transferred throughout the body. It's all a bit delayed and it's hard to predict how long its effects will last, or how strong they'll be."

Wes followed the smith back through the workshop, blinking against the brightness of the sun as they left the building. "And there's no way to avoid it? Or fix it?"

"A good sunblock can add a few minutes of initial protection and once a vamp hits the shaking stage, having a blood meal never hurts. A well-fed, well-rested vampire will always fight it off faster than a weakened one. But there's no cure yet." The smith handed over the package with a weak smile.

"Thanks." It felt odd to leave a conversation with a stranger on such a melancholic note. Wes tapped the top of the box. "My friend's going to love this."

As he made his way back to the car, the man called after him. "This vampire of yours, you take good care of them."

His use of neutral pronouns was a nice touch. It was so rare to not have someone impose their own assumptions about who Wes was and the gender of his partners—and he hadn't even been wearing his rainbow string of beads amidst his teal and gold ones today. Wes grinned, the expression feeling genuine finally.

"I will." He would. He had to. Without Wes, Vincent had no one else. Which was why Wes couldn't tell him, not about Vitalis-Barron or the terrible trade Wesley had almost made: Vincent's freedom, his life, for the company's downfall. But still…

This vampire of yours.

That felt so goddamned right—too right to not be true. Maybe he couldn't let Vincent in on the whole truth, but if he held onto this piece of it for much longer he thought he might combust from the pressure. As he settled into the car, he sent off the pictures he'd taken for Kendall. He didn't hesitate after, quickly typing his decision out just to make it real.

LordOfTheWin

I'm going to tell Vincent that I like him tonight. Wish me luck.

KendallCanoodles

I bet you ten bucks you don't need luck for this.

LordOfTheWin

Deal.

Wes was pretty sure he'd just lost ten dollars, and there was nothing he could do about it.

Vincent

The sun was still reaching for the horizon when Vincent banged on Wesley's door. He'd spent the day dashing from one shelter to the next as soon as he could bear it, too obviously suffering from sun-poisoning to risk the busy afternoon buses. The pain had finally lessened, but in its place came a feverish shaking. He tried to conceal the trembles beneath an air of exhaustion and a little anxious bouncing. Wes still looked worried though as the man ushered him inside.

Vincent didn't dare pull down his hood until the door had sealed behind him and the curtains closed. His shivers remained, vicious and aching, but in the safety of Wesley's four walls they felt almost survivable. For what felt like the first time since the library, Vincent breathed out.

The relief brought an uncomfortable wave of jealousy with it. He pushed it down. He was here to feed on Wesley with nothing to offer in exchange but his venom. Blood was more than he should have been expecting in the first place.

Wes narrowed his eyes, squinting in the dimness. "Are you hurt?"

"I'm fine," Vincent lied. Nothing good could come from worrying him.

"You're sure? You look like you're shivering a little." Wes reached out, and as his fingers slid against Vincent's arm, they induced a new kind of tremble, strong and warm and enough to soften the sun-shakes, if only for an instant. The old tremors crept back in as soon as it was gone.

"I just left my hood down a little too long. It's not bad, it'll pass." One of those things was true, at least.

"I'm sorry." His lips tugged down, but then his expression brightened. "You should feed! I know it's early but it might help your body cope with the sun-poisoning. Or, so I've heard." He looked almost embarrassed at the end, shrugging as he tucked his thumbs into his pockets.

It was cute. And far sweeter than Vincent deserved after all the irritation and jealousy he'd been letting stew lately.

He thought of the bag of blood Wes had found for him, his honest attempts to learn so far, the way he had been offering up everything he had without question. Even if he was still oblivious to Vincent's struggles at times, at least he was trying. Here, face to face with his earnestness and his eagerness to help, Vincent could feel his affection for the man outweighing everything else.

But a little fear still clung to it. A little fear that all those things would eventually be too much for Wesley. That the amount he had to try just to be friends with someone like Vincent wouldn't be worth his effort forever.

"I guess I could do with a snack. Just a little one, I promise." It sounded more like a plea than he meant it to and he added a crooked smile at the end. "If you want, I'll chase you around a bit later. You can hide first and try to fight me off with pillows or something."

Wesley's face reddened a little beneath the warm tan of his skin. "I never said I was into that," he grumbled, but he groaned after, pressing his hands to his cheeks. The dozen wrapped beads around his wrist slid ever so slightly down his arm and Vincent's gaze kept moving, following the gracious curve of his muscle to the delectable crook of his elbow. "Fuck, yeah, okay, that sounds like a blast, and not just for kinky vampire shit. I haven't had a proper pillow fight since middle school."

"I'm all for helping you reclaim your childhood." If it stirred up Wesley's scent and made him laugh and struggle playfully beneath Vincent, all the better. "Now, I think you'd better bare your neck, if you know what's good for you..."

Vincent swore that the more accustomed he became to Wesley's blood, the better it tasted. That seemed like the inverse of logic. Too much rich cake made the sweetness overbearing. Too many meals of a favorite food in a row made it less appetizing. Too much champagne made for a headache.

But this—their legs tangled beneath them as they sat in the center of the couch, Vincent's fingers in Wesley's hair and Wes's throat vibrating with soft, breathless sounds as Vincent drank Wesley in, drank him up deep and a little ravenous—this experience felt more wonderful every time. It was as if the fading of the initial butterflies left space for Vincent to take in even more of Wesley. And Vincent did.

It made it all the harder when he forced himself to lick the wound closed early, leaving the softest hint of a kiss afterward. As he let Wesley go, he could already feel the blood at work, settling his body into something almost useful again. And Wesley had known this. He'd figured it out and offered it up without reservation. Though at the moment it seemed to be benefiting the man, too.

Wes gave a long, happy hum. He flopped sideways across the length of the couch, not bothering to hide his erection as he settled his legs over Vincent's. Just bros for kinky biting, that was all they were. All Wesley seemed to want, anyway. But one of Wes's pant legs pulled up around his socks, and for a moment Vincent was pretty sure he understood the whole deal with women not showing their ankles in the old days. He swallowed.

Wesley looked up at him, a brow lifted. "Are my feet yummy?"

"They smell." Which was true, technically, they just didn't smell particularly bad. Kendall must have trained him well. When Wes tried to protest, Vincent caught his legs and pulled the man's feet into his lap. "Knees though…" He mimicked biting Wesley's kneecap with just his regular teeth.

Wes laughed and tried to jerk his legs away.

Vincent grabbed at the nearest one, holding it fast to his chest. "Want to wager on whether or not you're ticklish?"

"Fuck, never, that's cruel!" Wesley flailed.

Vincent wiggled his fingers into the soft spot of the man's kneecap until his whole leg jerked and he shrieked, falling off the couch in a series of curses and cackles. His laughter subsided, but he continued to lay there, smirking up in a way that did funny things inside Vincent's chest. When his gaze darted to Vincent's still trembling hands, the expression fell. It was like turning out a light, except the light was as much inside Vincent as it was on Wesley's face.

"Any better yet?"

"It's getting there." Vincent preoccupied his fingers by tying up the stray threads where Matthew Babcock's grip had torn a seam loose on the front of his jacket. If he could just pull himself together a little more, then Wes could stop worrying.

"Hey, Vinny?"

The string Vincent was trying to wind into a knot unfurled beneath his ungainly fingers, yanking the entire seam loose. It split from his shoulder down to his armpit, the pieces of fabric falling apart to reveal a slice of his worn gray shirt beneath. "Shit."

His throat knotted. This was the new jacket. The one he'd gotten with the money from Babcock. Babcock, who was now making it very clear that a job or even a safe place to charge his phone weren't in his future here unless he wanted to try his luck with a legal system that preferred not to recognize vampires as people under the constitution.

No matter how happy he was to be biting Wesley, the rest of Vincent's life was fucked.

"Dude, it's fine." Wesley sounded nervous. He hovered over Vincent, holding out his hands like an offer of peace. "It can be replaced."

Vincent had to get a handle on his emotions. He could not scare Wesley like this, not after all Wes had done for him; the blood and the moans and the laughter. It *was* just a jacket. Vincent could fix the sleeve with some patchwork or switch back to his old one.

But he couldn't fix the problem that had caused it and he couldn't go back to the way he'd been living. He couldn't keep living like this either, getting pieces of Wesley's bright, happy world and Wesley's bright, happy affection as his own life continued spiraling. Couldn't keep dreading the point when Wesley realized that Vincent wasn't any different from his old thrift store jacket, threads always just about to break, fabric forever in need of extra care. Couldn't keep stewing in discomfort while waiting to see if Wes's generosity and attention would wane.

"It isn't fine," Vincent whispered. He stood up, an accidental burst of his vampiric speed turning the motion so fast that Wesley stumbled back. Vincent's legs wobbled under him. A lingering tingle of sun-pain made him flinch, and he grabbed the arm of the couch.

"What's wrong?" Wesley looked so confused—so stupidly, ignorantly confused.

It was like he hadn't noticed the change a single shower could make in Vincent. Or how hungry Vincent had been since his busy work schedule had suddenly and mysteriously opened up since last week. Or how

Vincent had carefully made sure that all their ridiculous bets were never for money, even though he knew Wes's wagers with other people were a mile-long history of monetary transactions.

Just like he hadn't considered that standing for hours in the sun to experience a parade wasn't an option for Vincent. Just like he couldn't tell that the privilege he had from living in this wonderful little house with no job and no worries hadn't been slowly eating its way into Vincent's soul. Because it had. And Vincent didn't want to dwell on that, didn't want to risk looking at Wesley with anything but respect and affection, because Wesley didn't deserve his jealousy.

Wes had a dead mother. He'd grown up with just her and lost her too young. But he'd *had* a mother who loved him, who'd given him a house instead of kicking him out of one. Right now, with the most expensive thing Vincent owned falling apart under his fingers and Wesley staring at him like he was being turned a little monstrous by it, Vincent couldn't keep bottling it all up. Something had to slip.

"I lost my job, you know."

Wes kept staring at him. "I… shit, dude, I'm sorry." He held out a hand like he was going to pat Vincent's shoulder, but pulled it back before he could. He pasted on a weak smile instead. "That sucks, but it'll be okay. There are other jobs out there. I've filled out so many applications this week, I can help you. It's really not that bad."

"If you're not a vampire, maybe." Vincent raised his voice and the sound drew a flash of panic across Wesley's face but he still couldn't stop himself.

"Night shifts." Wesley spread out his arms and gave something almost like a laugh. "We'll find you someplace with good night shifts."

"Night shifts have day interviews. They stick them in courtyards and rooms with big windows on purpose." Vincent's whole body ached again, sharp, spearing pain working its way through his joints. The blood had been meant to help with this, he thought, distantly. Stupid vampire body making everything harder on everyone.

"There has to be something out there. A freelance gig? Or you could work for that taxi app?"

"I don't have a car."

"There's still plenty of random stuff that you can do from home, right?"

"That's not really an option for me." Vincent could feel the tremble in his words and it turned them meaner somehow.

A knot formed in Wes's brow. "But you have a place? Most vampires don't actually live in crypts and gothic castles, right?"

"I have… something. But it's not exactly set up with a home office." Vincent couldn't look at Wesley long enough to form the words.

"Well, fine." Wesley sounded almost as shaky as Vincent felt, his gaze leaping from Vincent to the window to the wall and back. "I have a house and a car. You can use mine. You can work from here."

It should have been a considerate, thoughtful offer—*was* a considerate, thoughtful offer—from a man who had no idea how quickly and thoroughly he would get sick of offering his space to Vincent and receiving nothing in return. "So we just pretend I live here, then? How is that supposed to work? Do I come over every night and eat your food and use your shower? Do I put you as all three of my references and my emergency contact? Do I address my taxes from here?"

"I don't know? Maybe. If you have to."

"Then say we do all that. Maybe it's fine at first, but what if I lose whatever gig I've found because they realize I'm a vampire or because sometimes— sometimes I just can't make myself do the work—and then what if I can't get another one, or maybe I do but people know I'm here and they start treating you differently because of me, and I'm miserable and you're miserable, and you just want things to go back to the way they were." The words seemed so easy suddenly, bursting out of their cages and ravaging through his chest in the process. "You've been so fucking nice about everything, but no one can give that much and not get anything out of it."

Wes flinched like he'd been hit. "I haven't been…" He swallowed. "I won't hurt you like that. I promise, I won't."

"Why won't you? You only wanted my friendship because I fascinated you: Vinny the Vampire with the intoxicating bite." It felt like a fire burning him from the inside out. But he had to say it. "Your life is all about having fun and being wild and spontaneous, and getting whatever the fuck you want, and I won't fit with that forever."

Wesley's face crumpled. He made a sound that could have been a laugh at any other time, in any other context, and turned himself in a bouncing, energetic circle too choppy and frazzled to be happy. "God. Fuck," he whispered.

Vincent cracked. "I'm sorry; that was shitty. I shouldn't have…"

"You're half right though." Wes laughed again. "You're right that I'm a disaster and kind of a junkie for anything that makes me feel good. I'm—" He closed his eyes, his head tipping back. "Fuck." He drew in a breath, then another, and looked at Vincent pleadingly. "But I care about you. Not your bite, but you. Just you. And I am trying to help. I know I've been a fucking mess at it, but doesn't that still count for something?"

Wesley cared. Vincent wanted to hold onto that and to all the things Wesley had done for him. He'd offered his blood, his home, his food, he'd even tried to take Vincent to a hospital when he'd passed out. He'd seen Vincent's scars, and he'd looked terrified by them. But he hadn't run. He hadn't demanded to know that there would never be more of them. That was something.

It had to be something.

"I hope it counts," Vincent admitted. "And I care about you, too, so fucking much. Maybe that's enough. I just don't know."

All the fire drained out of him, leaving only the shakes behind. He lowered himself, slowly, sloppily, back onto the couch. Wes kept watching him, his thick brow tight and his beautiful lips bunched together. Vincent's heart ached.

And that was another problem with Vincent spending all his time here, with betting his life on Wesley's good will: Vincent Barnes was fairly sure that he was madly in love with Wesley. Between his jealousy and his fear, that love had been clouded over, but it was still there, bright and hot and consuming in a way that made him doubt whether he could be in the same room with Wes for another minute without the unsaid weight of it burning him up.

If Vincent had to be here loving Wes and wanting him every night for the foreseeable future, then it would be less painful to walk into the sun.

Wesley settled on the floor in front of Vincent, looking just as worn and heart-aching as Vincent felt. "So what do we do then?"

"I don't know." If he didn't take Wesley up on at least part of his offer, he'd probably have to leave the city to get someplace Babcock's influence didn't reach. But he didn't want to leave. He *wanted* Wesley. Vincent rubbed the underside of his left forearm. He only realized what lines he was tracing after Wesley's gaze jumped to them.

Wes leaned toward him, his hands slipping over Vincent's knees. "Vinny…"

Vincent pulled his fingers into a fist. The tender way Wes was looking up at him now seemed to shoot daggers through Vincent's chest. "Wes." Vincent leaned his elbows onto his knees, dropping his forehead into his palms. "I do want this to work, I do. But there's something else..." He took a breath, preparing, and dragged his hands off his face.

Wesley was so close, his chin between Vincent's knees like the damned energetic, too-kind golden retriever that he was, staring up at him with so much worry that Vincent thought his chest would cave in.

Without thinking, he slipped his fingers against the man's cheek, hands still shaking, lungs tight and butterflies in his stomach and a rush around them as though his anxiety was centering them both in the center of a tornado. He lifted Wesley's head, and Wes let him. "I know you've enjoyed what we've been doing, and I won't ever judge you for just wanting to have some kinky fun, but I…"

The panic that was growing on Wesley's face terrified the words right out of him.

He swallowed. He had to say it. If they were going to be more to each other than this simple friendship, then he couldn't wrap his feelings up and bury them and expect them not to explode someday. "I—"

A banging came at the door.

Vincent startled back with nearly the same force as Wesley, his focus snapping toward the sound. It came again, three hard thumps like someone was trying to break the door down.

"This is an emergency!" a man shouted from beyond it.

A man who sounded an awful lot like Mr. Babcock.

Wesley's eyes widened, darting from Vincent to the door before he burst up and sprinted across to the foyer. Vincent cursed under his breath. He almost scrambled after him, but Wesley must have noticed the panic on his face, because the man shooed him toward the kitchen, mouthing something that could have been, "*Hide?*"

Vincent's stomach twisted. But if it was just Babcock out there, he wouldn't be any threat to Wesley, a human. It was Vincent they were after. But how the fuck had Babcock found him? Had Babcock been following him this whole time?

He slipped into the kitchen as Wesley opened the door, pressing his back to the wall and tipping his head as though that might help him hear better through the pounding of his heart.

"Hello?" Wesley asked.

"Are you alright, sir?" That was definitely Babcock's assistant, no doubt about it. "Is there anyone else in the house with you tonight?"

Wesley hesitated, but if his reply sounded off, Vincent thought it was only the usual amount of *why are you at my door asking that* confusion. "No. What's the emergency?"

"We're sorry to bother you, sir," Babcock said. "I'm Matthew from the Neighborhood Protection Agency. We have knowledge of a dangerous vampire breaking into your premises."

"There's no one here. I haven't heard anything, at least." Wesley managed to sound a convincing mixture of concerned and annoyed. He shuffled around, then grunted. "There aren't any police alerts out. What's this vampire done?"

Vincent's phone vibrated in his pocket. Fuck. He pulled it out, about to turn it to mute—if the 5% battery didn't die on him first—when he caught the message that had just come through.

LordOfTheWin

run

For once Vincent didn't want to run from Babcock. The thought of leaving Wesley alone as this man intruded into his home was agonizing. The thought of leaving Wesley without telling him how he felt, after Wes had looked like Vincent was about to emotionally murder him, had to be some other level of hell entirely. But this was what Wesley needed from him, and Vincent trusted Wesley.

He was going to keep trusting him.

As he slid his phone away, his fingers brushed against something coin-shaped at the bottom of his pocket. But every one of Vincent's pennies were accounted for multiple times over, stashed safely into his change baggy where there was no risk of losing any. His fingers shook with renewed vigor as he pulled out the bit of metal. It looked unassuming, dull and silver and lightweight.

Vincent realized what it could be—what it had to be—with mounting horror. Babcock had planted a tracker on him. That reshuffled the man around in his mind with agonizing speed. Babcock wasn't just a typical bias-driven citizen, or even a more aggressive one, willing to remove a vampire from the city if they happened to cross his path, but someone who knew intimately what he was doing. Someone who'd done this before. What had Vincent been helping the man with for all those weeks?

Who had he helped hurt?

Fuck.

"I guess you can look around if you want," Wesley was saying, his voice a little louder than before. "But I think I'd have noticed if there was a vampire in my house."

Double fuck.

Still crutching the tracker, Vincent sprinted across the kitchen to the window above the sink. It only squeaked a tiny bit as he pressed it open, popping out the screen and slipping through. No time to put it back, he closed the glass entirely and dashed across the darkening yard, diving over the low fence in a roll that brought him out of view of the house.

He scrambled around the dirt and weeds, catching the first rock he could find, and slammed it into the tracker. Once. Twice. On the third time the metal case popped apart, revealing bits of wiring. Vincent crushed that too.

The rock slipped from his grip. He gasped in a breath, hunching forward. Deep blue streaked the sky, the last hints of orange fading in the west, but his muscles ached and shook like it was in the grips of sun-poisoning again. He had to get somewhere safe, a place where he could lie down and wait for his body to figure itself out.

From the house, he could make out the sound of Wesley's voice, not in fear or anger, just casually guiding Mr. Babcock and his assistant around. He was safe. Of course he'd be safe. He was the kind of person Babcock probably believed he was protecting.

Still, forcing himself down the hill toward the cemetery behind Wes's house hurt almost as much as the sun-induced pain did. He started typing out a message to Wesley as he moved, half jogging and half stumbling: *I'm safe. Hanging out near the big mausoleum behind your house.* He lowered his finger toward the send button.

His phone went dead.

19

WESLEY

Matthew Babcock had come to Wes's door. Matthew Babcock had walked through Wes's house. Matthew Babcock had called Wes's vampire—his kind, thoughtful, adorably awkward vampire—a dangerous menace, a burglar, and a serial assaulter.

Because Matthew Babcock was hunting Vincent.

Wesley had never particularly liked the man during their email exchanges, but he'd never wanted to punch him in the jaw the way he did now. Instead of beating him to a pulp, Wes waved Babcock off with a smile that hurt his teeth, his fist pinched so tightly that he had to hide it behind his back to keep from giving himself away.

Neighborhood Protection Agency his ass. Wes betted the badges were printed in some Vitalis-Barron warehouse. Whatever the man said, he knew exactly who and what Babcock was, and it was no better than a modern-day vampire hunter.

The only thing that had kept Wes's ruse intact long enough to distract him was the fact that Babcock seemed to have no idea who Wesley was. It made sense. He'd never sent the man any pictures, and even knowing his full name would still bypass Wes's pseudonym-heavy social media accounts with their anonymous icons of his legs swinging over a five-thousand-foot drop. The fact that Wes had never introduced himself meant the hope he'd harbored that he might get into Vitalis-Barron at Babcock's side had probably sailed. Then it had been attacked by man-eating mermaids and sunk by a kraken, because there was no way Wes could stand to work with Babcock again now that he'd dangled Vincent in front of him by calling the vampire dangerous, treacherous, and cowardly.

And Vincent was absolutely, positively none of those things. The potentially drugged human being pushed into a car last weekend? That had been a fully consenting Wesley, still a tiny bit inebriated, but if anything he'd been the one who'd dragged Vincent back to his place not the other way around. But if Vincent was the vampire Babcock had been hunting, that meant Vincent had run into Babcock before. Vincent had been assaulted by Babcock before.

And he hadn't said anything.

A rush of anger shot through Wesley, not at Vincent but at everything that had taught the vampire that he had to bottle that hurt up. Wes opened their messages, writing so fast that it was a miracle his autocorrect caught all his typos.

LordOfTheWin
The hunters are gone now. You can come back.

He flipped to his emails, forcing himself to take a few long, deep breaths. The only contact he wanted with Babcock now was to kick him in the balls, but if he could draw the man's location out of him, at least he could tell Vincent where to avoid. Each word came slowly, painfully through a tunnel of anger.

Matthew,
I have a thing right now but let me know where you're at and I'll try to join you.
Wesley

He turned back to his chat with Vincent. No reply, not even the typing bubbles at the bottom. As he stared at his last message, Vincent's icon dim to one side, he remembered the way the vampire had looked at him just before Babcock's knock, like he was scared. Scared of Wesley.

"*I know you've enjoyed what we've been doing, and I won't ever judge you for just wanting to have some kinky fun, but I…*"

Wesley's brain filled out the missing words with ease: *I can't do it anymore. If I'm going to be working here, we have to stop whatever this is. I respect your kink, but seeing you this hot for me is uncomfortable. You're my friend, Wesley. I can't have any confusion there.*

And then he'd touched Wesley's cheek.

Wes's fingers hovered over the spot. That was a normal friend thing, right? A normal *I-want-to-end-whatever-this-is-and-just-be-friends* thing.

He could feel Kendall laughing somewhere in the back of his head. He wanted to call her and let her explain what the hell Vincent had been trying to do, but he was certain that he couldn't have a conversation with her right now without splitting into a million emotional pieces. Just sitting here, doing nothing, was already putting him on the verge of a breakdown. Besides, Kendall wasn't the person he needed to talk to now: Vincent was.

Vincent, who was alone out there somewhere. With a tracker. Being hunted by Babcock.

Shit.

Wesley snatched his jacket off the stair's railing, shoved his feet into his shoes, and threw himself into the night. His phone chimed on the way down the front drive, and he fumbled it open, heart slamming against his ribs. It was only Babcock.

In the Sunset Ridge neighborhood; I think you live around here? We traced the vampire to a house on Timmons Street but he'd already fled, and the tracker went offline shortly after. Scouting the surrounding area now.

Matthew

No more tracker; that was a relief, at least.

Wesley double-checked both directions to make sure that Babcock and his assistant weren't currently in his line of sight before turning at the street he'd always seen Vincent appear from. He stalled a block down. To the right the houses split off into a cul-de-sac, but otherwise this was the end of the residential area for at least a two- or three-minute walk as the road weaved around the cemetery and through the local shopping center. Vincent *had* implied he didn't have a standard place of living. And he was a vampire.

Wesley turned toward the cemetery. He jumped the little stone wall that surrounded it. Instantly it felt darker, the streetlamps all behind him or far to his left or right, their reach receding with each step he took. He couldn't use his phone light, not without the potential of alerting Babcock to his presence, so he stumbled blindly through the gravestones, apologizing to the ghosts every time he knocked one of his legs against something hard and dark.

He realized halfway through the cemetery that he wasn't entirely sure how he was supposed to be helping Vincent like this. Vincent clearly knew that Babcock was trouble. He'd already found and disabled the hunter's tracker. Unless Wesley was going to tell him about his dealings with Vitalis-Barron—something he was now certain would destroy any chance he had at proving he could be trusted not to fuck Vincent over in the long run—then it wasn't likely he could say anything about Babock that Vincent hadn't figured out himself. And if it came down to a fight, Vincent was stronger and faster than Wesley and probably a lot better at hiding.

He'd still been shaking though. As clearly as he'd been trying to hide it, the sun-poisoning was far worse than he'd admitted. Of fucking course it was; Vincent was the vampire Babcock had been trying to flush out. He must have been in the sun on and off all day. Wesley's chest ached for him. He couldn't just leave Vincent to suffer through that alone. Even if all he could offer was his support, as a friend or a boyfriend or their weird in-between thing, whatever Vincent needed, then he wanted to be there for that.

He just had to find the damn vampire first.

"Vincent," he hissed, ducking past the sweeping wings of an angelic monolith and creeping across a set of flat marble grave-headers like they were steppingstones. The ghosts he was apologizing to had better not have been real, because if they were he was going to be pissing so many of them off. He snuck around the side of the graveyard's three stone mausoleums, whisper-shouting again, "Vincent!"

Nothing.

He kept moving, but as he turned away, the roof of the furthest mausoleum clattered.

"Wes?" Vincent's voice was soft and a little wobbly.

Wesley's heart caught. "Yeah? Yeah it's me!"

A little choked sound followed. "I could kiss you right now."

"Please do."

He swore he didn't imagine the curse in Vincent's intake of breath and the moment of stillness that followed, but then the vampire said, "I wager you one piggyback ride that you can't climb this," like nothing had changed.

Wesley's hope plummeted. Maybe he was wrong about being wrong. Or maybe...

He just had to come out with it. Though if his actual coming out experience had been this hard he might have been in the closet still. Wesley gritted his teeth as he pulled himself up the side of the mausoleum and prepared to do the impossible. When he reached the top, the words died in his throat.

Vincent lay on the slanted rooftop, curled in on himself and shaking beneath the starlight. He'd wrapped his arms around his body and while the darkness hid most of his expression, what Wesley could see looked pained.

Wes dropped down beside him, pressing his palm to the vampire's shoulder. "It got worse."

Vincent gave a little laugh. "The after-affects keep creeping back up on me."

"Would more blood help?"

"Probably. But I'm not exactly fit to pay you back."

"Fuck that, Vinny." Wes settled onto the roof at Vincent's side. He scooped an arm under Vincent's back as he shoved his sleeve away from his wrist. "I meant what I said. I'm here because I care about you. All the payback I want is for you to feel better."

"Thank you." Vincent's voice sounded a little rough, and his trembling fingers were delicate as he held Wes's hand to his mouth.

Wes looked away, worried instinctively that maybe like this the fangs would nip right through his tendons. But Vincent's lips met the tender skin so gently that Wes breathed out. He barely flinched as his skin broke, sighing when the venom finally began to settle his mind. It was subtler this way, the whole process a lot less of a rush. There was something lovely about it despite that. Or maybe because of it. He was giving Vincent a part of himself not for the endorphins or the intoxication, but because he *could*.

And he wanted to give Vincent everything he possibly could for as long as the vampire would let him.

He stroked Vincent's hair with his free hand, watching the stars twinkle above them and listening to the quiet sounds of the night: the rustle of the nearby trees, the distant hum of the highway through a break in the hills, the chirp of the crickets, and the single coo of a mourning dove, not a sign of Babcock or his assistant to be heard. Despite all the stress and pain that had brought the two of them here, this felt right. It felt like where they were meant to be.

As Vincent finished, he let Wesley's hand go, but the vampire stayed laying against him. He fitted his head onto the crook of Wes's shoulder. It felt like it belonged there. "Sometimes I like to sit up here and stare at the stars right before I turn in for the morning," he said, his voice hushed.

"So you *do* actually live in a mausoleum?" Wesley gave him a soft poke in the side. "I thought that would totally be one of the things the media had made up."

"It is, mostly. I'm special." *Special* in his tone sounded like a curse, bitter and twisted. "And I'm kind of angry at you for having so much more than me. As though part of me blames you, like somehow you're the reason I'm living this way just because you happen to have a little old house and a fifteen-year-old minivan, when you aren't actually the problem at all. You deserve to have that kind of stability just as much as anyone, just like everyone deserves food and shelter and peace."

"Including you," Wes finished for him. "To be fair though, this is a fantastic mausoleum and the trashy minivan was my mom's. I had a pretty decent Honda Civic in college, but I sold it when I moved back in. The check got me a jump on the student loans." Wesley groaned. "And I really, really do need a job."

"Why don't you get one?"

"Because jobs are boring, obviously," Wes replied on instinct. Beneath the reflexive response, though, sat something that wasn't fun or snarky or easy, just true. He sighed. "Because when I do, then it becomes my house, and my debt, and my car, and I'm the adult, and my mom… my mom will never come home again." A knot formed in the back of his throat, but he spoke through it, staring at the stars and letting himself feel small, for once, to sink beneath the weight of the sadness he'd been trying to pave over all year, to not fight quite so hard. "Right now I'm taking up her couch and playing games like it's summer vacation and she's about to get back from a long work week. I know I am. I know I shouldn't be. It's been over a year. But I can't move on yet."

"How did she die?" Vincent shifted, turning a little onto his side and tipping up his chin to look at Wesley. "Is that okay to ask? I'm sorry, I shouldn't be prying."

"Pry, please. I want to tell you everything." Even if he couldn't, because it would probably drive Vincent to the hills if he did. But he could find a piece of the truth for him, at least—something he hadn't even found the courage to tell Kendall about yet. "Technically, no one knows. She vanished a little over a year ago, but she'd never be gone like this if she was still alive. There was a bus ticket purchased on her credit card without any sign of her at its destination, and her friends said she'd withdrawn since she'd switched back to night shifts, so the police finally decided she'd just bailed. But if she was unhappy, she would have told me, and she'd never have gone anywhere without letting me know. I think…" Wesley waited for his chest to tighten, for his brain to shout warning signals, for the world to tunnel in and the emotions to grow unbearable. But Vincent's solid presence and listening ear were like a stabilizer, grounding him in the feelings without letting them overwhelm him. "I think she went to Vitalis-Barron's research lab for one of their clinical trials, and it killed her, so they covered it up."

"Fuck." Vincent whispered. His fingers wrapped back around Wesley's and squeezed gently. "I'm sorry."

Something welled behind Wes's eyes. Relief, he realized. Reassurance. Vincent believed him, and cared, and Wes could let him. Wes didn't have to try to joke his way out of this. With Vincent, he could just be. That knowledge lodged in Wes's chest like a gentle, warm ache. "I can't prove it. I can't even prove she went there in the first place. They say their patient logs are confidential, and the police refused to look into it at all. Apparently just having a flier for their research studies was deemed insufficient evidence for a warrant. But she'd been really sick a few months before with something that never seemed to go away, and a lot of Vitalis-Barron's current research involves trying to use the vampiric immunity in order to heal humans. I know they're fucking over vampires while they do it, so what would stop them from being careless with their human patients too?"

"Oh." It was barely a breath, but Wesley felt it vibrate through Vincent. He wasn't shaking anymore. That had to be a good sign. "They're really that bad, are they?"

"Yeah." He thought of Babcock and cringed. "I went to an interview for a research position with them to try and gather more information. They didn't let me see anything useful, but I got the general vibe, and it wasn't good. Those people at my door earlier were with their laboratory. They claimed they were from some weird neighborhood safety group but they're definitely under Vitalis-Barron's payroll."

"I worked for them." Vincent sounded so hollow that it took Wesley a moment to register his words. "The job I lost, it was for that man, Mr. Babcock; bringing back information on people's habits and whereabouts, mostly at night."

"Ah, shit." Wesley's phone vibrated but whoever it was could wait.

"He's been distributing fliers about me so none of my usual haunts will let me in, and I found his tracker in my jacket. That's how he knew I was in your house." Vincent laughed, three bitter, wet inhales that could almost have been sobs. "The irony is—or maybe it's not irony, maybe that was his backup plan all along—is that it's been making those research advertisements trying to get vampires into their studies look almost appetizing. I never trusted Vitalis-Barron, but if they were my only option, I thought maybe it would be worth it. I could let myself be some asshole company's guinea pig for the money. But I didn't realize they were *killing* people."

"Promise me you won't ever go. If something happened to you there..." There was so much more he needed to add to that: *I almost brought you to their doorstep. I betrayed your trust and put you in danger and*

I could never live with myself if that happened to you again. But how could Vincent forgive him for that when Wesley couldn't even forgive himself? The more Vincent told him, the more desperately Wes knew he needed the vampire to keep trusting him, to keep accepting Wes's support, so Wes could be there for him, be everything he needed and more.

Vincent shrugged, the shift making his body rub against Wes's. "It sounded a little dull anyway. If I was going to give someone that much control, I'd rather it be a desperate human with a bite kink chaining me up in their basement or something. As a predator of the night, I have to maintain *some* dignity."

Wesley would have made a joke off that, but right now it seemed less important than usual. He squeezed Vincent's hand so tight the vampire stiffened. "Vinny, I mean it."

Vincent nodded in the darkness, his jaw rubbing against the side of Wesley's chest. "I won't do anything that foolish, I swear it."

"Good." He released a breath, and ventured, "Because if you try, I'll chain you up in the basement I don't actually have." The way Vincent chuckled at that made him feel daring. "Can I ask a terrible question?"

"Only if you're alright with all my answers being terrible answers."

"You won't scare me off. I already saw your fangs and I think they're sexy."

"Fair enough." Vincent went quiet, tracing his fingertips across Wesley's hand as he waited.

Wes swallowed. "Your scars…"

Vincent's tracing stopped. "You're not going to ask the whole question?"

"I'm kind of embarrassed to, actually," Wes admitted.

"You're embarrassed? Think of *me*."

"Yeah, but you're awkward like eighty percent of the time. This is a risk for me. It could ruin my reputation as an always-confident asshat." Wesley stopped himself short as his brain registered his own words. "Sorry, I should be more serious about this."

"No!" Vincent laughed, soft and at least eighty percent awkward. "This helps. It is serious, but it's also something that I can't allow too much hold over me, you know? Sometimes the only choice is between laughing and crying, and I used to do a lot of crying until there was nothing left of me. I like that you help me laugh instead."

"Well, I like that you help me cry, so we're even." He thought he could feel Vincent smile at that.

"They're from high school. At the time, it had felt like the only way to express some things I didn't have words for." Vincent breathed in, then out again. "Those feelings didn't stop there. I wanted to take a gap year before college to help, I don't know, figure myself out, I guess? But my parents told me they wouldn't pitch in for my tuition if I waited, so I went anyway. When I got there everyone acted so happy to be free and alive and young, and I was finally out from under my parent's noses, but it didn't change anything. I was doing everything I was supposed to be, but I still felt like the kid hiding behind the curtains hoping no one else noticed me, while also *needing* everyone to notice me at the same time, and not knowing what the fuck to do about it. Then I met a vampire."

"That was when you turned?"

"Not at first. I just wanted him to bite me, not the kinky way you like me to, but because it was painful and ecstatic and vulnerable and it made me feel like I was alive for a little while."

Wesley's mouth went dry. "I get that. Well, not exactly like that but the needing to feel alive because if you stop, for even a moment, then there's space for everything else to crash in, so you have to keep going, keep smiling, keep throwing yourself forward at top speed because when you don't you end up sitting naked in the shower hyperventilating into oblivion? I get *that*."

"Oh." Vincent wrapped his arm across Wesley's chest and held him. "But you're always so... you act like you're happy."

"I *am* happy. Except when I'm not. And then I kind of want to kill something or else die a little bit. Not in the big S way, just like, I don't want to be here for a while." Wesley snorted. "I bet you a hundred bucks this is what people get therapy for."

Vincent made a sound somewhere between a groan and a whimper. "I'd take that bet but it wouldn't be enough to pay for therapy in the first place. I checked, after I turned; I thought if I could at least fix that part of myself before I went crawling back to my parents then they'd accept me, but there wasn't anyone under their insurance who offered sessions at night, and everyone else costs a fortune."

"Why did you become a vampire?" Wes asked. "You didn't know how much it would suck, did you?"

"There wasn't a reason; it just kind of happened. I was so low at the time, and the vampire I'd been seeing brought a couple of vamp friends with him for this basement party that I barely even remember. They'd all been biting me on and off, and I'm pretty sure I ended up in a supply closet or a laundry room or something with one of them by the time I started passing out. I've been thinking about it a lot since then, and I don't know if they even realized what was happening to me, or cared enough to pay that kind of attention. I was in a bad place, and I might have chosen to turn if they'd asked, but I didn't really get that option, you know?"

Wesley felt like he had to give some sort of comfort, but Vincent's revelation was so awful and heart-wrenching that everything in him wanted to run back to the happier topics, to a place where the shitty vampires the media were based on only existed outside of their lives, in stories and jokes. While he tried to wrangle up the emotions into something useful, Vincent kept talking.

"It happened, though, and there's no way to take that back now. I cut all ties with them after. They would have helped me through it, I think—the vampire I'd been seeing originally would have, at least—but I couldn't bear it. It's part of why I never tried to find the vampiric community when I came back here, either. I was too nervous to approach them alone."

"If you ever did want to, I'm here for you. You could bring me with you, like your little human pet or something." He didn't think, just said it, and after it was out, he realized it was true. He wanted to go with Vincent, not to find another vampire to bring to Vitalis-Barron or even to fulfill his curiosity or expand on their kinky play, but just to help Vincent make friends and feel more comfortable with who he was. There had to be others out there like Vincent; vampires who knew what it was like to struggle to find their footing after they'd turned. People who could support him in the ways Wesley couldn't.

He didn't realize how quiet Vincent had gone until a car revved along the nearby road. The vampire picked himself up on one elbow, his arm still slung across Wesley's chest. His fingers found Wes's sternum through his hoodie fabric. "You'd do that for me?"

"Of course. I'd do anything for you, Vinny." He was pretty sure he would cut his chest open and give Vincent his bloody, beating heart if that's what the vampire needed. He'd do that, but not tell him the truth. Not about some things anyway. But maybe others... Maybe.

"I don't think actual vampires treat humans like pets though," Vincent was saying. "That's probably just a bad media trope. But maybe there's a kink community for it? Are you into that?"

"I don't know, probably in some variety? But I don't think I need to do it in front of anyone. You're enough for me."

Vincent just hummed, his whole body a little tighter suddenly.

"Hey, Vinny?" Wesley asked, before he could lose his nerve. "I have a question."

"Hmm?"

Wes slid his hand over Vincent's, casually, like a friend might. Or a boyfriend. He took a breath, and as he had with the freezing lake, he dove headfirst. "Are we dating yet?"

Vincent froze, for just a second, a second in which Wesley's heart ricocheted around his chest like it might burst out through his ribs and leave him dead in its wake. Then Vincent sat up and swung his leg over Wesley's hips. He settled there almost hesitantly, like the whole concept was new and experimental, but when he spoke, he seemed more certain and almost a little pleading. "Can we be? Please?"

"Fuck yes." Wesley breathed out in a flutter of relief. "Actually if you add it all up, I think we've been dating for like a week already."

"Damn." Vincent started shaking again, and Wes's panic spiked until the sound from Vincent's chest caught up with him: a pure, light laugh that put into song everything Wesley had been feeling. He laughed too, tipping his head back and cackling into the sky with the kind of joy no amount of adrenaline or intoxication could bring. The feeling didn't vanish as they quieted, the faint curve of Vincent's lips catching in the moonlight. He traced his fingers over Wesley's abs, and Wes could feel it flicking switches inside him.

Oh fuck. It hit Wes then—not the erection, though he felt that coming behind it—but the fact that, if they were dating, then Vincent probably wanted him the way he desperately wanted Vincent, and if they both wanted each other, there was nothing stopping them from *having* each other. Thankfully, Vincent was smarter than Wes, because before Wes could ask *do you want to touch my pingly,* Vincent spoke for him.

"I wager you one really explicit sex act that you can't kiss me faster than I can kiss you."

Wesley could barely form his reply through his breathless exhilaration. "De—"

Before the full word could slip free, Vincent's mouth covered it up, his fingers gripping into Wesley's hair. He kissed like he'd been thinking of this every moment since they'd met, kissed like they were two objects destined to come together from the start of the universe, the earth finally plunging into the sun. Wes's mind turned to stardust and his bones to light.

And Wesley Smith Garcia kissed his vampire back.

VINCENT

Wesley and Vincent were dating.

Of course they were dating. The moment Wesley had questioned whether they were, it seemed ridiculous that they had not been, and just as ridiculous that Vincent had been afraid to ask. He and Wesley were friends, yes, but they had always been something more than that.

Not only were they dating, but Wesley and Vincent were kissing, too.

That seemed equally right, Vincent straddling Wesley as his lips pressed Wesley's open, his chin twisted and his nose bumping into Wes's cheek. He gripped Wes's curls, pinning his head in place because he knew now—had maybe always known—that this was what Wes wanted. The man made a delicate yearning sound, soft and tight, and his mouth moved against Vincent's in desperate, urging gulps like he was trying to drink Vincent in all at once for fear he'd never have him again. His teeth tugged at Vincent's upper lip and Vincent's fangs caught on his lower, tearing as he tugged free. Vincent sucked on the cut long and hard, the bright taste of Wesley's blood blooming through his mouth. He moaned as he finally closed the tiny wound with his tongue, his nose bumping against Wes's.

Wesley gasped. His hands dragged up Vincent's thighs to clutch at his hips, one wrapping a little lower and further than the other. "Do that," he breathed. "Do that, but everywhere, to all of me."

"Eat you like a delicacy?" Vincent asked, dragging one fang along Wesley's cheek, his lips brushing along behind.

"Hell yes." Wes sounded rough, hoarse in the best possible way, like a dam about to burst. He went tight beneath Vincent as his skin finally broke, then loose again in a delirious sigh as the venom slipped from Vincent's fangs, shuddering when the cut closed over. One of his hands moved a bit lower, rubbing down the front of Vincent's thigh.

The building pressure made his dick ache. He moved his way along Wesley's jawline, nipping and sucking and slowly shifting the angle of his hips to ride toward Wes's touch against his thigh, just a little terrified to say what he wanted with more than body language. But he *did* want this, even if he wasn't quite sure what *this* was, other than to have Wesley—moaning, writhing Wesley—be a part of it.

Vincent nibbled at the crook of Wesley's neck, nuzzling and kissing just as often as he bit down. For a moment he lost track of Wes's hands altogether. He worried he'd finally have to tell the man what he wanted, but then Wes clutched his fingers around Vincent's ass with one hand and pressed the other in a rhythmic motion against the front of his pants. Vincent moaned into Wesley's skin. It should not have wrecked him that thoroughly, with the thick jean fabric still between him and Wes's palm, but all his nerves were alight in a way they never had been on his own and Wes seemed to know exactly how to rub to make Vincent's lashes flutter involuntarily and stars build behind his eyes.

He had to pay the man back somehow.

His cheeks flushed hot, then hotter still at the thought of what he wanted to try in response, but before he could psyche himself out of it, he reached between their legs, only fumbling against Wes for a moment before he dragged his nails up the bulge in the front of Wesley's jeans.

"Fucking—" Wes hissed, arching into him.

Their hips brushed like a spark.

And from somewhere below them and down the hill, Babcock's assistant said, "Did you hear that?"

Vincent froze. His heart hammered in his ears. Wes's fingers closed around his wrist. Slowly, he let Wes go, shifting off him. His erection still ached threateningly but the chills running up his spine at the sound of two pairs of approaching footsteps were far from sexual.

On this side of the roof, they had momentary cover, but as soon as Babcock and his assistant came around to investigate they were doomed.

Vincent slid off the edge, hooking his feet into the edge of the window below. He held onto the roof as he lowered himself to the sill. His dick protested the position, but he tried his best to ignore it. He had already broken the stained-glass window loose when he'd moved in at the beginning of the summer, and now he pushed it open with all the stealth he'd gained from years of breaking and entering. He helped Wesley to the sill, then inside, managing not to die of embarrassment as the front of Wes's pants brushed against his cheek, the man clearly still just as hard as he was.

They had been kissing, after all. Touching, even if there was still a layer of fabric between them. Vincent didn't have anything to be embarrassed about.

As Wesley tried to drop from the window, his phone slipped from his back pocket. Vincent caught it for him, tucking it away and closing the window. The hunters rounded the mausoleum.

Vincent and Wesley went still, backs against the cold wall. The shuffling from outside was laced with the low mutters of two people. A flashlight beam shot through the window, then rose to the rooftop. Wes's fingers closed around Vincent's. He squeezed. Vincent squeezed back.

"He can't have gone far," Babcock's assistant hissed.

"By now he might have found a chance to feed." Babcock sighed. "We'll look for another hour or so. I don't want to keep wasting time on this damn feral. They're not usually this much of a pain."

"Did you check inside?"

Babcock grunted.

Vincent pulled Wesley behind the ornamental stone coffin as one of the flashlights moved back around the mausoleum. The thick metal door only had a little intricately ornamented gap to look through, but Babcock rattled it so hard that Vincent worried he might break something. He lifted his light. Vincent checked that his bundled sleeping bag and spare clothes were still out of view of the door slit. The sarcophagus created a dark shadow over it as the beam passed, but Wesley's gaze still caught on the spot. He kept staring at it even as Babcock dropped the light, casting the mausoleum back into darkness.

"This one's sealed tight."

Babcock moved to the other mausoleum, but his rattling turned to background noise against the aghast expression on Wesley's face. As soon as the hunters were out of earshot, the man sank the rest of the way to the floor in a slump. Vincent dropped his head against the stone behind him, staring up at the ceiling so he didn't have to see Wesley. All the sexual tension they'd just built between them had been snuffed out, replaced by something Vincent liked a whole lot less.

"What?" he asked. He didn't have to see the man opening and closing his mouth, trying to form his awkward question into something that wouldn't sound so terrible. He knew Wes well enough by now. "Just say it."

"Vincent." He sounded like he was moving quickly from shocked to broken.

Vincent wished he'd go back, reverse them all the way to the roof where the most important thing had been their mutual understanding and their hands on each other. "I live in a mausoleum. We already went over that."

"Yeah, I know. I just thought there'd be like..." Wesley flung his hands out, bumping into Vincent's chest by accident. "I don't know."

"A velvet-lined coffin?" Vincent snorted.

"A TV or a mini-fridge or a—a *bed.*" Wesley shook his head. "God, Vincent. Is this why you look so grunge all the time?"

Vincent turned to stare at him. "You thought it was a fashion choice? Fuck."

"Yes? You're a vampire, how was I supposed to know what you were into." Wes cringed. "That's not fair, I'm sorry." He breathed out, running his hands through his hair as he turned his face back towards the nook where Vincent stored his sleeping bag, even if Vincent was pretty sure his human eyes couldn't see it without the nearby light of a phone. "But why didn't you tell me? I would have done something! I have a house. I have an extra room, you could have moved in!"

"*This* is why I didn't tell you," Vincent whispered.

"Why?" His tone was miserable. "Because I'd want you to be safe and happy? Because I'd want to take care of you?"

"Yes!" Vincent shouted so loud that his voice echoed in the small, hard-edged space, and the crickets went quiet outside. In the silence he could hear the echoes of all his jealousy. He would have moved into Wesley's house in a heartbeat; he would have stayed there forever if he'd been allowed. He dropped to the ground next to the man. "No. Not because you'd want to take care of me, but because maybe you wouldn't. I didn't want to know where I'd hit the limit to your kindness."

"Vinny," Wes muttered. He turned his head and leaned a little closer. His nose brushed Vincent's forehead, and he lifted his lips to kiss there softly.

As he turned back, Vincent slipped his chin onto Wesley's shoulder. His nose pressed against the man's jaw, and he breathed in Wes with a small, tight inhale. The flood of the man's scent calmed him. Wesley didn't just smell like Wesley anymore. He smelled like home. "I could have trusted you," Vincent whispered. "All this time, I could have just trusted you."

He swore Wesley stiffened, but in the same moment his phone vibrated again. Vincent pulled it out of his pocket. The screen lit up, revealing a notification from the Griffon app and a few emails, their content all hidden. Wesley quickly scrolled aside the emails and unlocked the phone to open the messages from Kendall. A soft chortle left him.

"What?" Vincent grumbled.

Wes pointed to the picture beneath Kendall's chaotic description of work drama. "That's the werewolf meme I mentioned yesterday."

Vincent squinted at it. "Do they *eat* the baby?"

"Metaphorically? The original was about feelings, I think."

As Wesley lowered the phone, another email notification appeared. With the screen unlocked, the sender and subject highlighted itself at the top: *Matthew Babcock. Vitalis-Barron Post-Interview Questions.*

Babcock. The name took the breath out of Vincent, but this wasn't entirely news to him. Wesley would have been in contact with Vitalis-Barron if he'd been trying to get into their research labs to prove his mother's death. He'd known who Mr. Babcock was. It made sense that he'd been part of Wes's interview process, and if Wes was still hunting for the truth of his mother's murder then he wouldn't want to give up that line of communication. That he hadn't told Vincent this outright made a knot form in Vincent's stomach, but maybe he had a good reason. Vincent hadn't told him that he was living out of a four-year-old sleeping bag in a mausoleum. Some subjects were harder to breach than others. Maybe Vincent just needed all the facts.

As Wesley noticed the notification though, he hissed between his teeth and tried to swipe it away. His fingers fumbled shakily over the screen. The phone dropped.

Vincent caught it before it could hit the floor, but the email app thread had already opened sometime in the shuffle, popping up to the most recent reply.

Leaving Sunset Ridge Cemetery now. You coming or not?

Matthew

As Vincent's fingertip rested on the screen, it jumped back up through highlights of the condensed thread.

> **Me**: No blood bags. He feeds straight from humans...
> **Matthew Babcock**: Not when we make it especially for them. He's that feral then...
> **Me**: Actually, scratch that. If I can get a blood bag from you, I'm pretty sure he'll...

It clicked slowly, numbly, a little like being shot: the whole thing over and done with, the wound having already torn him open, but his brain was not quite able to register the pain. He scooted back from Wesley once, then again. And suddenly it felt like his chest had been ripped apart.

The odd passing out after drinking from Wesley's blood bag, the vague memory of being in Wes's car, even the way Wes had practically begged him to come back when Vincent was about to climb out the window that first night. Had the spicy ramen been a set up too, to make him *need* the blood bag in the first place? What about the drinks at the Fishnettery? Their endless texting? The moans and the kink play and the heart-to-heart—what of it had been real and what had been *this*.

Wesley had tried to give him to Vitalis-Barron.

It didn't matter to Vincent why. It never mattered why to any human, not when it was a vampire they were targeting. Any reason was always good enough to fuck over a depraved and dangerous bloodsucker.

And Wesley—fucking Wesley Smith Garcia, Vincent's almost boyfriend, the person he thought he'd been falling in love with—Wesley had tried to fuck him over so thoroughly that Vincent couldn't breathe, couldn't think. He gasped, and he was on his feet somehow, his back bumping into the wall. Wesley's phone clattered out of his fingers. It settled at the human's feet, the soft light casting haunting shadows above his cheeks and in the hollows of his eyes.

There was so much they should have been saying or doing, curses to throw, bones to break, words and blows that would complement the shattering inside Vincent. But there was nothing to be said that could justify this. Nothing to be done that could take it back.

And Wes didn't try. He stared at Vincent, his mouth opening and closing, then snapping shut entirely. His throat bobbed. He closed his eyes and finally uttered a single word. "Fuck."

The air in the mausoleum had gone dead, forcing Vincent's inhales shallow and sharp. He found the sill of the window with his fingertips, then his palm. He had to get out of here, get somewhere safe. Somewhere without Wesley in it. His arms moved on instinct, as though it were a completely different person pulling his body up and through the window.

Wesley didn't call after him.

Vincent tried not to let that crush him all over again. Of course Wesley wouldn't call for him. Their relationship had been a lie; one long manipulation. Maybe it had turned into something more real by the end—*maybe*—but then Wesley had kept lying by not telling him how things had started. Wes had let him believe that he'd been trying to save Vincent when he'd passed out from the drugged—*drugged*—blood bag. Wes had convinced him that he was trustworthy and selfless, that he was the one person who might not see Vincent as a burden, but as family.

Well, Vincent hadn't been a burden to him, alright. He'd been a prize. A price. A thing.

Vincent felt bile rise in the back of his throat. He stumbled through the graves away from the mausoleum. His knees threatened to give out. He couldn't tell if the shakes rolling through him were more delayed sun-poisoning or just his body trying violently to reject everything he'd learned. Either way, he was weak and in pain and not safe out in the open.

He found his feet starting to move toward Wesley's home and he forced them away. Turning from the houses and the lights and the distant sounds of happy humans settling in for the evening, he headed into the quiet darkness of the forest. Babcock was still out here somewhere, Vincent knew, but that felt like a secondary problem to the one that was currently ripping his heart to pieces. It continued feeling like a secondary problem, right up until a burning heat slammed into him from the trees. As he shied away from it a wire sprung around his neck.

Vincent reached for it on instinct, his hands still trembling so badly that they seemed to blur in the dim monochrome of the night, but someone at the other end yanked. The wire tightened. He stumbled. Another yank dragged him to the ground. He wheezed against it, trying to get his fingers around the wire, but a second trap caught his ankle, pulling his body taunt and drawing the first cord tighter.

For a terrible, choking moment Vincent thought they might rip him apart like the old execution methods from days when vampires were more legendary horror than unhomed nuisance, but as his vision turned to spots and his consciousness began to slip, the metal noose loosened. He groaned hoarsely, barely managing to open his eyes as boots stomped around his head.

"Finally. Who knew he'd go down so easily in the end."

They grabbed his wrists. He tried to tug them away, but the searing that had originally stumbled him pressed into the center of his back. It felt like the terrible metal

Babcock had with him when he'd first confronted Vincent, slowly draining away his strength as it blazed against his exposed skin and made his spine ache. His attacker pushed him down with it and yanked his hands behind his back. A plastic cord tightened around them.

Someone else yanked at his ankles, binding them with a similar tie. "A lot of the feral ones are like this. They've got no support, so if you get them panicked enough they run right into the first trap you set."

"Babcock?" Vincent groaned.

His assistant slammed her boot into Vincent's stomach and he curled inward, whimpering. Before the pain had faded, she took hold of the metal noose still around his neck and pulled him to his knees with it. She stared down at him, her lips twisted. "No support, huh? That means no one's going to miss you."

The way that statement hurt, Vincent wished she'd just kicked him again instead.

21

WESLEY

The way Vincent's face had broken in the dim light of the phone screen felt seared into Wesley's brain, a brand that would never leave him. He'd dreaded the moment all week, actively avoided it, hoped that maybe it would never come while knowing that it had to. But experiencing the pain of it, seeing the horror and the fear splinter Vincent's expression and the stiff, scared way he'd fled from Wes had hurt in ways Wesley couldn't have imagined.

He could have called after Vincent. He could have apologized, or explained, or pleaded. Maybe he should have; maybe it would have helped. If it would have given Vincent even a little bit of peace, it would've been worth it. But when Wesley had finally managed to open his mouth, nothing but that single curse had made it past the bitter pain in his chest. He'd sat in numbed silence as Vincent vanished out the window, coat flaring behind him.

Wes didn't know how anyone had ever felt like this and lived through it. He was pretty sure that he didn't *want* to live through it. He dragged his knees up, shaking as he dropped his head onto them.

His phone's light timed out, leaving him suddenly in the dark. Tears slipped down his cheeks. It felt almost wrong to grieve the loss of their relationship after everything he'd done; this was his fault after all. He shouldn't have been allowed to weep over it, when his single-minded assholery had caused it in the first place.

Wes choked in a breath and screamed it out into his knees.

The screen of his phone lit back up. He wanted desperately to throw it across the mausoleum or delete the thread of Babcock's emails or delete everything entirely, his whole fucked up life, and go volunteer at a vampire help center someplace they actually had those. Someplace better than here, with people better than him. With people like Vincent.

God, Vincent.

We caught the bloodsucker a little way into the forest west of the cemetery. Last chance to help us bring him in! We'll celebrate with drinks and War Call after.

Matthew

Wesley's blood went cold. He sprang to his feet so fast that the world swam. His shoulder crashed painfully into the stone wall. He leaned there, typing without really seeing the words.

I'm coming now.

Babcock replied immediately.

I'll send Natalie to meet you at the edge of the cemetery.

Fuck, he had to hurry.

Wes scrambled out of the window, slamming his phone on mute as he sprinted for the forest. He tripped over enough gravestones to lose count, ending up with a long red scrape across his left hand that he couldn't quite recall the source of. He'd barely dove into the cover of the trees when the silhouette of Natalie stepped out, her phone screen lighting up the underside of her face. She leaned against a trunk.

Waiting for him.

That was one hunter taken care of, for the moment anyway.

Wesley crept deeper into the forest, wishing with every twig snap and leaf crunch that he had Vincent's skill at stealth. Or his eyesight. He found the only pinprick of light in the darkness and followed. It led him to Babcock, the man's back gratefully toward him and his metal stick tucked under one arm as he typed on his phone, his bright flashlight aimed at a hunched, kneeling figure.

Even half blocked by branches and shifting in and out of the bobbing light, Wes knew Vincent in an instant. He would know him anywhere: in the pitch black, at the end of the world, by the sound of his breath and the way Wes's heart tuned to it. The sight of him like this burned Wesley alive. His vision tunneled in. His toe hit a mug-sized rock. He picked it up, balancing it in one hand as he crept toward Babcock. The man's skull was all he could focus on, the rest of the world a hazy whirlwind drowned beneath the rush of blood in his ears.

This man had hunted Vincent. Had used him and bound him and hurt him. Was going to turn him over to Vitalis-Barron's experiments in exchange for a paycheck. He was the very incarnation of the company. If Wesley couldn't burn them down, he could at least damage a cog in their machine.

Babcock made an annoyed sound at his phone screen. He turned. His brow lifted. As their eyes locked, Wesley hesitated. But he couldn't stop. Someone had to pay for everything that had hurt Vincent, that had killed Wesley's mom, that had fucked over so many people for the profit of a corrupt corporation. If that someone wasn't going to be Wesley then it was sure as hell going to be Babcock.

Wes bashed the rock into the side of Babcock's face.

The man stumbled with a grunt. His stick fell first, disappearing into the bushes, then his flashlight slipped, tumbling across the ground and settling at an angle that cast them both in a stream of silver. Babcock blinked against the glow. His hand went toward his belt, but Wesley hit him again, slamming the rock like a bat into the man's shoulder, then once more straight at the center of his chest. Something crunched.

Babcock stumbled harder this time. He caught himself on the trunk of a tree, his gaze bleary and hair rumpled from its usual slicked-back state. Something dripped from the corner of his lips. He stared at Wesley in unfocused confusion, as though still trying to put the pieces of himself back together as he asked, "Who are… You… you lived at that house we tracked the vamp to…"

"I'm Wesley; you invited me here." Wes grinned, no pleasure in the expression. Well, some pleasure. Babcock could drown in his own blood, and Wes felt he would just keep grinning. "Yeah, that was my house. And that vampire you've hurt? That's someone I love."

Babcock's eyes sharpened, then widened, and his lips turned to a snarl. "Now, hold on." But he was reaching again, hand curling behind his back.

"Fuck that." With all his might, Wesley smashed the rock into Babcock's temple.

His skull thudded beneath it. He fell. As he hit the ground, his head made a second thump, sharper and wetter. He didn't move. Wes's arm shook, but he kept hold of the rock as he knelt, hovering his hand over the man's mouth, then pressing beneath his jaw. Nothing.

Oh. Wes had probably killed another human, and he felt… nothing. No, he felt good. He felt just a little bit righteous even. He definitely needed to get a therapist after this.

Wesley dropped the rock and scooped up the flashlight instead, rushing to Vincent's side. His lungs clenched and his throat went dry at the raw, red welts beneath the metal choker that looked like something made to catch dogs not people. A sob welled in his chest as he reached for the vampire.

Vincent flinched away.

Wes stopped. He lifted his palms. "Sorry, sorry, I know I—I'm not exactly the person you trust most right now. But I just want to help."

"Then help," Vincent wheezed. "Find a blade."

"Right." Wes scrambled to Babcock's body—it smelled like urine now; that meant he was dead, didn't it?—and patted along his waist. He found a gun hidden beneath the back of his jacket and a small knife hooked to his belt.

Vincent only cringed a little as Wes cut the ties on his ankles and wrists. He pulled the metal off his neck with an inhale so ragged it seemed like he might burst into sobs. His gaze darted to the trees in the direction of the quiet cemetery—Natalie must not have heard their commotion this far in—before jumping back to Wes, then to Babcock's body, tense and scared like a cornered animal about to flee.

Every instinct told Wesley to grab him. If Vincent ran now, he'd be alone, without safety or shelter or blood. He'd have nothing and no one again. And Wesley would still be here, with a dead body and no proof of Vitalis-Barron's crimes, forever wondering whether Vincent was alive, whether he was happy, whether Vitalis-Barron had snatched him away for their experiments and disposed of his body alongside Wes's mom.

Unless…

Wes didn't want to think like this. He should not have been considering asking anything of Vincent, much less something so dangerous. But Wes still needed to take down Vitalis-Barron, for his mother and for Vincent and for every other person they'd hurt. And he had something he wanted Vincent to have—something

Vincent needed far more than Wes ever would. This was likely the only way Vincent would trust him enough to accept anything from him. He had to put all his cards on the table, the terrible alongside the good, and let Vincent judge if they were worth it.

"One last wager," Wesley said, breathless.

Vincent didn't interrupt.

"I need to get into the Vitalis-Barron research building and you need enough security to restart your life," Wes explained. "So how about this: we hide the body in the brush, and you come to their lab with me now, before they realize Babcock is dead. We find the proof that my mother was part of their studies when she died, proof I can use to stop them from coming for you again and maybe even shut them down, and after we break out you can have my house." Not his mom's house, but his now. It had been Wes's for over a year, he just hadn't wanted to accept that.

He watched the shifts in Vincent's expression, the confusion and suspicion, but beneath that was something a little bit hungry.

Wes felt like shit to prey on it. He had always been the predator in their relationship. At least now he was being open about it. "The mortgage is entirely paid off, so you'd just have to deal with the property tax and the insurance. If you get a roommate or two, you shouldn't even need much of a job. And I'll even sign it over to you right now, in my own blood if I have to, so if we get to Vitalis-Barron and you want to back out, it's still yours."

"But you…" Vincent looked back through the woods like he could see the house from there. "Where would you go?"

Of course that would be Vincent's first thought—not of himself, but of how his gain might hurt someone else. Wesley didn't know if his heart could handle much more of this feeling: the painful mix of how very much he loved this overly compassionate vampire and how much he regretted taking advantage of that compassion. He tried not to let that all show as he shrugged. "I'm an adult with a college degree. I can get a job like everyone else and rent an apartment or something. I'm not a vampire."

Vincent grimaced. He rubbed at his wrists, his tight brow casting odd shadows in the beam of the flashlight. Facedown in the dirt, Babcock's phone lit up. Natalie had to be coming back any minute now. Wesley shifted between the soles of his feet, glancing toward the cemetery.

"Please, Vinny. I really need this. I don't have any other options."

With such ragged caution that it hurt Wes to watch, Vincent drew to his feet. He wrapped his arms over his chest, squinting at Wesley. "I risk my life for one night, we fuck Vitalis-Barron over, and I get the house?"

"One night, Vitalis-Barron gets fucked, and you get the house. Unless it looks too risky, then I pull you out immediately and you still get the house." Vincent would just have to trust that Wes would follow through.

The vampire ran his fingers over the welts along his throat, and his gaze went to Babcock's cooling body. He swallowed. "Deal."

"Deal." Wesley offered up his hand.

They shook.

22

VINCENT

Getting away from Babcock's horrible silver stick had revived Vincent's speed and agility, and he'd even stopped trembling about ten minutes after they left the woods, but his anxiety—that had to be what it was, since the sun-pain never returned—was wearing off into an ugly nausea that felt only a tiny bit better. At least his brain seemed to function at almost normal capacity, so long as he didn't think too hard about Wesley Smith Garcia: betrayer, manipulator, and violent protector.

"And that vampire you've hurt? That's someone I love."

He kept replaying Wes's words like they might change.

They could have been another manipulation, a lie in a long string of half-truths and avoidances. But Wes had fought Babcock for Vincent when he could have offered to shake the man's hand instead and slide into the research lab on his coattails. The only thing that had stood between Wesley and the goal he'd been working so hard for was Vincent's suffering. Wes hadn't been willing to permit that. It wasn't enough, at least not yet. But it was something.

The offer of the house was something, too.

Vincent stood in the front hall space, picking out each little piece of the room that had come from Wesley's mother: the family photos of a smiling Mexican woman with a beaming boy half covered in mud, the pin for *nurse of the month* on the minivan's lanyard that dangled from the garage doorknob, the little cherub-like action figures of her favorite animated characters lining the mantel beside Wesley's video game collectibles, the old rosary she'd saved from a religion that must have been important to her once. He found her, too, in the wear on the wood flooring, in a chip in the banister, and in a loose, feminine handwriting that marked the adventure map on the back of the couch. She had turned this place into a home for her and her son. And now Wesley was giving it away.

To Vincent. To the vampire he'd nearly handed over to a company he knew was running deadly experiments on them. But then he hadn't. And that also meant something.

If only for the first time since they'd met, Wesley stayed true to word, pulling his own house key off its chain and offering it to Vincent. There were no signatures involved, much less ones with blood. Vincent was grateful for that. If he had to smell Wesley's blood while still feeling his current range of conflicting emotions towards the man, he thought he might vomit. While simply possessing a key wouldn't hold up in any court, particularly when it was a vampire trying to argue for ownership, the sentiment still counted.

They climbed into the minivan in a silence broken only by the snap of their seatbelts, then the rumble of the engine. As they sat at a turn, the blinker's ritual click-click boring into Vincent's skull, something finally occurred to him that he should have asked back when they were still in the woods frantically covering Babcock's body with a tangle of dead brush.

"You have a plan, right?" He felt a little sicker with each word. "You know where Vitalis-Barron is keeping this information? And you have some kind of exit strategy, for both of us?"

"Si—yes! Kind of." Wesley's hands went tighter around the wheel. "I know where the front entrance is, and the back exit, and that the parking lot is really empty at night so there can't be that many staff at this hour. And I have Babcock's gun now."

"Oh my god." Vincent pressed his palms to his cheeks, focusing on the cold of them. "We're going to die. I'm going to die, and you're going to prison."

"You're not going to die." There was an edge to Wesley's voice that hadn't been there a moment before. It cracked as he continued. "But I might be going to prison anyway, since I kind of killed Matthew Babcock. Though technically, I think it was whatever he fell on, not me. It looked like there was some blood on the dirt under his head."

"A lot of blood," Vincent said, then cringed. "I could smell it."

"Right. So not entirely my fault. I'm a man-slaughterer, not a murderer."

"Which is why you tossed the murder weapon into the creek?"

"Man-slaughterer weapon."

Vincent closed his eyes, trying not to think of the way it had kept smelling of Babcock's blood until it sank into the muck. That only brought visions of the man's corpse, and of Wesley slamming the rock into his head.

"And that vampire you've hurt? That's someone I love."

Vincent breathed out, watching the rock drop in his mind, feeling the break in Wes's voice and the way the man's hands had shook as he'd freed Vincent. "Do you feel bad about it?"

"Killing Babcock?" Wesley hesitated, his gaze on the freeway. "I think I should, but I don't. He was going to bring you to Vitalis-Barron. I'm kind of glad he's dead."

"That's not at all hypocritical." They were cruel words—there was no comparison between Babcock and Wesley, even if their goals had been aligned for a few weeks—and as soon as Vincent said them, he wanted Wes to argue. To prove him wrong.

But Wesley only gave another broken, bitter laugh. "It's so fucking hypocritical!" His knuckles had gone a lighter monochrome in the dark of the car. "I should be with him, cooling in the forest. I deserve that. I fucking—" He made a sound like he'd been stabbed in the chest, hollow and pained, more an exhale than a true noise. His voice dropped to a whisper. "But first I have to take Vitalis-Barron down and make sure you're safe. Then I'll accept the consequences."

Vincent pressed his palm to Wes's hand, wrapping his own fingers around them on the wheel. "The only consequence you deserve, Wes, is therapy."

Wes sniffled, not quite an agreement, but enough for now.

Vincent drew back. Then fiddled his thumbs in this lap, counting the cars in the slow lane as they passed.

"Do you want to talk about it," Wes asked.

"What part?"

Wesley snorted. "The one where I suck as a partner and as a friend and as a person?"

"No, not really." Vincent truly didn't, not about that. There were only so many ways he could explain that

Wes wasn't the monster he made himself out to be while Vincent was still drowning in the weight of what Wes had nearly done to him, and there was only so much forgiveness Vincent could offer before he would start widening his own unhealed wounds. But there was one thing he needed to know now. "If I asked you a question, would you answer it honestly?"

"I'm never not going to be honest with you ever again." He released a shaky breath. "You don't have any reason to believe that, but it's the truth."

Vincent did believe it. He wasn't sure why. Perhaps it was just all the little-big acts combined, the saving him from Babcock, the offering of the house, the way Wes was speaking now, like he was a raw, flayed-open thing and every word was his blood oozing beyond his control.

"That's someone I love."

Vincent believed him. He just needed to hear it. "It was all real, right? What we said and did on the mausoleum roof, all the dates that weren't dates, what we felt. You really do—" *Someone he loves.* "You do care about me?"

"God yes," Wes said, and he sounded so thoroughly broken that Vincent couldn't bear to look at him in case what he saw there really was Wes's raw and bleeding heart, because if he did, he was fairly certain he'd have to find a way to heal it, even if it meant cutting himself back open to do so. The little sob the man gave turned suddenly to a laugh, tight and bright and aching. "Does that make it better or worse?"

I don't know, Vincent thought, and couldn't say it.

∾

By the time they pulled the car into the vacant dirt lot for the lake beach next to the Vitalis-Barron research compound, they had a ragged half-assed plan. If they weren't working against Babcock's death here, Vincent would never have agreed to it. As it was, he twisted unhappily against the old cord Wesley had wrapped round his wrists and scowled at the massive building complex with its large, sterile windows and perfectly manicured landscaping. The gate guard seemed confused by their lack of vehicle, but Wesley flashed a little card he'd been given at his interview and bemoaned how his excitement had led him not to check the gas level in his car.

"What was I supposed to do? Pull into the gas station with a half-conscious vampire whining in the front seat?" Wes laughed.

Vincent hissed softly under his breath and played up his shaking, stumbling act as the guard waved them through. He carried on with it all the way through the nearly empty parking lot despite the building's dimmed lightning, its main doors sealed shut for the night. It seemed Wesley had been right: they really didn't staff the complex much after hours, keeping with the current trend of having as few shifts as possible that a vampire might sneak their way onto. Wes led them toward a locked side entrance. He held up his card to its scanner and it buzzed, popping open for them.

Its foyer could not have been any more standard: a gray rug over tiled floor with a receptionist behind the desk. As the woman stood, three people in uniforms who looked somewhere between guards and secret agents stepped in from the next room. For a moment Vincent was certain they'd already been foiled, but the guards smiled and greeted Wesley professionally.

"You're new?" asked the more senior of the agents, her voice gravelly.

"First catch." Wes grinned his larger-than-life smile, not less intoxicating than the first day he'd turned it on Vincent. It covered his lies as easily now as it had then. "Got him right as he came stumbling out of the woods. I think he's the one Matthew Babcock has been tracking. You know Matthew, right? I haven't been able to get a hold of him since, and I didn't want to leave the vamp just hanging out there and risk the sun-toxins wearing off."

"Right, Matthew Babcock! You're Wesley? He mentioned you might be showing up soon."

Wes just kept beaming. "The one and only."

"Wesley Smith?" The receptionist repeated. "Come right this way, I have your employment file ready to sign, then we can schedule you for onboarding tomorrow."

Panic twisted inside Vincent at the thought of being taken away from Wesley, dragged into the depths of the research lab alone. He fought to hide the emotion from his face, tipping his chin down and pinching his eyes closed like he was in pain, while every muscle in his body prepared to run. He'd known this was a terrible plan. God, how had he agreed to this?

Wes made such a disappointed sound that even knowing it was fake, it was hard to hear and not feel sorry for him. "Ah, Babcock's been gearing me up for this for weeks; I was hoping I'd get to see the whole process of my first sign-up for myself."

The receptionist's brow lifted, but she nodded. "If Babcock has been mentoring you, then I don't see why not? You already signed the initial NDA at the end of your interview, and we will need some information from you about this vamp before we officially process him." She looked at the gravelly-voiced agent. "You don't mind, Myers?"

Myers huffed. "That would be easier for us anyway. Then we don't have to put the specimen in holding overnight."

Specimen. It made Vincent's spine crawl in a way that not even the nastier slang for vampires could. He wasn't a monster here; he was a rat, a numbered thing to be dissected and the pieces thrown in the trash after.

Wesley barely seemed to notice his discomfort, even as Myers replaced his blinding with a pair of cuffs that clipped just out of Vincent's reach, but that detachment was for the best right now. He had to play the part. And contrary to everything the man had initially done to try and force Vincent here, Vincent found he trusted him in this. Even if he didn't look like it, this was hurting Wes too.

Myers led Wesley down the hall, Wes making a show of half-dragging and half-pushing Vincent along. Vincent's gaze caught on the security cameras in the corners, and he had to force himself to keep walking. It didn't matter if they were on video or not. Vitalis-Barron would know their identities no matter what. They were only getting away with this if they succeeded in dismantling the company.

As Myers directed them into an elevator, the other security returned to their stations near the foyer. At least that was good—two less humans to fight their way through later. Myers held down three different elevator numbers, then tapped the alarm button with the ID card strapped to her belt. They began to descend. And kept descending.

A nauseous sensation grew in Vincent's stomach. He leaned forward, focusing on the sound of his own breath. Wes's thumb slid over his arm just out of Myer's line of sight, rubbing gentle circles. The soft touch soothed him, if only a little, and the thoughtfulness of it soothed even more.

The elevator dinged four stories down, and the doors opened. The hallway walls were as stark white as the floor, the only ornamentations the metal and glass of doors and equipment. It seemed like something out of a video game: too harshly screaming *evil lab* to be real. But then, it was likely the people who had approved this particular lab hadn't been particularly moral themselves. Maybe the stereotypical statement of villainy was the point.

At least here the cameras vanished, and the halls seemed quiet and empty, the lights having to boot up from status mode as they progressed. That left its own weight in Vincent's gut. Clearly Vitalis-Barron worried far more about humans breaking in than vampires breaking out. While good for him and Wes, he feared what state their vamps had to be kept in to justify it.

Myers steered Wes into the first room on their left. The small, stark chamber had two cushioned chairs on one side of a metal table, thick cuffs welded across from them. Scratches pointed toward the bindings like warning signals. Vincent stiffened, but Myers only had him deposited beside the stool on that side, barely paying attention to him as he shook and huddled away from her. She drilled Wesley on the state of Vincent's pathetic life, jotting his answers into a tablet she'd collected from a metal rack outside the room. There wasn't much drilling to be done.

"He's been living in the cemetery, yeah. Babcock's already cut off anyone that might have wondered where he's gone. Honestly, from what we could tell, he's got no one and nothing." Wes shrugged at the end.

It was true. It was true, and Vincent knew it, but hearing it out loud so bluntly and totally made his jaw ache and his eyes burn. He choked back a whimper.

"We love these ones," Myers hummed. "No clean up, just snatch and go."

She asked about his state, the last time Wes figured he'd eaten, and whether Wes knew how long he'd been turned for. Wes made up his answers quickly after she implied they had ways of getting the information out of Vincent if he didn't—*sun-poisoning*, he said, *36 hours since his feeding and two years since he'd turned.* Vincent hoped they didn't have an easy way to prove him wrong. Myers brought them back out, tablet tucked beneath her arm. Vincent felt better just having Wesley's hand returned to his arm, even with his grip so tight and his manner less than friendly.

"That's someone I love."

Vincent didn't have nothing after all.

They turned from one sterile corridor to another, passing dim rooms with sleeping scientific equipment, all the researchers cleared out for the evening. As they walked, Wesley slipped in a few questions about protocols and methods, which Myers answered with so little hesitation that it amazed Vincent. But then, he supposed, Wesley had just bound and delivered them a person to torture in order to get this job. Anyone willing to go to those lengths had to be pretty deeply sold on working here.

"You collect all this data on the lab tablets, right? Is that very secure?" Wes asked, "I thought all this science stuff was supposed to be pretty secretive." From anyone else it might have sounded probing, but between Wesley's easy smile and the nonchalance of his voice he seemed like nothing more than a good-natured jock unaware of his own ignorance.

"All of the technology on this level of the basement connects to the private server that's only accessible from here. Nothing gets in or out. Trust me." Myers motioned toward Vincent and winked, her smile cruel. "Our research is locked up tight."

Wes chuckled with her, and the way the laughter crawled over Vincent's skin took him a moment to push past, to find the man beneath the act, the one who'd lain beside him on the mausoleum roof and stared at the stars. That was the man he'd come here with. That was a man who would probably hit Myers over the head with a rock if she turned away for too long—which worried Vincent in its own way, but one that made him want to help Wesley more, not less.

"You have great timing, we've been running low on specimens," Myers said, waving her badge in front of a massive, two-panel metal door. It unlocked with a *thunk*, and it seemed even she had to put her weight into opening it.

Inside, the long white room continued to the left and right. Three rolling metal tables with straps had been lined up neatly and a lab technician at a bench-cart parceled out small samples of badly-smelling blood into little plastic pouches. Beyond them were the cells. Built into the wall, each four-foot by four-foot chamber was brightly lit, their only furnishings a little toilet system in the back corner.

There were so many—over two dozen, their glass entrances swaying in Vincent's vision, doubling and tripling as his chest tightened. Only eight were currently occupied. Each sickly-looking vampire looked so hollowed out and twisted that they seemed more like the monsters from the myths than the humans they'd once been. It took Vincent a moment to recognize the fourth from the end, their cotton-candy hair now stringy and oily and their dark skin an ashen gray. They lay in their shirt and boxers, curled on the white floor beneath the blinding lights, an arm over their head as they breathed raggedly.

Vincent shook for real now, his pain and horror turning to anger. He'd given Babcock all the information the man had needed to designate the cotton-candy haired artist as a vampire and let Vitalis-Barron set up a story to justify their disappearance. He had participated in this torture without even knowing it. Not only had Vitalis-Barron been treating his community like disposable lab rats, but they'd made innocent people—the people most likely to be vampires themselves—complicit in the work.

"I don't keep up with the specifics of the research," Myers said, continuing toward one of the empty cells, "but whatever the nerds have been up to recently, these specimens aren't lasting very long under it. We need all the new bodies we can get."

Vincent wanted to burn the whole place to the ground.

The lab tech stopped Myers to ask if the "new specimen" had been deprived of blood long enough to start him on the feeding regimen that round.

Wes's hand tightened around his arm and he caught the tiny pulse of his jaw just before his eyes met Vincent's. *"Leave?"* he mouthed.

Everything in Vincent screamed yes, run, but he couldn't just escape this and forget about the vampires here. He couldn't sit in Wesley's house knowing this lab would keep torturing their way through people like him without remorse, and that when he'd had the option to do something about it, he'd chosen to cower instead. Maybe the two of them, with no solid plan and no training, wouldn't be able to bring down a company this size in the end. But Vincent was sure as hell not leaving here without trying to bring down something. If that meant he died as sickly and pained as the vampires he'd accidentally condemned to those cells, then so be it.

He checked that Myers was still focused on the lab tech and shook his head before pointing to the dying vampires with his chin. *"Save them,"* he mouthed.

Wesley's expression hardened. His hand darted between Vincent's, undoing the fastenings at his wrists as his gaze went to Myers's belt. To her ID access badge.

Before Vincent could find a way to reply, Myers turned to wave them forward.

Wesley gave a low whistle under his breath. "This place must be hopping when you've got all the cells full. Looks like I've got some work ahead of m—e!" While his head was twisted toward the empty cells on the far side of the room, he caught his foot in the lab tech's cart, tipping it over as he tripped into it. The open vials of blood splashed across his jacket and sprinkled on his face and neck.

In the midst of the commotion, Vincent swept his hand out, unclipping Myers's ID badge so fast that his arm blurred. He pressed it into Wesley's back pocket and took a step away after, holding his wrists as though the bindings still held. His head felt light, the danger of what he'd just done hitting him only now that it was over.

"Shit, I'm so sorry," Wesley said, his cheeks flushed beneath the splatter of blood and palms outstretched as Myers cursed.

"It's fine," she muttered, helping the lab tech right the cart. She glanced at Wes and her nose wrinkled. "There's a bathroom down the hall, sign over the top. Don't get any of that stuff in your eyes or mouth."

"Right, sorry." Wes bounced backwards with a sheepish smile and fled so awkwardly out the room that Vincent felt like he was looking at himself in a mirror.

As the door closed behind him, all the remaining warmth seemed to desert the space, leaving it a terrible, lifeless place. Vincent swallowed. Myers grabbed him. He flinched, stumbling over his own feet with each harsh shove she gave him toward the empty cell.

Run. He had to run. But he couldn't, not yet. Not until Wesley—

And then he was inside, the glass sealing closed behind him. He forced himself to breathe. Either Wesley would come back for him, or this was where he'd die.

Wesley would come back for him.

23

WESLEY

Wesley deserved some kind of award for what they'd just pulled off. Maybe a *stupidest plan ever doesn't fail—yet* award, or an *idiot fumbles through life on sheer charisma* award. Definitely a prize for *man doesn't break cover despite wanting to look back at the vampire he's madly in love with one last time.* It wouldn't be one last time though. He was coming back for Vincent.

Right after he figured out where the damned server room was.

He tried to ignore the fact that he'd seen no references to the kind of nefarious human studies that might have killed his mom. Perhaps the human deaths had been accidental. This was still the place that regularly handled the deaths of their lab participants and had the security set up to keep it all under locks. This would still be where they held those records. They would have known what they were doing was too illegal to keep in the labs upstairs. If his mom's information was in their system, this was where it had to be.

Wes turned away from the restrooms, walking until he found a little safety map with the emergency exits and fire extinguishers highlighted. He scanned the setup. There were a dozen obvious laboratories and an area that was definitely the prison he'd just let them lock Vincent in, and there, at the center of the research floor, was a small room only identified as 340. Either that was the server room, or Wes was fucked.

God, if this worked, he was never going to half-ass anything again in his life. Maybe he'd even start going to Mass. At least for Advent and Easter.

He swiped a tablet from a metal basket as he jogged, glad that at least the night shift down here seemed to be just Myers and the lab tech from the prison room. Room 340. He held his breath, and pressed Myers's ID to the lock. It clicked open.

A row of tall, cabinet-sized computers blinked in the darkness. Wes flipped on his phone light and pulled an external drive from the belt loop of his pants. The handle of Babcock's gun pressed awkwardly into the small of his back as he squatted beside a strip of ports, hunting for the size that fit.

"Here goes." He shoved his drive in.

Nothing instantly shut down on him, which seemed like a good sign. He used a cord from a nearby box to hook the tablet into the same computer server box. Did they have a more specific name than that? Wes was pretty sure his business degree had never covered industrial espionage.

He inserted Myers's access card into the side of the table. The device made him input the woman's pin code, and he congratulated himself for having watched her fingers closely when she'd first entered it. He clicked into the server's main file system.

When he tried to open the human research trials folder, a popup appeared asking for an additional password. Fuck. For some reason he'd figured getting direct access would bypass that kind of security, but that seemed foolish now. He clicked back out, looking through the rest of the folders, different veins of research, protocols and certifications, then there: specimen records.

Even the humans they'd killed had to be in there, if they'd been willing to cover up their disappearances the same way they had their vampires'.

Adrenaline fluttered in Wesley's chest, like the moment before launching off a cliff. He could have copied the entire folder over, looked through it later in the safety of his home. But he had to know. He opened it. At the top appeared a massive spreadsheet, individual files below it. Files with names.

Aaron, Eric.

Ackerman, Tina.

Aguilar, Daniella.

Ahmed, Jarrell.

Wes scrolled down, and down, through D's and F's and then to G.

Garcia-Serrano, Jessica.

He sucked in a breath, held it, and popped up the file. It was dated the day before her alleged bus ticket had been purchased. At the very top beside *status* it read *deceased* in big letters, with a death date of three months after they'd taken her. A full four weeks after he'd held her funeral.

She'd been alive. She'd been alive in these labs when he'd buried her coffin.

Wes's chest seized. It was all he could do not to scream, not to sob himself into another oblivion. He leaned forward instead, pressing his head to the computer box and breathed. And thought of Vincent. Vincent was back in that cell still, waiting for him. There would be time to mourn later. Right now he needed to finish this and save his vampire.

But as Wesley steadied the tablet screen, his gaze slipped down the document. Beneath the status of her death was her age, and beneath that they had another descriptive classification. Another piece of his mother written out like it could define her, scientifically determine who she'd been, and let her be discarded for it. It read *presumed date of turning* with a day that had to have been seven or eight weeks before they took her and the qualifying note of *information received from patient under duress.*

Date of turning—what did that have to do with his mom?

She wasn't. She hadn't been.

Her complaint of feeling sick had started around that time and when they'd talked she'd mentioned how she'd liked the transition to night shifts a lot more now than when she'd worked them in the past and... oh. The pieces had already been there, everything already in place, the light on even if he didn't want to acknowledge it.

Why would Vitalis-Barron have wanted his mom this badly, if she hadn't been a vampire?

Wesley felt as though his soul was boiling, and in one fell swoop it turned to ice as he realized what this meant, now, presently, to him and to Vincent and to this company who'd done such harm to the vampiric community without anyone even knowing or caring: this would not be enough to topple them. Maybe if he had a really good lawyer he could force a settlement or if he went to the press he could embarrass them out of a percentage of their profits. Even if the majority of the people living in San Salud were uncomfortable with having vampires as neighbors or employees, most of them would still find outright imprisonment and experimentation offensive if it was shoved in their faces blatantly enough. But there was nothing *technically* illegal about the inhumane treatment of people the law didn't even consider human in the first place.

Wes could barely stop from launching the tablet across the room. Instead, he made himself leave the document, and drag the contents of its entire folder onto his external hard drive. He watched the little completion bar go up and the transfer ping as successful before shoving the drive back into his pocket. Then he did throw the tablet, letting it smack and clank into the server boxes.

It did nothing for his mood.

He wiped his face as he left the server room, smearing blood and tears across his cheeks. With Myers's ID in one hand and Babcock's gun in the other, he stormed the empty, sterile hallways heading for the vampire prison room. Someone else already held open the door, her back to him and her shoulders shaking.

"He's dead!" Babcock's assistant screamed. "I found his body under a fucking bush."

"I'm sorry, Ms. Deleon," Myers replied, her voice wary. "This must be difficult for you, but we have protocols in place that need to be followed. Have you informed Dr. Blood?"

"Yeah, and she won't even let me call the police on it, because some newb we've been helping already brought in the vamp who murdered him." Natalie pulled something long and silver from her jacket. It took Wesley's brain a moment to process it: Babcock's metal stick. In its presence, every vampire immediately cringed away. "That vamp, he's the one. He's the fucking—"

"Ms. Deleon," Myers interrupted her. "He will suffer under the research just like all the others. Matthew Babcock's death is a tragedy but—"

Natalie stormed into the room. "He killed one of ours, he can suffer *now*."

"That isn't what we're here for, Ms. Deleon."

Wesley crept after the enraged hunter, catching the door before it could seal. Myers stood between Natalie and Vincent's cell. The vampire leaned against the back wall, his arms wrapped around himself and his eyes closed, his breathing so shallow that for a moment Wes was scared something had already happened to him. Off to one side, the lab tech quietly inserted a miniature blood bag into the first cell through a wall compartment. The vampire within grimaced and slowly edged toward it.

Myers watched the hunter approach. For a moment, it looked like she would reach for her belt—for a weapon or a radio, Wes didn't know—but then her lips curled.

"I have to find our new recruiter," she said, stepping aside, but she kept watching Natalie as she passed. Her voice turned to a hiss. "When I come back, I want you gone."

"Don't hurry," Natalie snapped. She hit the button for the sliding glass door of Vincent's cell. He flinched, but as the barrier rolled up between them, he only huddled further into the corner.

Why didn't he...?

Waiting. He was waiting.

For Wesley.

Well, Wesley was here, and he was going to set the world on fire before he let anyone hurt his vampire again. "I have dibs on that one, actually," he shouted, throwing the door wide. "As it stands, I still owe him a daring escape."

All three of the room's human occupants turned, confusion on Myer's face and a vengeful understanding on Natalie's. With a grin, Wes slammed off every one of the lights, casting the blindingly bright room into darkness.

24

Vincent

Vincent had barely a moment to dwell on how much he absolutely adored Wesley before the darkness fell, the room turning to monochromes in the sliver of incoming hallway light. The humans all stumbled. Myers fumbled at her waist and the lab tech froze in terror as Natalie cursed and tried to slam closed Vincent's cell door again. Vincent ignored every alarm in his head that told him not to go anywhere near her burning silver stick and forced himself to scramble past her before the sliding glass could descend. He kicked the weapon from her grip, giving it a second boot to roll it across the room.

As the metal clattered farther and farther away, his skin stopped sizzling and his strength returned. His heart in his throat, he dove past each of the other full cells, hitting their door buttons one by one. He staggered to a stop at the end, glancing from where Wes stood in the doorway across the long chamber and back at the vampires. If they were too sick, if he had to carry each of them out, if—

But the cotton-candy haired vampire stumbled from their cell first. The others came close behind. They launched themselves at Myers and the lab technician, fangs sinking into flesh with hisses and grunts. The subtle tang of blood saturated the air in moments.

The cotton-candy haired vampire pushed by them, tackling into Natalie, teeth bared and snapping at the hunter's throat. Natalie kicked them back and barreled toward the exit so fast that by the time Vincent thought to follow she was already pelting past Wesley as he floundered with his gun like he was trying to figure out how to cock it. Straining against the brightness of the hall, Wes finally managed to shoot Babcock's gun after her. He cursed as it bucked in his hands. Natalie shrieked and a door slammed down the hall.

The cotton-candy haired vampire crawled onto their hands and knees. Their hungry gaze fixed on Wesley.

"Vinny?" Wes whispered, one hand on the door and staring into the lab like he wasn't sure if he needed to start running too.

Vincent moved toward the vampire, his palms up, trying to get their attention in the calmest way possible. "He's a friend. You can't feed on him."

But a famished growl sprang from the cotton-candy haired vampire, and two of their starving companions let go of the unconscious lab tech to follow suit. Their focuses fixed on what Vincent knew from experience would be Wesley's strongly beating heart and the gentle throb of his pulse through his throat as he swallowed, ignoring Vincent's words as though they were another language entirely.

Instead of backing away, Wes stepped forward, squinting into the room with his hand outstretched. "I won't leave without you, Vinny."

Which meant Vincent would have to leave without *them*, without the victims Vitalis-Barron had tried to turn him into.

The rest of the emaciated vampires lifted their heads from their dying prey and slowly turned on Wes like a pack. A pack of people, good people probably, but starving, tortured people who had been pushed so far from their natural state that all they could see in Wesley was the blood they'd been denied. They weren't monsters, but right now they would be monstrous, if given the chance.

The cotton-candy haired vampire sprang at Wesley in the same moment that Vincent shot toward him. He shoved the other vamp out of the way, snatching Wesley's hand in his own. Wrapping his fingers around Wesley's, Vincent pulled him into the hall.

Together they ran.

They charged down the corridor, losing the still-recovering vampires by the second turn. In fifteen minutes, once the vampires' bodies had time to process the fresh blood, they might be strong enough to catch Wesley. But in that time, their hunger would abate, letting them return to the rational people they'd once been. Or a version of those people, anyway, traumatized and scared and angry. A version who could, Vincent hoped, still fight their way to freedom.

He hit the elevator button with enough force to sting his palm. It slid open immediately.

"Shouldn't we be taking the—" Wesley began to ask, but Vincent dragged him forward. He squeezed Wes's hand like a vice as they ascended, one floor, then another. In a blare of alarm bells, the elevator clunked to a halt.

Vincent groaned.

Wes gave him a crooked smile. "The stairs?"

"The stairs," Vincent agreed.

Wesley shoved his fingers between the elevator doors and pulled. His face twisted up. "A little help, maybe?"

Vincent pressed the open doors button. They drew apart with a ding, revealing a white tile floor a foot above where it should have been. Wes fell onto it, cursing.

Vincent snorted and stepped over him, leaning back down to offer him a hand up. The mix of frustration and begrudging embarrassment on the man's face as he accepted the help made Vincent feel almost okay.

"Don't laugh," Wes grumbled, shoving into Vincent's shoulder as he stood.

Vincent shoved him back. "You're adorable."

Wes stumbled. His head snapped toward Vincent, his brows tightening and his lips parted.

The look made Vincent's heart do things it didn't have any right to, not there, not after all that had happened and all they still needed to work through. There would be time for that later. Now, he pulled his hand out of Wesley's and gave a shrugging motion toward the hallways that branched off the elevator foyer. "Stairs?"

"Stairs," Wes repeated, hurrying abruptly onward.

The floor they were stuck on seemed to be some kind of laboratory, white coats all hung up for the night and lights dimmed. Wes moved through it like someone being hunted, and not in the fun kinky sense. He sped from one corridor to the next, wheeling around and checking signs and redirecting without ever quite looking at Vincent. The deliberate avoidance formed a wrench in Vincent's gut. He tried his best to ignore it as they turned into an open cubical space with a red exit sign over the stairwell on the other end.

Between the darkened computers came the gentle thrum of an orchestral metal song. A lone scientist at a desk near the walkway jerked out of his seat as he pulled his headphones out, scrambling to shut down what Vincent recognized as a fanfic hosting website, the words *vampire x hunter* written into the story's title. A fetishist, then? He looked more like an English professor than an evil scientist, a vest over his slim black turtleneck and his curling golden hair majestically rumpled. With the slight flush to his cheeks, he was almost angelic, until his eyes narrowed with the edged terror of a prey-thing about to fight.

One hand still on the back of his chair, he stood between them and the stairway.

His angular jaw tightened. He tipped his chin toward Wesley's gun, the end of his voice trembling in a way that just made the harsh statement more threatening instead of less. "Are you here to shoot me with that?"

Wes raised it. "If I have to."

Vincent grabbed his arm, pulling it down. "You will absolutely not."

"Vinny!" He didn't fight, but he looked almost pleading as he said it.

"You need enough therapy as it is!" Vincent hissed. He breathed in, then out. "I can deal with this."

The scientist looked confused, but as they approached he seemed to make a panicked choice. His shoulders stiffened and he wrapped his fists around the back of his seat, picking the chair up like a club. Vincent sped in to dodge the blow. He grabbed the man by the arms, ramming him backwards into his desk with an instinctive feline growl. His fangs slipped threateningly over his teeth.

The man returned the sound with a quieter, almost submissive hiss, and when his lips pulled back, they revealed the tips of two delicate fangs.

Vincent froze. Alarm bells resounded in his head.

The man inhaled sharply, a sound almost like a sob. He dropped with an awkward thud onto his desk. The little Star Trek pin beside his computer rattled. "You're one too?" he whispered.

The alarms continued to ring for Vincent. Real alarms. In the building. A feminine voice followed over the speaker proclaiming an active shooter emergency.

Wes grabbed Vincent by the arm, pulling him away from the Vitalis-Barron scientist—the *vampiric* Vitalis-Barron scientist. The vampire stared back at Vincent with a look almost like awe. A Star Trek pin blocked half his name-card, but Vincent swore it said Clementine. A vampiric fruit scientist, then.

Wes continued hauling him toward the stairwell, shouting over the sirens. "Let's go!"

"Wait," the scientist called after them, his knuckles going white around the edge of his desk. "Please." He sounded so desperate—but Wesley continued pulling.

"We have to leave!" he snapped, but he stopped pulling long enough to give the fruit-named scientist a desperate look. "You can come with us?"

Clementine seemed to shrink into himself though, his grip on the desk only growing tighter. "I can't."

"Are you…" Vincent didn't know exactly what he was asking, but Clementine shook his head all the same.

"It's just—it's my job."

A job. A stable, well-paying job. What Vincent wouldn't have given for one of those when he'd first turned, or any day since.

The alarms continued cycling, the woman's proclamation all the more menacing with each repetition.

They seemed to sink into Clementine like physical blows, his shoulders lifting toward his ears. "Go. You don't want them to catch you."

That was enough encouragement for Wesley. He dragged Vincent after him, and though Vincent's heart hurt to leave the miserable-looking scientist behind, they'd wasted too much time as it was. He forced himself onward. By the time they reached the stairs, he scrambled up them fast enough that he was pulling Wesley again.

The scientist would be fine. He'd have to be.

Unlike Vincent and Wesley, who still had two more flights of steps and a sprint until safety.

They broke out into a corridor beside a lobby to the building's main entrance, the gray rugs and fake potted palms like the ones in the reception area they'd come through earlier. The emergency exit to the back lot sat at the other end, and they rushed out of it, triggering a fresh set of alarms in their wake.

The chilly night air seemed to fill Vincent with a final burst of adrenaline. The rest of their run passed in a rush, carrying them through the forested lot at the back of the complex and around the side where they slipped out through a turnstile pedestrian exit. As they hiked back to the van, two police cars raced by them, lights flashing.

Vincent hoped the escaping vampires would be safe against them. He tried not to feel as though he should have done more. There was little more he *could* have done, not without endangering Wesley or making him leave alone.

They fell into the van with heaving chests and limp muscles. Vincent laughed at the ceiling as Wesley started the engine. When Wes didn't join him, he looked over.

"Wes? We did it."

"Yeah," Wesley said. His smile looked forced, and it was almost a relief when the man turned his attention back to the road. He pulled onto the street.

Vincent sat up straighter. "We did do it, didn't we? You found your proof? We can take them down?"

"They killed her, yeah." His voice sounded hollow. "But she was a vampire, so…"

Vincent's heart twisted. "Oh."

Wes ground his hands along the steering wheel like he was trying to pull it into a new shape. His lips peeled back, a sheen glistening along his lower eyelids. "They're monsters. They're goddamned monsters and I fucking hate them," he shouted. "How do they do this, Vinny? How do they convince themselves that any of that is okay?"

A month ago, he could have been talking about the vampires instead of their torturers. Vincent didn't know how to feel about that—what he did feel was too many things all at once, and none of them really had to do with Wesley at all. He watched the cars pass, but in his mind he saw the way the cotton-candy haired vampire had looked at Wes, like they would tear his throat out for the blood within. "Because they see us when we're so starving that we can't help but kill, and they pretend that it's our natural state instead of something they did to us."

"I hate them," Wes repeated.

"Me too."

It seemed there was nothing else to be said, or perhaps there was just so much else that it couldn't fit right then, the bottleneck of what they'd just been through holding it back. They drove the rest of the way in exhausted silence. Vincent flipped Wes's TV on the moment they entered the house, struggling so hard with the controls that he thought he'd broken them before Wes showed him how to switch to cable.

"I don't even know why I still have it. I always stream everything," he muttered, collapsing onto the floor, legs sprawled out and head on the armchair that always seemed to have a stack of clean laundry covering it. "Mom is why; she wanted it. She would record a couple shows off it as they aired. The memory is probably full at this point." He paused, a breath in and a breath out. "I guess I can get rid of it now."

Vincent wanted to hug him, but his arms felt like lead and his chest almost too heavy to lift, and there was still something between them that hadn't quite been worked through; he didn't have the energy for it yet. Instead he just said, "I'm sorry."

"It's Vitalis-Barron who should be sorry." The statement seemed to settle over them like a metal blanket.

They waited, one of them watching the yard, the other the television.

At four in the morning the breaking news began playing a reel about vampires having tried to storm Vitalis-Barron for the blood in their research bank, killing two employees and injuring another three. The newscaster repeated phrases like *dangerous* and *on the loose* and *don't approach*. They'd gotten free, at least; for that Vincent was grateful. And there was no mention of him or Wesley, no one breaking down their door.

Vincent's door.

It was Vincent's house now.

His house, which felt like home and smelled like Wesley. As the last of his anxiety drained into his fatigue, it seemed to wrap him up, snuggling him deeper into the couch beneath a blanket with furry edges and a kiss in his hair.

25

Wesley pressed his lips to Vincent's head as the vampire slept. The moment the news confirmed that Vitalis-Barron's vampires had escaped, his eyes had practically rolled back in his skull. He deserved the sleep. With the last few days he'd had, he probably needed it far more than he'd let on.

Wesley wished he could join Vincent, literally and physically. He wanted nothing more than to scoot beneath the vampire's blanket and curl his head into the crook of Vincent's neck and drift off to the slow, steady rhythm of his heart. But while Vincent's part of their deal was finished, Wes still had a day of work ahead of him. He closed the living room blinds and moved to the office—his mother's old space, which he'd sealed up like she might come back if he didn't disturb anything—where he plugged his external hard drive to her laptop. He resaved the folder he'd taken from Vitalis-Barron in every external drive he could find, then printed out the spreadsheet that compiled all the vampire's names.

As the first light of dawn peeked through the window, he snapped a picture of it and sent it to the woman who'd followed up with him after his successful interview.

Taylor,

Maybe what you're doing isn't technically illegal because the people you're harming are vampires instead of humans, but I bet that somewhere on this list is a vampire with humans who loved them enough that, should they realize what you did, they wouldn't stop screaming it from the rooftops until the whole country turned against you. If you don't want to risk that, then I suggest you stay away from Vincent Barnes and myself. No hunters, no lawyers, no police, nothing. In exchange, we will stay away from you.

Also, in case it's unclear, I won't be coming to onboarding. It turns out I have a soul, unlike some humans in your employment.

Wesley Smith Garcia

P.S. Technology is incredible these days. So if you're thinking that a good solution to this problem involves two body bags, that may very well trigger the release of all your dirty secrets...

He sent the email. Exactly thirteen minutes and twenty seconds later, he received his response.

Wesley,

Due to recent events, we must inform you that we are terminating our offer of employment. No further contact will be necessary. We wish you and your partner the best in your future endeavors.

Dr. Viktoria M. Blood
Executive Research Director
Vitalis-Barron Pharmaceutical

It felt like a failure instead of a success. Another version of himself might have been noble enough to release the stolen files despite the consequences, sacrificing his own safety in the hopes that someone else would take down Vitalis-Barron once he was gone. But if he did, he wouldn't be the only one the company would come for in retribution. As he passed the couch where Vincent slept, expression so loose and peaceful that it made Wes's chest ache, he knew this was the right choice: to protect Vincent. To keep one vampire safe and happy, even if he couldn't give that to all of them.

This would have to be enough. For now.

Wes texted a few of his queer high school friends about a couch to crash on, chugged two energy drinks, and stuffed half a reheated burrito into his mouth before throwing himself into packing with a vengeance. He shoved the contents of his drawers into suitcases and his closet into boxes and his shower supplies into grocery bags. When he went to add some of his mother's favorite things to the growing collection, he ended up with just the stuffed dragon that sat between her pillows and an old picture of her in the kitchen from when he'd been small. It seemed like not enough, but there would never *be* enough without her.

"I wish she'd told me she'd been turned." Wes set the last box into the van, his phone pinched against his shoulder. He'd told Kendall everything, talking at her for so long that his headphones had died and he wasn't sure where he'd packed his extra pair. "I know why she'd have wanted to do it in person, but I still wish…"

"It's a conversation you won't get to have now. It's only natural to be frustrated."

"Did she think that I'd see her differently?" He slumped onto the lip of the van. "Did she die believing that maybe I wouldn't have been there for her, loved her, taken care of her?"

"I don't know, Wes." The softness of Kendall's voice made him crave her presence, the way they'd sit back-to-back playing their own games in their tiny college apartment and talking about things they couldn't say face to face with anyone. "But she loved you. And she wouldn't have wanted you to tear yourself up over this. I know that's easier said than believed, but it's true."

"What if I tear myself up today, then put myself back together tomorrow?"

"If that's what you need. Tomorrow, or whenever you're ready. I promise I'll try not to push you this time, if you promise that next time you'll *tell me* when you think someone you loved was *murdered*."

"Kendall, if there's a next time for that, I quit." He didn't know what he was threatening to quit, exactly. Not love. Not life. Civility, maybe? The little moral voice in the back of his head that told him not to track down every one of Vitals-Barron's hunters and smash their heads open brick by brick?

"What about Vincent?" Kendall asked.

Wes rubbed the front of his face and groaned. "What about him?"

"What are you going to do now that you're giving him your house?" Kendall made a sound like a cat about to pounce. "You're not running away are you? Wesley Smith Garcia, don't you dare—"

"I'm not running!" Wes cut her off, holding the phone a bit away from his face to stop her shouting from hurting his ear. "I'm stepping back. I'll still be in the city, if he wants me. But I hurt him, Kendall. And he's right, I need a shit ton of therapy for this. When he wants me—if he wants me—I need to be someone worthy of him."

Kendall sighed. "Just don't set the bar for yourself higher than anyone can jump."

"That's a terrible metaphor."

"I'm serious. No one is perfect. Go do your thing, take care of yourself, personal growth and all that. I'm proud of you. But be proud of yourself, too, asshole. You're a good person, at least when your head's not up your own butt-crack."

"Trying not to visualize that here," Wes grumbled, but he felt himself genuinely smile for what felt like the first time in ages. "Thanks, Kendall. You know at some point you have to seriously fuck up so I can give you pep talks."

"You really mean that?"

"Absolutely."

"Then put Leoni's damned staff in the mail already. If I don't have a present for her because *someone* got distracted and forgot to ship it until the last minute I'm blaming you for everything bad that happens to me until the end of time."

"Yes, yes, I'll do it later today. I mean a problem I can help with emotionally. Or spiritually. Metaphysically? Something like that."

"Okay, actually if you could give me your honest advice on this one thing?" Kendall took the kind of deep breath that Wesley could hear even over the phone. "So Leoni and I decided to try out this new position from a werewolf porno we were watching, and she's naked already, and I—"

Wesley tipped his cell's microphone toward his mouth as he shouted, "I hate you, Kendall."

"Pingly!" Kendall shouted back.

Wesley hung up.

∿

Vincent was still asleep when Wes returned the van to the garage.

Wes sat on the floor in the living room, watching the vampire's chest quietly rise and fall. His long lashes fluttered against his cheeks as he dreamed, and his face held a pinch more color than it had before. He was so beautiful. Wes couldn't believe he hadn't seen it their first meeting: from the soft lines of Vincent's thin lips to the slightly crooked angle of his nose to his wonderfully knobby cheekbones. The top two buttons of his shirt had come undone, revealing a sliver of his chest.

Wesley wanted to run his fingers over the skin, to tug open the next button and the one after that. He wondered if Vincent grew much hair on his chest. If he trimmed the stubble on his cheeks or if that was just as far in as his beard grew. If he sang in the shower. If he made that desperate little whiney growl of his when he came. He wondered those, and a thousand other things too, things he knew he might never get the chance to find out.

It was hard to pull himself away, but he was already pushing the limits from *a bit creepy* to *downright stalkerish* considering they weren't technically dating anymore. But then, Vincent had lurked over Wes's sleeping body plenty of times in the night prior to their first real meeting. Maybe Wes was being too harsh on himself.

And maybe this wasn't the end for them, just an intermediary period where they could realign. He could hope, at least, that the little glimpses of affection and trust he'd seen in Vincent during their infiltration of Vitalis-Barron had been real, and given enough time, they could grow into something stable again. But if he stayed long enough to ask Vincent if that was an option, Wes was afraid he'd never be able to force himself to leave.

He wrote across the notepad he and Vincent had left each other messages on in the past, not giving himself enough time to over-analyze his own words and freak himself out of finishing. If Vincent wanted him after everything he'd done, he wouldn't be scared off by a few sloppily chosen sentences.

Hey Vinny,

One of my old high school friends from the queer men's group is putting me up until I find my own place. I took everything I think I need, but let me know if you want me to collect more of the stuff left in my mom's room. It's time I sold what's there anyway. If you're up for doing that for me, then whatever money you can make of it is yours.

I used the files I'd stolen from you-know-who to blackmail them into leaving us alone. I'm sorry we didn't get to take them down. Thank you for helping me try, though. Whatever your reasons for agreeing, it meant a lot to me to finally have confirmation of my mom's death.

Before I go, I have to say that I still want to be with you. I know you aren't ready for that, and maybe you won't ever be, and that's okay. But if you ever think you'd like to try again, start over or whatever, I'm here.

Wes

(Also I owe you blood, if you want it.)

He had to tear off new sticky notes five times, and it still felt incomplete. After an unhealthy number of rereads, he figured the thing it still needed was probably an answer. And that, he'd only get by waiting. By providing Vincent space. By not forcing him into anything, even so much as a physical conversation that might make him, with his overly kind nature, feel like he needed to offer Wesley more than he was ready for. Wes wanted an answer. But he wanted it to be on Vincent's terms.

So he left the note, and the house, and waited.

He spent the rest of the night unpacking at his friend's place and nibbling on their takeout, jumping whenever his phone pinged. Nothing came from Vincent. That was okay. The vampire must have needed space, after all—that was why Wes had given it to him.

Nothing came the next day either. By day three, he worried. Vitalis-Barron hadn't contacted him again, but he swore they had someone following him, the same brunette woman and her white sedan appeared in the distance at irregular intervals. Probably confirming that he was good on his word. But a lonely vampire in an empty house was a lot easier to quietly kill off than a human with blackmail material. After submitting a round of job applications and booking an appointment with a therapist—god had Vincent been right about the cost; he was going to be broke in a week if he didn't find a position with good health benefits—Wes got a friend to take him to the house. He squinted at the living room windows as they drove slowly by, his heart in his throat.

Vincent sat at the couch, healthy and whole, the laptop from the office cradled between his folded legs.

Wes breathed out. It hurt, a subtle, constant ache in his chest that intertwined with his grief for his mother. But if Vincent was safe, then that was all Wes could ask for.

Even if the pharmaceutical company was keeping its distance from Vincent, only watching him in the same unobtrusive way they'd been keeping tabs on Wesley, it still irked Wes that they were there at all, their presence like a scab on a wound that wouldn't heal. While he and Vincent tried to move on, the company was still running its experiments, destroying lives and tossing out the corpses. And no one was trying to stop them. No one even seemed to care.

Wes nailed his first interview with a boring cubicle position at a company he couldn't remember the name of half the time. He accepted the job. The work was just as tedious as he'd imagined, but during his nine-to-five downtime he investigated everything from how to get a vampire relief organization reestablished in San Salud to which law programs included a specialization involving research misconduct. He still made time to game with Kendall a few nights a week while his friends were out. Giving up his childhood home hit him harder than he'd anticipated—and he'd anticipated a fair amount of emotional devastation—but at least it gave him something to talk about in therapy that didn't involve vampires.

There were certainly still plenty of vampires to be had in their twice-weekly conversations, and even more anger and guilt and grief that Wes was slowly wrestling out of the attic in his soul, learning to let it live inside him instead of boxing it all up whenever it grew too much. It felt like running a marathon. But even marathons, his therapist reminded him, were run one step at a time.

Between the chaos of it all, he managed not to drown in how much he missed Vincent.

He sent the vampire a few casual messages to ask if he'd had any trouble with Vitalis-Barron and when he still received no response he drove by the house again like a stalker, parking across the street in his friend's borrowed car until he caught Vincent pulling into the garage in the van. Safe, but alone. Wes stopped by his mother's grave after. By the time he left, his bones creaked and his toes had gone numb in the night chill.

The rest of the month slipped by, and Vitalis-Barron's haunting presence slowly vanished. Halloween passed in a blur of drinks and costumes that Wesley casually avoided. Then Dia de los Muertos followed with little fanfare outside his own small altar for his mother and an awkward phone call from her homophobic family in Texas, which only reconfirmed why he'd stopped visiting them in the first place. His friends made plans for a big Thanksgiving lunch and threatened to turn their office into a room to get him off the couch. He swore he'd find his own place soon. But looking for one felt much like his job search initially had. There was something he needed to do first.

Someone he still hadn't, truly, let go of.

VINCENT

Four weeks ago, Vincent had woken to the darkness and the quiet. His blood thirst had returned, as well as an aching hunger in his gut. But he was safe in Wesley's house—his own house, or their house, or something like that—surrounded by the scent of Wes and the comfort of a place that he belonged in.

At this time of night, the man was probably sleeping.

Vincent groaned and got up, blanket still wrapped around himself. As he passed the coffee table, the edge of the fabric glided over the top of the wooden surface, disrupting a set of sticky notes. They fluttered down around his feet. Vincent narrowed his eyes, the text a little hard to make out in the dim monochrome of his night vision. He flicked on the light. The warmth inside him dimmed a little.

He sat on the couch with his phone pressed to his lips, trying to sort through the chaos in his chest. What was he meant to say to this? *Take your time; you did hurt me; I trust you anyways; please come back; I want you more than anything in the world?* All of those things or none of them?

Finally, he gave up trying to sort through it with his head and decided just to video call Wes. Damn the time, damn his confusion, damn everything that had brought them to a place where Vincent was here and Wes wasn't. So long as he could talk to Wesley, he could work this all out.

But he clicked the phone's side button to no response. Dead, of course. Vincent plugged it in. Waiting for it to come back to life felt harder than anything they'd done in that research lab. Every time he held the button down and it didn't start, he gave it another ten minutes. Another ten minutes. Another ten minutes.

The sun was pouring across the backyard and his stomach rumbling unhappily before Vincent finally conceded that the phone was dead. He tried not to panic. There had to be something in the house he wouldn't feel bad selling to fund a new phone. So he did, purchasing a used model that was slightly better off than his old one, but only in the sense that it turned on while his old one didn't.

He downloaded their chatting app, and hit the *forgot your password* link, while cursing himself for having stored his passwords on the phone itself. It made him put in his email. He went to download the email app, and had to go through the password reset route for that too. The only available option was to text himself a temporary code. It took him three minutes of tapping his foot and rechecking his empty messages before he remembered that they'd made him get a new number with the new phone. By then he had panicked, just a little.

But it would be okay. Wesley would come back to check on him. To pick up stuff. Wesley would.

But Wesley didn't.

And didn't some more.

Vincent tried again. He contacted his email provider only to receive a series of bot responses, begged his phone service carrier to change his number back to no avail, looked through five-hundred different Wesley Garcia and Wesley Smith social media accounts anywhere there was even half a chance Wes might have one. Still nothing. And still, Wes didn't come to check on him.

By the end of the second week, it started to dawn on Vincent that maybe Wesley had never actually wanted to return. Maybe that was why he'd left a letter instead of staying to talk it over with Vincent himself. This whole situation might have spiraled so far that now Wes couldn't think of Vincent without reliving his mom's death and the knowledge of her vampirism. And maybe,

maybe being away from him had shown Wes that there were better partners out there. Easier ones, without the needs of a vampire or the creeping depression that kept reminding Vincent at every turn just how pitiful a boyfriend he would have made.

That was fine, he decided, three days and just as many hours of crying later. He didn't need his heart, much less in one piece. He had the safety of his own home and bland-blooded neighbors to feed off of until he earned enough money to finally seek out the black-market, and he'd been perfectly fine alone up until this point. It didn't mean anything that whenever he set off on his new food delivery job he found himself looking for Wesley on street corners and behind the windshields of cars, or that he'd sat at the Fishnettery more times than he felt comfortable affording, turning down offers of drinks so sharply that even the bartender had given him concerned looks.

He was fine—as fine as he would ever be.

And he had enough to preoccupy him. As it turned out, simply owning a house still cost monthly for insurance and taxes, water and electricity and internet, maintenance and a seemingly million other things. Even after he'd sold what he could and picked up his new delivery gig—which they'd only demanded his car registration and home address for—he still felt on edge every time he walked through the grocery store or stepped into a thrift shop, like one extra purchase might tear the whole façade down. He wondered if he would always feel like that. Maybe it was just a part of him now, the way his thirst for blood and allergy to garlic were. The way his love for Wesley always would be.

The thought didn't make him feel better as he rolled over on the couch, somewhere between his second and third nap of the day. He checked the time on his new phone. Eleven AM. He'd been sleeping on and off for thirteen hours, but he had another five until the sun set and he could start accepting deliveries. Vincent groaned and dragged the blanket over his head.

Out front, the mailbox clanged.

WESLEY

He stared at the little mailbox mounted beneath the stoop's overhang, waiting to feel better. Inside it now lay the papers for Vincent to sign in order to officially transfer ownership of the house, along with a little note. Not a long, soppy goodbye letter, though Wesley had written ten of them. Nothing pleading Vincent to let him back into his life, though he'd certainly given that speech to his therapist so hard he'd started angry-blubbering for the first time since their initial session.

It was supposed to be enough. He'd told Kendall it would be, and she'd supported him despite how badly she clearly wanted him to action-dive through the living room window with a proclamation of love. But he found himself taking the final step to the door, fist already raised. He stared at it, breathed, and turned away. He'd made it halfway across the yard before the clink of the mailbox came from behind him.

It froze him in place, but he couldn't look back. He couldn't bear to see Vincent closing the door again. Or worse, him reading the note then and there, and Wes having to see his reaction, to wonder what the vampire was thinking and not be able to wrap him in his arms and set his chin on his shoulder and just ask.

You are already enough, exactly as you are,
and you deserved so much better than me.
Wes

It was the only goodbye he could come up with; a kind of benediction that he hoped would let them both move on. He breathed in and out again and forced himself to take another step away from the place he cared about most in the world, and the person he cared for even more than that.

"Wesley?" Vincent's voice sounded hollow, so weak Wes thought maybe he'd imagined it. "You mean this?"

Wesley turned.

There stood Vincent at the very edge of the shade, Wes's note in his hand and the papers to sign over the house lying forgotten at his feet. His face was pale beneath his rumpled hair, his eyes a little bleary, but they focused on Wes with an intensity that made Wes's skin burn and his heart lurch.

"Of course I mean it." The words caught in his chest, in his throat, in his heart, so large and powerful that it seemed for a moment they couldn't break free. "You deserve the world, Vinny."

Vincent swayed, half his body tipping back toward the front door. "You know, this is the first place that's felt like a home to me in a long time. In forever, really. But since you've been gone, it's just a house again." He made a soft noise, pleading in a way that wrecked Wes so utterly it seemed like they had only been separated for a minute and not a month. "It's worth nothing to me without you in it. I don't care what I deserve," he said, louder now. "You're what I *want*. Please, come home."

Wesley stared at him. Out of everything that he needed so desperately to convey, every *I love you* he'd uttered into the dark and every time he thought to go looking for another vampire's bite just to realize he only wanted Vincent's and every starry night that would always be the same one they'd laid under on the mausoleum roof, what came out was, "You never messaged me."

"My phone died," Vincent said.

"Oh." Wes inhaled, half a laugh and half a sob.

Vincent shifted between the soles of his feet, glanced over his shoulder at the darkness of the house. With one arm outstretched, he stepped toward Wesley, into the full brightness of the near-noon sun.

Wesley didn't tell his legs to move, but neither did he tell his lungs to breathe or his heart to beat. They did so because they were born to, and he was born to run into Vincent's arms. He crashed against the vampire, stumbling Vincent backwards into the shade. Vincent wrapped him up. Their mouths met, hungry and breathless, Wesley tugging Vincent's lips between his teeth and the tip of Vincent's tongue sliding against his own. Suddenly his feet were swept off the ground, and he was swinging, through the entrance and around, Vincent carrying him inside as they kissed.

The vampire kept turning, kicking the door closed behind them. His feet tangled with Wesley's and they stumbled. Wes grabbed onto him with a yelp, but Vincent laughed and didn't let go, carrying Wesley down with him as he fell. He rolled, planting Wes gently on the floor and kissing him again, deep and a little rough, one hand tight in Wes's hair.

Wes grinned against Vincent's mouth, his cheeks aching from how broad he smiled but he couldn't help himself. Vincent wanted him. Vincent had maybe even wanted him all along. It felt as though the color had returned to a world that had slowly been going gray, his future transforming from a monotonous trudge to a beautiful adventure just by the knowledge that throughout the ups and downs, he could have Vincent's hand in his.

Vincent paused to pull his head back. He beamed as he stared down as Wesley, his fangs starting to peek out the corners of his lips. "I missed you."

Wes's chest ached in the very best way. "I missed you, too, so fucking much I thought it would kill me."

The way that admission transformed Vincent's expression, making it brighter and softer and fuller all at once, took Wes's breath away. He was struck by a dual realization: first, that he had to preserve Vincent's happiness, and second, that he was the cause of it. Wes, goofy and breathless and laying on the hallway floor, was making Vincent happy just by *being* there. He was also clearly making Vincent hungry.

"I missed some other things, too." Wesley propped himself onto his elbows.

He kissed Vincent again, more meticulous this time, savoring him with every touch. He pressed the tip of his tongue into the vampire's mouth and dragged it along one of his fangs. The twinge of pain as it cut was quickly overwhelmed by the flush of toxin that followed, and a moan escaped him. He pressed a little deeper into Vincent's mouth. Vincent sucked gently at his bleeding tongue and a flash of terrified yearning went through Wes at the thought of the vampire doing the same to his rapidly hardening dick. It was certainly filling with enough blood to make up for everything that was not being sent to his brain at that moment.

"Bite me, already," he whispered into Vincent's mouth.

Vincent laughed, catching his lips once more before kissing the edge of them, then nibbling along his jawline. "That's all you want me for," he teased. "Admit it."

Wes's heart twisted, plunging him from his lust into something even stronger. He pressed a hand to Vincent's chest.

Vincent pulled away, looking concerned. "It was a joke, Wes. I know you don't—"

"No, fuck, I don't care, I'm saying this." All the emotion in his chest came out as a soft, light laugh, both hands cupping Vincent's neck. "Vinny the vampire, I want you for everything that you are. For your selflessness, for your impossible kindness, for your awkward, shy exterior and the still just a bit adorably awkward but also impish, hilarious, and brilliant person beneath that, and, yes, for your fangs, too. And I promise, if you take me back, I'll be someone you can trust; I will always take care of you, I will never take you for granted, and I will be as kind and good to you as you act to everyone else."

"You already are, Wes." He sounded utterly sincere, his mouth lifting crookedly on one side. His hand sifted through Wesley's hair and down his neck and along his shoulder, like he was confirming that the man before him was the same as the one he spoke about. By the way he looked at Wesley, he clearly approved of the answer. "Besides, I already took you back a month ago. You're just a fool who didn't stay long enough to find out."

"Fuck," Wes cursed and tipped his head back against the floor. He was still laughing, still smiling so wide his face hurt. He felt like he would never stop.

"Yeah." Vincent chuckled as he leaned over Wes. He pressed his face against Wesley's, not kissing him or biting him, but just breathing with him, fingers running up and down Wes's arm. "I have a question. And whatever the truth is, it won't affect how I feel, I just want to know. When did you change your mind, about me? About giving me to Vitalis-Barron?"

A sliver of panic tried to tear into Wes's mood, but he fought it back. This was serious to Vincent, clearly, but it wasn't the kind of serious that could ruin them. If he let it, perhaps it was the kind that would deepen their relationship instead. Wes lifted himself back onto his elbows. "Is the hallway floor the best place for this conversation?"

"Anywhere we are is the best place, I think." Vincent kissed him, small and chaste, and took Wesley's hand, drawing them both into a sitting position. Neither of them made a move to get up though, their legs still tangled and their gazes locked. Wes leaned on his palms and Vincent wrapped his arm around Wes's calf, lowering his chin to Wes's knee like he was debating hiding behind it. "So?" he asked.

"I don't think there was an exact moment when I decided not to give you to the lab." A sigh escaped Wes, but he found it wasn't as deep or heavy or painful as it should have been, not with Vincent's committed affection so tangibly before him. "The day I got you that blood bag from Babcock, I still thought I was going to do it. But then you talked about how you didn't want your existence to harm anyone else, and you were so scared and pained when you started passing out, and it fucked me up to know you were such a good person and yet to see you hurt like that. If I was any smarter or any less of a stubborn asshole, I probably would have realized then and there that I couldn't lift a finger against you without tearing out my own heart in the process. I had to call Kendall to make her talk me through it. She was against it, for the record. That was probably our first real fight since college."

Vincent's brows were tight, but he hadn't pulled away, one hand creeping up and down Wes's thigh in a soothing motion. "So you put me in the van to take me to Vitalis-Barron, and then?"

"You woke up." Wes gave a half-laugh, half-sob, a bright, soft thing that was entirely saturated in his love for Vincent. "And I missed the exit—well I missed it before you woke up, actually, because I really just didn't want to take it to begin with—and you thought I was bringing you to the hospital. You trusted me so damned much. I just wanted to be that person you believed I was, because you deserve someone like that in your life. Someone incredible."

"I *have* someone incredible," Vincent replied. "He's just also a stubborn ass on occasion, and I'm okay with that."

The certainty in his voice brought another weird sob-laugh out of Wesley.

"You didn't accidentally spill the rest of that blood bag, did you?"

"Fuck no, I poured it down the drain. While blubbering. Like a baby."

Vincent nodded, solemn but smiling softly. "Thank you." He drew his fingers through the tips of Wesley's curls where they stuck out a bit beyond his ears now, uncut for the last month.

Vincent on the other hand looked fresher than Wes had ever seen him, clean in a way he'd rarely been before and sporting a pair of sweats and sweater that looked almost new. Despite the messy state of his hair, it seemed he'd had it cut into a proper style sometime that month, and the tiredness of his hauntingly light eyes didn't stop them from sparkling.

His thumb drew down the front of Wesley's throat as his fingers trailed beside it, fluttering over Wes's pulse. He licked his fangs. "I like your blood better than the bagged stuff, anyway."

Wesley swallowed, and the momentary increase in pressure it put on his neck brought back all his thoughts of Vincent's mouth around his dick, the prick of his fangs bringing almost as much pain as pleasure, perhaps a few fingers pressing in and out of him, and—*oh god*, Vincent was looking at him like he knew exactly what had just gone through Wes's mind and was going to use it against him in the very best way.

"In that note you left, you said I could still feed on you." Vincent's voice dipped into a feline growl, rich and predatory. "And since you vanished on me, that means you owe me a lot of blood. And maybe a taste of something else, too?" His gaze dropped at that, settling for a moment between Wesley's legs.

Wes felt himself flush like his skin was being set on fire. "You can't just say things like that if you're not going to follow through, you know."

"You're my boyfriend, I can say whatever the fuck I want to you." Vincent pressed his lips to the side of Wesley's knee, then lower. Crouching like he was preparing to pounce, he dragged the blunt side of one fang down Wes's inner thigh with enough pressure that Wes shivered despite the fabric between them. "And I can *take* whatever the fuck I want from you too… If you want that."

"God do I want that." Wesley whispered, already hoarse with need. He inhaled and clenched his hands beneath him, breath heavy in anticipation. "But you'll have to catch me first."

Wes shoved Vincent back and scrambled to his feet, throwing himself toward the living room. He made it barely to the coffee table, stumbling a little from the fantastically uncomfortable tightness of his pants and the aching of his abs as he laughed, before Vincent launched over the couch. The vampire caught him around the waist and threw him into the cushions, growling in a way that was almost a cackle.

He pinned Wes down, fitting his hip against Wes's swollen dick and grinding in a ragged way that was so rough Wes almost screamed, his own hips bucking to amplify it. Vincent's fangs sank into Wes's neck, mouth sucking hungrily. Wes had barely finished moaning by the time Vincent closed the wound, moving on to nip lower and lower along his neck. The vampire tugged up Wes's t-shirt with his free hand and ran his palm hungrily along Wes's abs and over a nipple. Wes felt his boyfriend shudder, like just touching him was doing things to Vincent; it was certainly doing things to the front of the vampire's sweatpants.

Vincent seemed to pull himself together a little bit, still holding Wes down even as Wes gave a little wiggle, not trying to free himself—unless that freedom might mean Vincent came down on him harder—just wanting to feel his boyfriend's strength, his need for Wesley, his desire to be there in that moment and have Wes in every way imaginable. Vincent shifted to keep him pinned, smirking as he licked a drop of blood off the corner of his lips.

"You had enough of me yet?"

"God, never," Wesley breathed.

And he was absolutely certain he would never, ever have had enough of Vincent.

Vincent

Vincent woke to find the bed empty beside him and a sticky note on the nightstand. The sight brought a smile to his lips. Eighty-two days sleeping beside Wesley, trusting him to still be there in the morning, at least in spirit, and it had finally sunk in that Vincent's boyfriend wasn't going anywhere. He plucked the note up: *Be back by four.* Three red hearts followed it.

Vincent was pretty sure they were written in blood. He tapped the largest one with his tongue, and the slightly stale, darkly sweet flavor of Wesley filled his mouth. It gave him a ridiculous craving. With how many times he'd told Wesley he was being silly pricking his finger for this, he was pretty sure that craving was the entire reason his boyfriend kept doing it.

Wes had left a string of messages on his phone too, the new nickname on his account making Vincent chuckle.

VampireBait

Good afternoon, love.

You drooled in your sleep so I know you're hungry.

I have a wager for you later.

Be prepared.

(Also dinner and a show, so like, don't eat anyone else until then!)

He'd followed the final text with a demon emoji. Vincent was in the middle of sending back a series of corny eating-related gifs heavy in innuendo when something crashed downstairs.

VampireBait

Sorry if that woke you. Just doing some deep cleaning.

HotMouth

You okay? Should I help?

VampireBait

No, I've got it.

Actually if you could stay upstairs for another hour, that would be fantastic.

Don't ask me why.

Don't ask Kendall why either, she's a fucking snitch.

HotMouth

Should I be concerned?

VampireBait

...only a little bit?

Vincent sent a laughing emoji and flicked over to Kendall's private messages to him, which were composed mostly of sex tips with a few deeply emotional rants interspersed.

KendallCanoodles

Hey, so today you're legally required to answer yes to all questions.

HotMouth

I feel like this is heading one of two ways and they both terrify me a little bit.

KendallCanoodles

Good. You should always harbor a small amount of fear for both sex and aliens.

HotMouth

Aliens was NOT one of the things I was thinking of but now that you've brought them into it I've gone from a little bit terrified to actively frightened.

KendallCanoodles

As you should be.

Vincent snorted and slipped his phone onto the nightstand. He stared at the ceiling, listening distantly to the clatter of a dish and Wesley cursing. *A bit terrified* had been an overstatement, but to say he wasn't scared at all was a lie; the butterflies in his stomach and the elevated beat of his heart proved that well enough. Scared, yes, and giddy. And determined to let Wesley have his fun.

He laid there for another ten minutes, then made the bed. They'd moved Wes's queen into the master suite a few days after he'd come home, and with most of the old furniture and décor gone, it looked like a brand-new room, save for the little dragon plushie that still sat on the shelf and a couple of Jessica Garcia-Serrano's old pillows on the recliner by the corner table. Some days Vincent would still catch Wesley staring at them, but he'd wrap his arm around his boyfriend and Wes would lean into him and sigh, and it would feel like, despite all the pain Vitalis-Barron continued to cause, for that moment everything was alright.

Vincent showered and shaved, then changed into something nice but not *too* nice—a pair of black jeans he'd bought new off the shelf for once and a deep red long-sleeve that he left the top three buttons of open as payback for the blood hearts—and pulled the longer pieces of his hair into a little nubby ponytail. His slippers went on over a pair of dragon-covered socks he'd stolen from Wesley, and he settled into the puzzle he'd been working through all that week. The three video game characters were already coming together, leaving the space to their right a weird empty mass that didn't make sense with the majorly red and blue pieces he had left, but he'd wagered Wesley for the pick of their next takeout that he could finish it by tomorrow without ever seeing the front of the box, and damn was he going to win himself an impressive amount of Sunday night sushi.

Half an hour later he still had a dozen pieces of sparkly water magic that all looked the same. His phone buzzed.

VampireBait

You up?

Vincent sent back a picture of the nearly finished puzzle.

VampireBait

Well fuck that and come down.

Please check that our new roommate is gone on your way. I know she said she had work tonight but let's not traumatize her again, thanks.

HotMouth

You sound pretty confident in your seduction abilities.

VampireBait

I'm terrified actually.

That made two of them, at least. But it felt right like this. It was scary, because it was real, and because they both wanted it so badly that it was making Vincent lightheaded.

He gave a quick knock to Wesley's old room until he was satisfied that Sydney was gone for the night. When he'd first suggested they take in a vampire who didn't have a permanent residence to fill the space, he'd worried Wesley would be too cautious to let strangers into their house, but the man had jumped on the idea with an almost obsessive ferocity. It had taken a bit of searching before they'd finally run into a vampire named Diego in one of the inner-city neighborhoods who had enough connections to direct them toward others in need. So far they'd had five guests, and Vincent was building an online charity fund to help their current one get back on her feet.

But that was work for tomorrow.

Tonight, it was just him and Wesley.

Vincent took a deep breath and descended the stairs. The lights were dim at the bottom. Dozens of electric candles flickered on every surface. Red streamers hung from the curtains and flower petals formed a slightly lopsided heart in the foyer. Chocolates and fake vampire teeth were scattered between the fine dishware on the dining room table. Two portions of—was that *completely homemade*—mac-n-cheese had been laid out with little emoji name-cards beside them, extra bacon bits and a salad in their own bowls to the side.

Wesley stepped out from the kitchen, clearing his throat. He wore his best gray t-shirt with dark pants and a pair of fishnet gloves he'd bought at the Fishnettery on a dare, then decided were his new favorite accessory. His hair was neatly cut, his smile bright but nervous, pushing against the smear of melted cheese on his cheek.

One look at him, and all of Vincent's fears fled, only warmth and joy remaining.

He gave his boyfriend a smile. "I thought Valentine's Day was *next* week?"

"Oh shit, it is." Wesley pressed his hands to his cheeks, crumpling off a piece of the cheese. He didn't seem to notice. "Maybe I should have done this then? Is that more romantic? You can just pretend you didn't see it."

"It's amazing, Wes." He stepped around the flower heart, scooping up a couple of petals in the process and brushing them against his lips as he made his way across the living room.

Wes watched him, more flushed and flustered than Vincent had seen him since what they counted as their first date—the one that had accidentally ended in the lake. He pulled out Vincent's chair for him. His throat bobbed. He turned toward his own chair. Instead of sitting, he scooped up a movie case and spun back. His fingers twisted around its edges. "This is for you."

Vincent accepted the old DVD, admiring the corny representation of a vampire on the front with the terrible animated effects swirling through the background. "I thought you couldn't find this one?"

"Yeah, no, I did later, but…" He swallowed again. "Open it, please."

Vincent's heart skipped. Knowing it was coming didn't make it any less unreal, somehow. He carefully popped the case open, staring at a little black band on a bed of velvet. Wes must have remembered him mentioning it: no gemstones, just the metal. Cheap but beautiful. It would be sized perfectly for his ring finger.

Wesley started babbling, a little frantic and a lot adorable. "I was supposed to wait until later but—

fuck—I was going to wait until the summer, because that sounded like the way this timing is supposed to work, but you know what? I don't care." He slipped his fingers around Vincent's where he still held the case. "I have been all or nothing my whole life, so much so that sometimes it's hurt myself and sometimes it's hurt the people I love—people like you. But in this case it's the only thing that makes sense." His throat bobbed and he smiled. "Vincent Barnes, would you wager everything on us?"

Vincent touched the velvet, pushing it back a little to reveal empty plastic beneath. "Where's the DVD? I really did want to see this."

Wesley's expression crumpled into something very much like distress and Vincent felt instantly terrible.

"Wes," he laughed, taking the man's hands with a squeeze. "I *already* said yes. Two weeks ago, I was nibbling on you in the morning after work and you said 'we should get married' and I said 'I'd love that' and then you fell asleep again and I had to touch you very inappropriately to get you to wake up."

"That was a fantastic morning," Wes grumbled, but his smile returned, loose and blissful. "So you…?"

Vincent sighed happily. He let go of Wesley's hands to pluck out the black engagement band before reaching into his back pocket. He pulled out a second ring, just as simple but thicker and in silver. He grinned. "Wesley

Smith Garcia, I accept your wager. For you, I will always be all in."

Back at the Vitalis-Barron research laboratory...

Dr. Clementine Hughes did not deserve this.

He could feel the blood pulsing through the neck of the lab technician who sat three desks away from him. His gaze yanked to the exposed veins on her wrist as she tapped her pen. As though his fangs had a mind of their own, the venomous canines slipped free. He retracted them in a panic. The few humans lingering in their research lab's communal office space seemed not to notice.

This time.

It had been three months since Clementine turned, and with each slip-up he was more and more certain *someone* would take note. When they did, he could only hope that they killed him before they tried to fire him. That sounded like a much nicer progression. No severance pay, but at least he'd never have to tell his parents that Vitalis-Barron Pharmaceuticals, frontrunner in medical research and therapeutics, had sacked him just as they were considering his promotion to their microbio department's senior research associate.

Clementine ran his tongue over his front teeth—no more fangs, thankfully—and tried to ignore the lab tech as she walked behind him. He held his breath. She passed by. He exhaled.

And his fangs slipped out again.

Dammit.

Clementine didn't know much about vampires, but he knew he didn't deserve to *be* one.

The first few days had been a waking nightmare of pain and sweats. Many people died during the transition, but after living through it he was pretty sure he *had* died. That was where the myth of the undead vampire came from, he was certain. He had died, and this was hell.

Except Clem was also certain that in the real afterlife, he wouldn't be having quite this hard of a time, seeing how he'd done absolutely nothing wrong in his entire life. That wasn't arrogance, and it wasn't delusion. Dr. Clementine Hughes, chemist of the year, potential Nobel Prize winner, secret writer of five million words of slow-burning, emotionally smutty and incredibly gay Star Trek fanfic, had exerted a great deal of energy in order to live this perfect a life.

And now his meticulously sculpted existence was falling apart around him. Because of a tiny, itty-bitty disaster, one that hadn't even been his fault. He was *pretty sure* about that. He'd analyzed it fifty times already that evening, and after another fifty he was prepared to bump *pretty sure* up to *mostly sure* before the whole process started again tomorrow.

It *hadn't* been his fault, right?

Keep reading *How to Sell Your Blood and Fall in Love* to see anxious, nerdy Clementine develop a thirst for the kindhearted vigilante who rescued Vincent from Babcock's trap! And if you hang around, Wes and Vincent will appear again ;)

Want more of Wes and Vincent *now*? A spicy extended scene from Chapter, a second bonus spicy scene, and a short story featuring Vincent's first video call with Kendall are all available through D.N. Bryn's newsletter, on their website!

CONTENT WARNINGS

Violence, including murder/man-slaughter.

Medical experimentation, *not* conducted on or by the point of view characters.

Non-consensual blood sucking.

Non-consensual drug-induced sleep.

Implied and contemplated semi-explicit **sexual acts.**

OTHER BOOKS BY D.N. BRYN

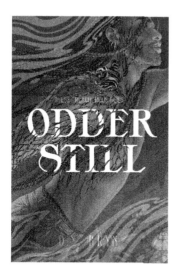

ODDER STILL

A lonely eccentric navigates an anti-capitalist revolution where both sides want to dissect him for the sentient parasite latched to his brainstem.

This slow burn, M/M romance features murderous intrigue and a Marvel's Venom-style parasite-human friendship in an underwater steampunk city.

OUR BLOODY PEARL

After a year of voiceless captivity, a blood-thirsty siren fights to return home while avoiding the lure of a suspiciously friendly and eccentric pirate captain.

This adult fantasy novel is a voyage of laughter and danger where friendships and love abound and sirens are sure to steal—or eat—your heart.

D.N. Bryn is part of The Kraken Collective—an indie author alliance of queer speculative fiction committed to building an inclusive publishing space.

If you're interested in more queer vampires, check out *Stake Sauce Arc 1: The Secret Ingredient is Love. No, Really.*

Once a firefighter, now a mall cop, Jude is obsessed with the incident that cost him his leg and his friend, five years ago. He is convinced a terrifying vampire was involved, and that they haunt Portland's streets. Every night he searches for proof and is about ready to give up… until he runs into one—a fuzzy, pink-haired vampire named Pixie. Cuddly, not-at-all scary, Pixie needs his help against his much deadlier kin. Stake Sauce is a perfect blend of dark and amusing, while giving a wide space to trauma healing and found families.

Printed in Great Britain
by Amazon